# THE NIGHT THE LIGHT WENT OUT

## A CAPE MAY HISTORICAL MYSTERY

### A.M. READE

PAU HANA PUBLISHING

Pau Hana Publishing

Print ISBN: 979-8-9872901-8-7

Ebook ISBN: 979-8-9872901-7-0

Printed in the United States of America

*This is the first book I've written from start to finish without my dog by my side, so this one is for her.*

*To Orly, the greatest dog in the whole world.*

# ACKNOWLEDGMENTS

⁓

There are several people I would like to thank for their help in bringing this book to fruition, and the first of these are two women whose generosity played a role in its evolution.

In 2022, the group Authors for Ukraine held an online auction with proceeds going to help Ukrainians in the days, weeks, and months following the invasion of their country. I am proud to have participated in the fundraiser. My contribution to the auction was an opportunity to name a character in an upcoming novel, and I was delighted when Marisa Young submitted the winning bid. Marisa chose the name Deborah, whom you will meet very soon. I wish to thank Amy Patricia Meade (people often confuse us because our names are so similar!) for her tireless work in organizing the auction.

Carole Grandy Sick won the opportunity to name two characters in a 2023 auction benefiting the Cape May MAC (Museums, Art, and Culture). Carole and I spent a lovely afternoon talking about Cape May, its history, its beauty, and my ideas for this book. The names she chose are George Moore and Abigail, and you will also meet these characters shortly.

I can't thank these women enough for their generosity and for the spirit of community and peace they share.

I would also like to thank my editor, Jeni Chappelle, who has made this a better book with her recommendations, advice, and guidance. I am delighted to count myself among her clients. You can find Jeni at www.jenichappelleeditorial.com. To Jeni's wisdom I added the invaluable suggestions and insights from members of my superb critique group.

Finally, thanks to my husband, John, who is always my first reader and offers his unwavering support of my dream of writing.

# PREFACE

~

At the southern tip of the New Jersey cape, where the waters of the Atlantic Ocean meet the Delaware Bay, there stands a lighthouse which has been guiding mariners and providing a reassuring beacon for the people on land since 1859. The only time the light has fallen dark was during World War II.

Prior to 1859, there were two other documented lighthouses in Cape May. The first, built in 1823, stood 88 feet above the water and was, of necessity, constructed on the shifting sands of the New Jersey coastal plain.

Relentless high tides and years of pounding surf were responsible for the erosion of that light's foundation. The 1823 lighthouse was thus dismantled in 1847 and its foundation bricks were moved to higher ground to provide a footing for a new lighthouse.

The 1847 lighthouse did not last long. It was "rough and rudely built," according to an 1851 inspection report, and its keeper was ill-supplied and untrained. As a result it, too, had to be dismantled. The replacement lighthouse was completed in

1859 and, at the time of this writing, has been standing for 164 years.

Despite there being no official record of a lighthouse in Cape May prior to 1823, there is a good deal of compelling evidence to suggest that such a structure was indeed in operation years before that.

First, maps from as early as 1744 show a light marker at Cape May (which was called "Cape Island" until the 1860s).

Second, in 1785 the Pennsylvania Board of Wardens purchased land on Cape May for the "purpose of erecting a beacon thereon for the benefit of navigation." That site is believed to be in front of present-day Congress Hall.

Third, in July of 1801, an advertisement appeared in a Philadelphia newspaper touting the beauty of the Jersey Cape and the accommodations and services available in Cape May. Among the descriptions of the enticing features in the growing resort area was the following statement: "[t]he situation is … in sight of the Lighthouse."

Fourth, there is genealogical evidence that a birth was recorded in 1815 (or possibly 1817) "in a lighthouse at Cape May, New Jersey."

And finally, Philadelphia, Pennsylvania, was (and still is) a critical destination in maritime trade. Ships from New York, Boston, other parts of New England, and Great Britain would have had to sail into the Delaware Bay and up the Delaware River to reach Philadelphia. It is highly likely that there was a lighthouse in existence in or near Cape May to safely guide those ships through the Bay and up toward Philadelphia before 1823.

It is in that lighthouse, long forgotten and officially undocumented, where this story takes place.

# CHAPTER 1

*I*t's hard to believe each day has the same number of hours. Some days seem to run by as if hitched to a wild horse.

Others, like Monday, the third day of September in the year of our Lord 1821, seem never to end.

The sound of a wagon racing past my house woke me earlier than usual that morning, its wheels rattling loud enough to rouse the dead. I pulled the bedroom curtain aside to look out the window and was met with the sight of swaying trees, black against a graphite sky. The wind had strengthened overnight. The wagon was already out of sight.

Sleep eluded me after that. I had been dreaming about Evelyn again and I knew from experience that the memory of her lovely face would permit me no further rest.

I made myself coffee and sipped the bitter brew while I pulled on my woolen shirt and trousers.

The last thing I did before heading out the back door was to pin on my badge, the only visible sign of my position in Cape Island. On days like this, when I was tired and in no mood for petty complaints from people in town, I contemplated not wearing the badge at all. But I always erred on the side of duty and fastened it to my shirt.

I walked to the stable where I kept my horse, Aces. I fed and watered her, then led her outside to the grassy paddock where she would remain until evening. I usually took her along with me wherever I went, but she had been lame for several days and I was resting her.

After mucking out the stable, I headed to work. Walking down Decatur Street in the dark, I saw no evidence of other folks who might be awake so early. Only me and that wagon driver, I supposed. Twice I had to hold onto my hat so it wouldn't blow off my head, so gusty was the wind. It felt good, though, after the hot summer we had endured. Before we knew it, there would be snow on the ground and it would be uncomfortably cold walking this early in the day. I was determined to enjoy the cool wind while I could.

Still, wind like this meant weather was on its way, and it wasn't uncommon for strong storms to crop up at this time of year. Once the sun rose, I planned to visit several farms where the elderly owners might welcome some assistance preparing for bad weather.

I unlocked the door to the tiny, one-room building I used, in part, as a cell. On occasion I held people in there for a short time before arranging their transport up to the jail in Cape May Court House. Other times, I let menfolk from town spend the night in there if they needed to sleep off the effects of too much drink before returning home to their angry wives. And several times, when a husband had raised a particularly heavy hand to his wife, I had slept in the cell to allow the woman to stay in my home while she waited for her man's ire to cool.

There was no one in the cell at present, so I had the small room to myself. When I became the sheriff's deputy three years before, I built a rough desk hewn from a downed tree and placed it next to the cell. Locks on the drawers kept my papers private. I sat behind the desk and unlocked the top drawer. The calendar I kept in there was blank for the day, which meant I had no duties to attend to on behalf of the sheriff or the court on that Monday morning. I leaned back in my chair and stared at the ceiling, my fingers intertwined behind my head. As long as I didn't have anything particular to do, I might as well wait for the sun to rise. I wished I could go back to sleep, if only for a short time.

The worst thing, I knew, was to sit idle. When I had nothing else to engage my mind, my thoughts always drifted to Evelyn, the unborn child she was carrying when she died, and the house in Cape Henlopen, Delaware, where we planned to raise our family. Such musings made for long days.

A hurried knock on the door mercifully interrupted the dark path my thoughts were beginning to take. "Come in." I leaned forward so all four feet of my chair were on the floor.

The door flung open and a breathless man strode into the small room. It was Joseph Whitman, a farmer from the outskirts of town. "Deputy Moore, old Abe Bradford is drunk as can be out at my house. He showed up a short while ago. He's a mean one when he's drunk. My son's watching him so he doesn't hurt anyone until you and I can get back there."

I was already on my feet and reaching for the key to lock the door behind me.

"Can I ride with you? Aces is lame."

"Of course."

I hurried after Joseph and jumped onto his horse behind him. I was well acquainted with Abe Bradford's tendencies when he'd taken too much drink—rum was his beverage of choice.

Joseph's horse was a fine, strong animal and he got us to the farm in less than fifteen minutes. Joseph tied him up while I started toward the house at a quick clip. Joseph caught up to me and we found his son watching over a snarling, cussing Abe

Bradford around the back of the house. Abe's hands were tied to a post with thick rope. Joseph's son had a bloodied lip and his left eye was starting to purple and swell.

"I had to tie him up after he hit me," the young man said.

"You all right?" Joseph asked him. He nodded.

Joseph turned to Abe. "It's a lucky thing the deputy is here or I'd have my hands right around your neck for striking my boy." Then he spoke to me. "Deputy, what'll we do about this fella?"

I instructed him to hook the wagon to his horse. When he had done that, we dragged the spitting mad fellow and hoisted him into the back of the wagon. Though his hands were still tied, I thought it best to tie his feet, too. I sat in the rear of the wagon with him while Joseph drove us back to the cell. He helped me haul Abe inside, where I untied Abe's hands and feet, narrowly escaping injury from the violent kicking and fist-swinging that ensued. I slammed the cell door shut behind me and locked it with a metallic *click*. I exhaled deeply and thanked Joseph for his help. Before he returned to his farm, I made him promise he would fetch the doc to look at his son's injuries.

Abe was still snapping at me after Joseph left. I didn't reckon I needed that so early in the morning. I pointed my finger at him and said, "Abe, go to sleep. You can't leave here until you've sobered up. And depending on what the doc says about the injuries you caused to Joseph's boy, you may be going straight up to Cape May Court House to see the judge."

I let Abe brood on that for a while as he quieted down. I made notes in my logbook about my trip out to Joseph's house and by the time I finished my account, the sky had brightened. I left the small building and headed out on my patrol. I would attend to Abe after he had some sleep. I left the door to the office unlocked so one of my neighbors, Daniel, could look in on him.

I was raising my hand to knock on Daniel's door when I heard footsteps pounding. I glanced up and saw Titus Fuller running across the road in the distance. I knew it was him even from far away—he always wore a red homespun shirt his mama made for him. He waved to me enthusiastically.

Titus, along with his younger brother and sister and their parents, were slaves living on a farm just outside of town. A New Jersey law enacted in 1804 decreed that although slave parents wouldn't be freed, any child born into slavery after the date the law was enacted would be free in a certain number of years. Under the law, Titus and his brother would be free when they reached the age of twenty-five, and his sister the age of twenty-one. I knew the siblings were all born after 1804, but I didn't know their precise ages. I often wondered how many more years they would have to wait. No matter the number of years, it was too long.

I returned Titus's wave with a broad smile as Daniel opened his door and invited me inside. I asked him to take Abe some food and water later in the morning. I paid him to do that on occasion—it helped me because I didn't have to prepare extra food for people in the cell and it helped Daniel because he appreciated the small amount of money I gave him.

Besides that, I trusted him. I had even provided him with a key to the cell in case of emergency. After speaking with him, I visited several farms to help the older farmers stable their live-stock and remove debris from around their houses. I went home for a quick dinner at noontime, then returned to the cell to see if Abe was ready to go home.

He was sleeping soundly, snoring like a contented sow, so I figured I'd let him rest a while longer. It couldn't hurt, and his wife would thank me for making sure he was cold sober before sending him home. I left the building and looked skyward. Clouds the color of slate scudded by. The wind was strength-ening and weather was barrelling in, so I made haste and headed toward the lighthouse. I hadn't visited the lighthouse keeper and his family in several weeks.

# CHAPTER 2

*H*enry Brewster had been the lighthouse keeper for years, long before I arrived in New Jersey. He was approximately forty years of age, with a short stature, a wide nose, and a raspy voice that sounded as if he had caught a chill standing too long in the rain. I knew him to be hard-working and serious.

His wife, Abigail, was a winsome and fetching woman who, I suspected, had known wealth at one time. She spoke with a refinement that seemed out of place in Henry's home, and whenever I saw her there was a book nearby. She always had a kind word for me. The last time I saw her, though, only a week earlier when I had chanced to meet her in the general store, she looked wan and tired. Her face was thinner than I remembered, but when I asked after her health, she would only say she had been feeling slightly unwell for a few days. She assured me she was much improved. A woman of lesser breeding might have regaled me with repellent details, but not Abigail.

Henry and Abigail had a son, Jeremiah, who had grown up at his father's side, learning the job of lighthouse keeping. I was fond of Jeremiah. He was a young man of curiosity and intelligence, and like his mother, he always had a kind word for me. The same could not be said for everyone in Cape Island.

It was early afternoon by the time I reached the lighthouse. The wind increased in strength during the time it took me to walk the few miles from town. I cast my eyes across the vast Delaware Bay where it joined forces with the mighty Atlantic Ocean. Whitecaps tumbled on the water, a telltale sign of bad weather moving toward the cape. Great gusts of wind blew in from the south, forcing sand from the nearby dune to eddy in the air. I shielded my eyes with my hand. The sea grasses at my feet bowed and dipped, their heads craning toward the north. Thick mists of water whipped over the small bluff cradling the foundation of the lighthouse and cottage. A piece of seaweed, still bright green and slick with salt water, assailed my face and slid down my cheek to land on the ground and somersault away. Seagulls wheeled in the sky overhead, rushing inland from the open sea. I was old enough to recall the Great Storm of 1806—it had started in much the same way, though I'd experienced it from the other side of the Delaware Bay. Hard to believe fifteen years had passed since that awful storm.

I walked up the sandy path leading to the Brewsters' cottage and knocked heavily on the solid wooden door. I waited for several moments, then knocked again. There had to be someone inside—Henry would surely be preparing for the coming storm. The original staircase to the top of the light was outside the tower, but after the small wooden keeper's cottage was added to the structure, a new circular staircase had been built inside the tower so the keeper wouldn't have to go out-of-doors to reach the light. Perhaps the family was working in the tower.

After an eternity, I heard a voice on the other side of the door. I had to strain my ears to hear over the wind.

"Who's there?"

"It's me, Deputy Moore."

An iron bar scraped against the door, which swung open on

well-oiled hinges. Jeremiah stood before me, his giant frame
filling the doorway. I knew him to be approximately twenty
years of age, but his large size and grizzled beard made him
seem older. His long, dark hair was disheveled.

"Good afternoon, Jeremiah."

The young man nodded, his piercing blue eyes scanning the
sky. "Afternoon."

"I've come to see if you and your father need any help to
prepare for the storm. I'll be glad to lend a hand if necessary."

Jeremiah made a gruff noise. I blinked in surprise—this
ungracious young man before me wasn't the good-natured
person I had grown accustomed to.

"Mind if I come in? Get out of this wind?"

Jeremiah seemed to consider the request, then took one step
backward and inclined his head toward the living area
behind him.

"Thank you." I stomped my boots on the planks outside the
door before stepping through the low entryway. I ducked my
head reflexively. That was one thing I didn't like about coming
out here to the lighthouse—the ceilings and doorways were so
low that a man of my height feared he might bang his head by
standing up straight. It was a wonder Jeremiah wasn't always
nursing an injury to his head. The young man was taller
than I.

Jeremiah closed the door with a loud *thump* and brought the
iron bar down over the latch. He preceded me into the parlor of
the small dwelling, then disappeared into his tiny bedroom
tucked under the tower staircase. The parlor was typically quite
dim, but that day it was even darker—I could see from where I
stood that the kitchen shutter was closed, and I suspected the
shutters outside the bedroom and stairway windows were, too.
Normally they stayed open to let in the light and the breeze, but
with the storm brewing over the water, either Jeremiah or
Henry must have gone out-of-doors earlier to secure them over

the windows. A small amount of gray daylight filtered down the stairway from the tower.

Several oil lamps in the parlor burned with a cozy glow, but the room was warm and stuffy. I took off my coat and hung it on a peg on the wall. I turned around and gave a start when I saw a figure leaning against the doorway of the main bedroom.

"Abigail? Is that you? Are you ill?"

Henry's wife swallowed audibly and lifted a limp hand in greeting. "Hello, Deputy. I am a bit unwell, but I should think … I'll feel better before long. Would you care to sit down? I'm afraid …" She took a deep breath. "I'm afraid I'm not much of a hostess right now."

"Don't fret about me, Abigail. You need to get off your feet."

I moved toward her. The poor woman needed help. I was about to call out to Jeremiah for assistance when he emerged from his bedroom.

"Jeremiah, please help me. Your mother is ill."

"What do you want me to do?"

"I want you to help me make her comfortable."

The young man came over to stand beside Abigail. I took one of her arms and instructed Jeremiah to take the other. "Over here," I said, gesturing with my head toward the fireplace, but Abigail let out a sound of protest.

"Please, I'd like to … lie down in my room."

I could see her a bit better now that I was standing so close to her. I caught my breath at the change in her aspect. In contrast to her thin, pallid appearance at the general store, her entire body was swollen—her fingers like sausages, her neck lumpy and thick.

Jeremiah's eyes met mine in the dimness. I had a feeling I knew what he was thinking—it was improper for me to accompany his mother into her bedroom. Nevertheless, I moved with small steps in that direction. Under the circumstances, her health was more important than propriety.

He acquiesced and helped me lead her to the side of the bed. An oil lamp sat on the bedside table, its flame low and meager. I let go of Abigail's arm and watched as Jeremiah helped her lie back against the feather pillows. She groaned as she shifted onto her side.

Jeremiah followed me from the room. In the doorway, I turned around and glanced at the ailing woman again. I nodded my head toward the other side of the parlor, indicating I wanted to talk to Jeremiah privately. A moment later I faced him and asked in a low voice, "She's gotten much worse since I saw her last. Should I fetch the doctor?"

"Says she don't want the doctor."

"But—"

I was interrupted by a terrific clattering noise from the kitchen. I am not typically a man who scares easily, but the sound gave me a start. I wondered what caused it—if I knew Henry Brewster, the man would not set foot in the kitchen to prepare a meal, no matter how sick his wife was. It had to be someone else.

A woman appeared in the kitchen doorway. It was Deborah Archer, who lived on a farm up the road. I had forgotten the Brewsters paid Deborah and her husband, Kit, to deliver supplies to the lighthouse every week.

"I dropped a kettle," she said.

"Hello, Deborah." I dipped my chin toward her.

"Good afternoon," she said crisply.

"With the storm brewing, I wanted to check on Henry and his family, see if they need my help for anything."

"Kit and I have brought all their supplies and Kit's helping Henry now. You needn't have come all this way."

"Part of the job." I smiled at her, but her countenance remained impassive. Dressed in a gray day gown with an ivory homespun pocket tied around her waist, she was thin and angular. Wisps of graying hair escaped the cap she wore. I knew she and Abigail shared a friendship borne of necessity, being the only two women this far out on the cape.

I looked over my shoulder. "Are they up in the tower?"

Deborah nodded.

Jeremiah was still standing in the parlor, listening to us talk. I turned toward him. "May I go upstairs and talk to your father and Kit?"

"Do what suits you."

I wanted to ask Jeremiah what was troubling him, but that would have to wait. I needed to make sure Henry had everything he needed in advance of the storm. I'd been up to the top of the lighthouse before. It was a heady experience—I could see miles in every direction. Today it would be interesting to see the storm approaching over the water from such a height.

But I had climbed only as far as the first of four landings on the steep, circular wooden staircase leading to the tower before men's voices reached me. Henry and Kit were headed down. I retreated and waited for them in the parlor.

Kit reached the bottom first. "Hello, George," he greeted me. Never did a man's voice suit his physical appearance so aptly. Kit was tall and rugged, with a deep, booming voice and an enviable head of dark brown hair. "What brings you out this way?"

"Hello, gentlemen. Henry, I came out to see if there's anything I can do to help you and the family with this storm coming. No telling how strong it'll get."

"Thank you, Deputy," Henry said. "Kit and Deborah brought sufficient provisions for the next week and we're battened down. Care for any coffee? I think Deborah made some."

"I believe I will."

Deborah emerged from the kitchen a minute or two later with a tray of tin coffee cups, a steaming pitcher, and a small jug of molasses. She set the tray down on the table where the Brewsters ate their meals and poured coffee into each cup. She passed them out to the men, including Jeremiah, who accepted his with a murmur of thanks. He added a hefty portion of molasses and took the coffee to his bedroom.

I gestured toward the main bedroom and spoke to Henry in a low voice. "I saw Abigail a week ago and she said she was feeling better. I'm sorry she's ill again."

Henry shook his head. "She felt better for a few days, but she's been sick again since Friday last. She's been back and forth to the privy a thousand times if she's been once."

"Jeremiah says she doesn't want the doc to come out."

"Naw. She says she'll feel better 'afore long. I b'lieve she's prob'ly right. She's been using the privy less and less since yesterday morning." Henry paused. "Will you excuse me, George? I need to run up to the tower."

"Certainly."

I spoke briefly with Kit while I finished my coffee. "I need to head back to town before the storm hits. You and Deborah ought to be getting back home, too."

Deborah spoke up. "The deputy's right. It looks to be quite a storm."

The sound of retching coming from the bedroom interrupted us. Deborah and Kit and I exchanged glances. I looked toward the stairs, hoping to hear Henry's footsteps descending, but he was still up in the tower. I considered shouting for him, but as I moved toward the stairway, the retching became worse. It sounded as if Abigail was being torn apart.

I turned away from the stairs and went to stand in the bedroom doorway. I paused only a moment before saying anything. It wasn't my place to attend to Abigail, but I was concerned for her. From what little I knew of her, I suspected she had a delicate constitution.

She groaned.

"You all right, Abigail?"

"I'm fine, Deputy." She inhaled noisily and retched again. "No need to ... worry about me." Abigail's words were followed by strident gagging and wet gurgling. It lasted for several long moments, then she could be heard taking deep breaths. It was a worrying sound.

"Maybe I should send the doc around," I suggested. "He can head out directly after the storm moves through."

"Don't trouble yourself or the doc ... it's just a bit of sour stomach ..." Her frail, shaky voice wavered as she breathed deeply between words.

"If you say so." I intended to call on the doctor on my way back to town whether she wanted me to or not. If Abigail had indeed been sick like this for several days and refused to consult with the physician, then it was up to someone else to make sure it got done. I didn't like to see a woman suffer.

I retrieved my coat and stuffed my arms into it. I was eager to get out of the hot, airless cottage. "You all take care in this storm. Looks like it'll be a big one." I was reaching for the iron latch on the door when a shout rang from the lighthouse tower.

# CHAPTER 3

"*B*oat!" Jeremiah burst from the room below the stairs at his father's call. I had never seen him move with such urgency. He leapt toward the door, but turned around as Henry came into view, trundling down the stairs on his short legs. Henry shouted, "There's a boat broken apart out there. Sailors in the water. I'll need all hands. Jeremiah, you get rope from the barn. Kit and George, come with me. Be quick." He grabbed a spyglass from a shelf next to the door and bolted outside. Jeremiah, Kit, and I followed.

Henry ran full tilt around the cottage before disappearing from sight. The strength of the wind didn't seem to slow him down in the slightest. Jeremiah raced toward the large outbuilding behind the lighthouse. When Kit and I had descended the shallow bluff and caught up to Henry, he was standing on the shore, scanning the water with the spyglass pressed to his right eye. The sky had grown darker and the wind howled with biblical force. The water heaved angrily, the waves rising and falling to impossible crests and troughs. The storm had strengthened by a surprising degree even since I arrived at the lighthouse.

"There they are," Henry shouted, pointing slightly to the southeast. I squinted, trying to follow his finger.

"I see them," Kit yelled. He grabbed my shoulder. "There." He pointed in the same direction as Henry.

I caught a glimpse of a piece of wood sticking straight up out of the waves, but it disappeared as soon as I tried to focus on it. "Is that part of the boat?" I yelled. A gust of wind roared off the water, threatening to topple us into each other. I stood with my feet wide and anchored my heels into the sand to stay upright.

Kit nodded grimly. "Henry, what do you want us to do?" he yelled.

Henry motioned for us to step closer to him. He shouted so we could hear him above the noise from the wind and the waves. A moment later Jeremiah appeared at a loping run around the corner of the cottage carrying a thick, coiled rope in his arms. The full force of the wind must have hit him hard, because he stopped abruptly and staggered a moment before putting his head down and barrelling toward us.

"We can't take the lifeboat out. It'll be more a hindrance than a help." Henry's bushy brows furrowed. "I saw at least three people. I'll tie the rope around my waist and swim out to reach them."

Kit wore a dark frown as he looked down at Henry. "That's foolish, Henry. You'll drown as sure as I'm standing here."

"Just do what I tell you to do!" Henry roared. Kit looked taken aback. Henry pointed to Jeremiah. "Hand me the end of the rope." Jeremiah fumbled for the end of the rope and thrust it at Henry, who quickly tied it around his waist, securing it with a tight knot. He faced us. "I'm going out there. Kit, tie the other end of this rope to that iron ring." He pointed to a large iron ring stuck into the outer wall of the cottage. Jeremiah heaved the coil toward Kit, who found the other end of the rope and ran toward the ring.

"God's teeth, hurry!" Henry barked. "Jeremiah, go back to the barn and bring all the rope you can find. One of you'll have to get into the water if I can't get to everyone out there."

Jeremiah turned and ran to do his father's bidding. Henry tore off his boots and threw his spyglass to the ground. As soon as Kit tied the rope to the ring, Henry didn't waste a moment before running headlong toward the violent water. He plunged in, his knees high-stepping until the water was too deep to walk. Kit and I watched as he dived under the waves, then emerged several feet away, his muscular arms powering through the rising and falling surf. Every few moments he would stop and splutter as the briny water hit him full force in the face. Henry was remarkably strong. He continued plowing his way forward, stopping briefly several times to look around. Whenever a sailor's head or limb was visible above the surface of the water, he would continue swimming in that direction. There seemed no end to the length of that rope.

Two of the sailors seemed to have recovered their wits— they lifted up their arms weakly and attempted to swim toward Henry. Waves thundered and wind howled as Henry reached them. His legs must have been churning with profound stamina under the surface of the water, because he was able to stay in the same place without being bandied about. He gestured toward the shoreline and shouted something to the men, then scanned the water again.

The two men took hold of the rope that trailed away from Henry's waist. Hand over hand, they inched their way toward us while Henry continued to tread water, sweeping his gaze over the dark, seething expanse.

From the shore, I could just make out the third man. He disappeared under the water several times. Henry couldn't have seen him because the waves around him were too high.

Jeremiah had returned with armloads of rope. "I'm going out there," I yelled to him and Kit. Jeremiah tossed one end of a rope to me and handed Kit the other end. Kit ran to secure it to the iron ring. I dashed into the churning surf, but as I got closer to the two swimmers approaching shore, they let go of Henry's rope and made grasping motions at me. One man grabbed my left arm while the other took hold of my right. They must have thought the water was shallower than it was. I started sinking. I kicked mightily, trying to get my head above water and shouting at them to let go, but drowning men are desperate souls. They will clutch at anything nearby. I took in great gulps of salty water as the waves closed over my head several times.

Finally I could no longer tell which way was up and which down. I could not see daylight. My body tumbled in the rough sea as if I had no will of my own. There was no breath left in me. I felt my muscles loosen. I heard myself crying out weakly, "Help!" as I sank deeper into the sea.

Then something exploded in the water next to me, dragging me into the air. I spluttered and choked, shocked to find Jeremiah's arm around my chest. The two men who had been grasping my arms were several yards away.

I looked behind me. Kit, too, was in the water now, running clumsily toward the two men, who were close enough to shore to be standing on the sea floor.

"Jeremiah! I'm all right! Go help your father." Now that no one was trying to climb my limbs to avoid a watery grave, I was able to catch my breath and twist my body toward shore. Jeremiah didn't need to be told twice. He immediately let go of me and cut through the water with strong, sure strokes toward Henry.

I was soon stumbling through the swells at the shoreline. Kit was attempting to haul both shipwrecked sailors out of the water.

All I wanted was to lie down on the sand and rest, but I

couldn't do that. I was the sheriff's deputy. It was my job to help. I tripped toward Kit and grabbed one man's arms while Kit grabbed the other's. Together, we struggled and huffed as we pulled their drenched bodies to safety.

As soon as the men were out of the water and lying face-down on the stretch of sand separating the sea from the base of the bluff, I turned back to locate Henry and Jeremiah. To my great relief, they had reached the third sailor. With one arm Henry held the sailor across the chest, so the man could lie on his back and catch his breath. With the other arm, he cleaved through the angry water. Jeremiah swam alongside them. I knew he would be able to take over if Henry exhausted himself or the man became wild with panic, as his fellow crewmen had done.

As soon as they were close to shore, I charged back into the water. When I was only a yard from Henry, I reached for the sailor just as Henry let go of him. Jeremiah floundered onto the wet sand, then immediately turned around to help his father. He was so much taller than Henry that he practically lifted him right out of the water. I pulled the third sailor to safety away from the pounding surf.

Once on land, the man fell to his knees and crawled forward, finally collapsing in a heap. His companions were still panting. They both looked up at the third sailor and let their heads fall onto the sand again.

I finally disgorged the salt water I had taken in and turned toward the rest of the group, wiping the back of my hand across my mouth.

"Was there anyone else in the boat?" I asked.

The first two sailors shouted "no" in unison while the third shook his head as if it were made of cast iron.

"We need to get indoors," I yelled into the wind. One fat raindrop pelted my face. The first two sailors struggled to their knees while I pulled on the arms of the third sailor to help him stand. As I did so, Henry, who had been kneeling next to me, gazed closely at the first two men whose lives he had saved. He inhaled sharply. Jeremiah walked forward and stood next to his father. He stared at the third sailor blankly, then turned to the other two and spit an oath too rude to repeat. He and Henry exchanged a look of utter dismay.

# CHAPTER 4

*I* did not have time to wonder why Henry and Jeremiah seemed aghast at recognizing two of the men they had rescued. We all needed to get inside as quickly as possible. Talking among ourselves was nearly impossible as we made our way up to the cottage, so we used our energy to lean into the wind rather than to speak. The raindrops fell harder and faster, stinging my face.

I was acquainted with the two sailors. Otto Schuhmacher farmed a small plot of land a few miles distant from Cape Island. He was shorter than I, thin and wiry, a coarse man. I knew him to be quick to anger. He had the weathered skin of someone who spent his life working out-of-doors. His hair, which was the color of wet sand, was always unkempt and his hoary beard was customarily filthy. He was about forty years of age, at least ten years older than I.

Otto's cousin, August Schuhmacher, ran the smithy in Cold Spring, not far from Cape Island. He was barely tolerated among the folks on the cape due to frequent complaints that he thought it good fun to instigate fights. It was my understanding that the cousins, who were about the same age, had come to the cape with their families when they were children. They hailed from hardy German stock who had traveled to the area from parts north in Pennsylvania. With his tall, lanky frame, August looked nothing like his cousin. He wore his beard short, but had thick brown hair and unruly eyebrows.

I was not familiar with the third man. His hair, the color of jet, gave him a devilish look. He was diminutive and portly, with hands the size of bear paws.

I suspected Henry and Jeremiah knew of the reputations of Otto and August and were dismayed at the prospect of having the cousins together in the lighthouse cottage. But they had no choice. Otto, August, and their companion had nearly drowned and would need to rest and recuperate indoors, at least for a short time.

The force of the wind pushed us through the door and into the warm cottage. Henry told Jeremiah to accompany him up to the lighthouse tower to scan the water for other people or boats, and the two men departed with haste. I motioned the three bedraggled sailors into the parlor. I asked each of them several questions to assure myself none of them were seriously hurt. Thankfully, their only injuries were minor cuts, bruises, and some ingested seawater.

Deborah hurried into the room from the kitchen. "Mercy me!" She bustled around, moving chairs and bringing stools from the kitchen so the men could sit. She placed two split logs on the already-blazing fire. "This will soon warm you. We need to get all of you out of your wet clothes before you take sick."

Her eyes widened. "Otto and August, is that you? Why, I barely recognized you in this low light. What were you doing out there in such weather?"

Without waiting for an answer, she turned to me. "I know this is improper, but you'll have to go into the bedroom to find dry clothes for Otto and—what is your name?" She addressed the man with the impossibly black hair.

"Philemon Grebbes."

She turned back to me. "And for Mr. Grebbes. Look in Henry's bureau. Otto and Mr. Grebbes look to be about the same size as him." She inclined her head toward the bedroom where Abigail lay.

I knocked on the door frame and heard a feeble, "Come in."

"I'm sorry, Abigail, but I need to get some clothes from Henry's bureau for the men he rescued."

She groaned, which I took for permission to enter. I reached over the half-eaten bowl of soup on the bedside table, nearly knocking it to the floor, and grasped the handle of the oil lamp behind it. Peering closely at the lamp, I turned the knob on the side of it to increase the height of the wick and the flame. In the flickering of the stronger light, I glanced at Abigail and was alarmed by what I saw.

Her skin, which had heretofore borne the look of fine porcelain, was an unsightly yellow. Somewhere in the back of my mind, a grim memory surfaced—a somber memory of a different woman with yellow skin. I shook off a rising feeling of dread and turned away.

I was moving toward the bureau I assumed to be Henry's when he burst into the room. I hadn't even heard him coming downstairs.

"I'll get the clothes for Otto and that other man, Deputy. It ain't right for you to be in here." His voice was only made raspier, I noted, by his foray into the water. He frowned and I left immediately, chastised by his brusque rebuke.

He came into the parlor wearing dry clothes several minutes later, then shut the bedroom door behind him. He carried a bundle of clothing under each arm—dry things for Philemon Grebbes and Otto, and his own wet things.

Over the next half hour, Kit and August and I obtained dry clothes from Jeremiah, and the four of us took turns using Jeremiah's room to change. I suppressed a grin when we were all assembled in Jeremiah and Henry's clothes. I had to roll up Jeremiah's trouser legs because his pants were a bit too long on me. August had to do the same, and roll up the shirt sleeves, too. Kit looked almost natty in Jeremiah's well-fitting green trousers and an ivory shirt. Otto fit neatly into Henry's clothes, but it looked like Philemon might burst out of his garments.

Deborah had amassed a pile of wet clothes from all of us. "Deputy, would you please help me string a rope across the kitchen? I'll need to hang these clothes quickly so they dry." She shook her head and made a *tsk, tsk* sound. "There's sand everywhere. Poor Abgail would not like that. I'll have to sweep it up."

I left my seat and accompanied her to the kitchen, wondering why she didn't ask her husband to help her. Deborah was one of the people who made no secret of her disdain for me when I became deputy, and I disliked having to speak to her. It was best when she and I could avoid each other.

Kit watched us go, a wary look on his face. I had heard the rumors that he disciplined Deborah harshly, but I had not seen evidence of it. If those rumors were true, perhaps she was glad of someone to help her besides Kit. With the light from one of the oil lamps, we rummaged through the kitchen shelves until we found a length of sturdy rope. With her help, I tied one end of it around a hook next to the kitchen door and the other end around an iron nail that Abigail used to hang a cooking pot from the opposite wall. Together we hung up the clothes in silence, then I returned to the parlor.

The heat had become intolerable in the keeper's cottage, and with the moisture from the clothes and everyone's hair rising in the air, the small space was stuffy and damp. I imagined this must be what a jungle felt like. I had read stories about jungles, and they were always described as suffocating places where the moisture in the air was palpable.

Eventually I tired of the silence. I turned to Philemon, the black-haired stranger.

"Where do you hail from?"

He glanced sidewise at his two companions. "Up north."

"What brought you to these waters with Otto and August?"

"Fishing."

"Oh? I do a little fishing myself. What were you fishing for?"

The three sailors answered simultaneously.

"Scup."

"Chub."

"Bream."

"Did you catch any before the storm blew up?" They nodded. I chuckled. "At least those fish got another chance."

Otto and August and their friend did not think my comment was humorous. They scowled in response and I stopped talking. Some men take their fishing too seriously.

While all the men sat silently in the parlor, Deborah busied herself in the kitchen. I hoped she was preparing food, because I was hungry after the work of rescuing the sailors and would appreciate some sustenance before leaving for town. I poked my head into the kitchen and found her behind the wet clothes. She stood at the long wooden worktable against the back wall, chopping vegetables. Two kettles bubbled on the cast iron stove. They smelled good. Holding an oil lamp aloft, I peeked into them.

"I smell beef soup and mushroom soup. Delicious. You'll all enjoy a good meal later," I said, trying to show her how personable I could be. "Deborah, I'm going to head back to town soon. There are people who might need my help in the storm. And my horse is still in her paddock, so I need to stable her. There's a man asleep in the cell, too, so I have to do something with him. Do you think I might have something to eat before I leave?"

She set her knife down and sighed.

"I can't get a moment's peace. Yes, I'll feed you. Go back to the parlor and wait for me in there. I'll bring in enough for everyone. What are you going to do about your clothes? They're still soaking wet, you know."

"I'll wear Jeremiah's clothes for now, but I'll be back after the storm to retrieve my own trousers and shirt." A sense of urgency was beginning to rise in my chest—this storm was strengthening rapidly and I had a bad feeling about it.

"Well, you do what you see fit to do."

I returned to the parlor, my mood growing rapidly more foul. Talking to the woman left me unsettled and peeved. After three years, hadn't I done enough to prove I deserved my post?

Still, when she came into the parlor with a loaf of bread and a crock of butter, I thanked and praised her profusely for her kindness. We all partook of the bread and butter, then I stood to leave. I put my hat firmly on my head and bid everyone goodbye and good luck in the storm.

"You sure you want to leave, Deputy?" Henry asked. "The storm's bound to have gotten worse while we've been indoors."

"Thank you, Henry, but I have a job to do. I'll check back after the storm passes." I opened the door cautiously.

In an instant, thick raindrops hurled themselves at me while the wind roared and whipped the hat from my head. I yelled out in surprise and watched in dismay as the hat flew away, dipping and tumbling in the wind. The other men crowded into the cottage doorway to get a look at the storm.

I nodded goodbye to them and stepped outside. No sooner had I left the shelter of the cottage doorway but the wind knocked me right to my knees. Flying sand stung my eyes and I squeezed them shut as I struggled to stand upright. Henry and Kit took hold of my arms and dragged me back toward the cottage.

There was no way I could make it back to Cape Island in this storm.

And the worst part of it was, this was only the beginning.

# CHAPTER 5

*H*enry and Kit led me to a chair in the parlor. "Sit here. I'll tell Deborah to fetch some water from the kitchen to bathe your eyes. You need to get that sand out of there," Kit said.

A moment later I gratefully accepted a bowl of water and a soft rag from Deborah's hands.

"Do you need help?" she asked. Her tone made it clear she hoped I did not.

"No, thank you." Squinting in pain, I wiped my eyes again and again until I could feel them becoming clearer and the pain lessening. Deborah refilled the bowl several times. Finally, I immersed my face in the water and opened my eyes, moving my head gently from side to side. That seemed to get the remainder of the sand out.

Kit stood nearby, watching. "Well," I said to him and Deborah. "You two won't be able to get back to your farm. It looks like we're all in here together until the storm lets up."

"Hopefully it won't last long," Kit said. Deborah glanced toward him and nodded.

I rubbed my temples. There was no way to get a message to

town—I hoped Daniel, my neighbor, remembered that Abe Bradford was in the cell. And I hoped he realized Aces was still in her paddock. I had to admit to myself that I worried more about my horse than I did about Abe.

It wasn't just the worry over Aces and Abe that had me concerned, though. I didn't relish spending the duration of the storm in this house where I knew a current of discontent throbbed below the surface—and it wasn't simply because Henry and Jeremiah didn't want the three men from the boat in their house.

I was a relative outsider in this county, having lived in Cape Island for only three years. I hailed from Cape Henlopen, across the Delaware Bay. Normally the people of Cape Island became easily accustomed to outsiders and eventually thought of them as friends and acquaintances, but it was different with me because of my job.

Most of the people in the area assumed someone from within their own citizenry would take on the job of deputy after the previous lawman became too ill to serve. But in fact, the sheriff chose me *because* I was an outsider. He wanted someone who would command more respect from the people hereabouts. He thought they would be less inclined to give in to temptation, whether it be moral or legal, if the new deputy wasn't a good friend or close relative of anyone in town.

I agreed the idea was a good one, but I hadn't expected the fiery opposition that arose among folks of Cape Island and its environs.

Those folks included people in this lighthouse. Deborah was one, of course. I supposed I would know before the storm was over whether Kit shared her opinion. Otto and August were two more. Henry and his wife and son had never made me feel unwelcome so I assumed they didn't oppose my presence in town, though I couldn't be sure.

But despite being stuck in the cottage with people who

opposed me, I had a job to do. I had to keep them safe. I had to prove to them that I was worthy of the position I held.

And that is precisely what I intended to do.

I looked up from where I sat, noticing once again how very warm it was. "Is anyone else as hot as blazes?"

Deborah frowned and turned from where she was clearing bowls and utensils from the table. "I should think you'd take a few logs off that fire if you're too hot." She was the one who had added more wood to the fire when all the men came in from rescuing the three sailors, I thought irritably. She moved toward the kitchen and spoke over her shoulder. "And maybe turn down a couple of the oil lamps."

Henry began lowering the wicks in several of the lamps while I reached the long iron tongs into the fire and carefully removed the largest log, setting it on the brick hearth. I repeated my movements with another large log, then replaced the tongs.

"That should help," I said.

"It is pretty dang hot in here," August said.

"Now it's too dark, though," Philemon said. I didn't say anything aloud, but I agreed with him. The logs left in the fireplace burned low, and the room was significantly darker now. A small amount of gray daylight filtered down from the lighthouse tower, but it wasn't nearly enough to see clearly. My eyes were adjusting well enough to discern facial expressions, but not much more.

Henry sighed. "Do you want to be cooler, or do you want to see everything in the room?" His voice was tinged with impatience.

"No need for a sharp tongue," Philemon said. "I was only observing."

"Well, observe to yourself," Henry muttered.

"I didn't ask to be brought in here," Philemon said.

Jeremiah snorted. "I s'pose you preferred drownding?"

I fought the urge to correct the young man's grammar while Philemon shot him a baleful look. I hoped Philemon's temper wouldn't prove to be as dark as the color of his hair.

"All right, gentlemen." My voice was firm. "It looks like we're going to be here until the storm lessens. It's mighty kind of Henry and his family to let us stay in the cottage, so let's be grateful for the hospitality and keep our uncharitable thoughts to ourselves." I hoped not only that Philemon would heed my words, but that Henry and Jeremiah would, too. It was, indeed, hospitable of them to allow the rest of us to stay at the cottage for the time being, but it was also the keeper's duty to provide shelter and assistance when necessary. This cottage didn't belong to Henry Brewster—it belonged to his employer, the Treasury Department of the United States. Henry had a responsibility to help. And there could be no doubt his help was necessary under the circumstances. This storm was only getting bigger.

Philemon grumbled something under his breath, but thankfully no one asked him to repeat himself. I had no doubt his words would have set off another angry exchange.

The minutes dragged by and Otto suggested a game of cards to pass the time. Henry found a deck in his bureau drawer and handed them to Otto, who dealt. The three men from the boat, plus Kit and I, now sat close together around two tables we dragged next to each other in the parlor. Henry declined to play, watching the rest of us with hooded eyes, while Jeremiah retreated to his bedroom.

For a long time the only sounds were the slap of the cards, occasional voices requesting a new hand, Deborah's movements in the kitchen, and the howl of the wind as it shrieked around the lighthouse and the cottage.

The card game had gone on for almost an hour when there was a moan from the bedroom. Henry looked up from where he sat in a corner. "Abigail, you all right in there?"

She moaned again in response. Henry pushed his chair back from the table and went into the bedroom. We could all hear the chamber pot being moved on the floor and Abigail retching. Henry returned a few minutes later.

"She all right?" I asked.

"What's wrong with her, anyhow?" August's eyes widened. "I don't want to be catchin' nothin' while we're stuck in this house."

"I reckon we better not be sick as dogs when we leave here," Otto said.

Henry ignored them, but answered my question. "She just needs rest. She'll be all right."

I wasn't so sure.

"Sometimes only another woman can help a lady in distress," Deborah said as she bustled through the parlor. She stood in the doorway to the bedroom. "Abigail, what can I do to help you? Can I bring you some food or drink? More of that soup? You need to keep up your strength."

"No," came the anguished voice from the bed. "No, I have some ... left in here."

"Very well." Deborah sighed and returned to the kitchen.

Even though the fire was lower and Henry had turned down the lamps, heat still hung in the room like a velvet drapery. I wiped the sweat running from my brow and down my neck. I glanced around and noticed rings of moisture under the arms of the other men. Their foreheads glistened. Unpleasant odors emanated from all of us.

"I'm afraid I'm out, gentlemen." I lay my cards face-up on the table. "You all keep playing."

The men nodded and returned to their game while I leaned my head against the chair back and closed my eyes. I was dog-tired, as I had been awake since that wagon woke me before dawn, and the energy I had expended to help rescue the men from the churning waters had left me feeling quite spent.

# CHAPTER 6

*I* must have fallen asleep, because when Abigail's scream echoed through the small cottage, ricocheting off the walls, I jerked my head up, uncertain for a moment where I was.

Strange shadows danced on the walls from the low firelight, because only a scant amount of remaining gray daylight filtered down from the tower into the parlor. Through the fog in my brain, I saw the men around the table and recalled immediately everything that had happened since my arrival at the lighthouse hours before.

Jeremiah was coming down the stairs. He froze at his mother's scream. The other men—even Henry—were all staring at the bedroom door, as if terrified to get up and face what they might find behind it. I bolted from my chair, knocking it to the floor. I rushed into the bedroom, not caring how improper it was. I yanked the oil lamp from the bedside table and turned the wick up as high as it would go.

Abigail lay on the bed, writhing in pain. She clutched her abdomen. Sweat shone over all her visible skin, which had alarmingly turned several shades of yellow darker than it had been even a short while ago. "Make it stop!" she screamed.

"Let me get Henry," I said. I turned to run out of the room.

"No. No, please, you … mustn't. I don't want … him in here. He—" Abigail gasped and screamed, the horrible sound enveloping the room.

"He what?" I was stunned.

But by now everyone was crowded into the doorway behind me and Abigail didn't answer me. I touched her clammy forehead. "What's the matter, Abigail? Can you tell me?"

"Help me!"

"Deborah, come in here," I said. She stepped into the room, her eyes wide. "Lift up her frock and rub her stomach."

"What?" She looked at me as if I were witless. "That won't help a bit."

"Just do it. Please." I had no idea what else to do. "Henry? What should we do?" I asked. Henry stood just inside the bedroom door, looking ashen. He shook his head. I couldn't imagine why Abigail didn't want me to fetch him a moment ago, and I glanced at her quickly to see if she heard me speak to him. She gave no indication that she had. Her eyes were squeezed shut in pain.

Deborah did as I asked, though reluctantly. She gingerly lifted the hem of Abigail's nightgown and placed it around Abigail's midsection. She commenced rubbing Abigail's stomach. As she did so, the three sailors and Kit receded into the parlor.

"This isn't doing Abigail a whit of good, Deputy," Deborah said, the corners of her mouth turned in a deep frown.

"We can't just let her lie here like this," I snapped.

Abigail now clutched the sides of her abdomen, begging for the pain to stop. She used swollen, trembling fingers to tug her nightgown down over her stomach. Deborah stopped rubbing her stomach and stepped away.

Because my job requires me to help in emergencies, it was not uncommon for me to find myself in dire situations. I had attended sick houses with doctors on many occasions. I had even been present a few times as the patient succumbed to illness. But I had never seen a patient in pain the way Abigail was. Under ordinary circumstances, I would have run for the doctor, but in this storm it was impossible.

Abigail let out a long, tortured scream. Out of the corner of my eye, I saw Henry and Jeremiah in the doorway, their faces white with shock. They seemed rooted to the spot, unable to move further into the bedroom. Deborah put her hand on Abigail's forehead but jerked it away with a look of horror when foam began to erupt from Abigail's mouth. Deborah turned to me and opened her mouth as if to speak, but as she did that, Abigail's body shuddered and went motionless.

Deborah's mouth hung in the shape of an "o," as if she were trying to scream, but no sound came out. She reached out a tentative hand to touch Abigail's forehead, then drew back again. "Get a looking glass." Her words were so low, I had to strain to hear them over the sound of the wind.

I scanned the room quickly, then glared at Henry, who was still standing in the doorway. "Where's a looking glass?" I demanded. I was disgusted with the man, refusing to come near his wife in the moment of her greatest need.

He finally roused himself to action. He jerked open Abigail's top bureau drawer, pulled out a small glass, and thrust it at Deborah. She bent her head down to Abigail's chest, then held the mirror above the poor woman's mouth. She watched the mirror with fierce intensity for a full minute before placing it face-down on the coverlet. "There's no breath."

Abigail was gone.

Deborah looked closely at her friend's eyes, still anguished in death, and closed them with her fingertips.

I closed my mouth when I realized it was agape. My mind

reeled. How was it possible that Abigail had died before my eyes? Just a week ago she was feeling better. She and Henry both said so. How had she so quickly and so ferociously become ill again?

Henry now bowed his head as he stood over his wife's body. I watched him, my thoughts warring. I felt sorrow for the man and his son, but my blood burned with anger. Neither one had done anything to help her as her life ebbed away. It was unthinkable.

What were we to do now? I knew I wasn't the only one who didn't relish the idea of a corpse mere feet from where we all sheltered in the parlor. But there was no alternative. We couldn't even start preparing her body for burial. It was too dark, too stuffy, and too crowded in the small cottage, and there was no question of preparing the body out-of-doors. We would have to wait until the storm blew itself out to sea.

I shuddered. The echo of Abigail's scream reverberated in my ears. Suddenly the prospect of remaining in the cottage for the duration of the storm seemed even more dreadful.

If only I had known at the time that Abigail's death would not be the last.

# CHAPTER 7

*J*eremiah had retreated from the bedroom doorway and was presumably in his own room when Henry, Deborah, and I returned to the parlor. Deborah walked straight to the kitchen without another word. I closed the door behind me. I gazed around at the men in the parlor, who were as silent as stone, looking at their hands or the floor. Finally Kit looked up and addressed Henry. "Is she …?" His voice died.

Henry nodded his head slightly. "She's gone." His gaze didn't leave the floor. Kit murmured his condolences while the three sailors remained silent. Henry took a deep breath and nodded, then walked with heavy steps to the stairway leading to the tower.

I cleared my throat. "There's no way to get back to town right now to fetch the doctor. The storm's too great. We'll leave the bedroom door closed."

I sat in the chair farthest from the bedroom where Abigail's body lay. My thoughts were muddled and scattered. There was silence for several minutes before Otto, stroking his foul beard, spoke up. "What did she die of?"

"I don't know. We'll need the doc to answer that." My jaw clenched reflexively. I wondered if the close quarters we were sharing for the duration of the storm would result in the rest of us getting sick with whatever killed Abigail. It worried me—the men in the parlor hadn't seen Abigail's face. It had been a mask of unspeakable pain. And something else—was it fear? Fear that her disease would spread among those in the house? Fear of dying? Fear of something I couldn't name? The very thought of dying in such agony was chilling.

Another worry tickled the back of my mind, too. Something that flitted through my thoughts when Abigail insisted I not summon Henry. Something I was not ready to face.

The only sound inside the cottage came from the kitchen. I looked through the doorway to see Deborah vigorously scrubbing a large pot. She sported rings of perspiration around the neck and under the arms of her frock. Her hair had escaped her cap and hung limply around her face. Her pocket hung ponderously around her waist. I always wondered what females kept in those mysterious pockets.

"Are you all right?" I stepped into the kitchen.

She turned around with a start, placing her hand over her heart. "Oh! You startled me, Deputy. My nerves seem to be suffering, to tell you the truth. I'm trying to keep my mind and hands busy. I've seen people die before, but seeing Abigail pass in that way ... I never witnessed such a thing."

"Maybe you should rest."

Deborah shook her head. "I don't want to rest. I'll just see Abigail's eyes if I try to close my own. Besides that, where would I rest? Certainly not in the parlor with all those men."

"I'm sure Jeremiah wouldn't mind you using his bedroom."

"I'll stay in here, Deputy," she said primly.

I returned to the parlor, where Philemon had commenced pacing the perimeter of the room. It was unnerving. Kit sat in a corner away from the other men. He held an open book and was tilting it toward the oil lamp burning next to him, though I fancied his eyes were following Philemon's movements.

"What are you reading, Kit?" I asked.

Kit held his place with his finger while he turned the spine of the book toward me as if I could read it from where I stood. "It's 'Precaution' by James Fenimore Cooper. Good book, though I confess I'm having some difficulty concentrating just now because of ..." He nodded toward the room where Abigail's body lay. "I found it on a shelf over there." He pointed to a corner of the parlor. "I'm sure Henry wouldn't mind lending it to you sometime."

I had heard of the book. I had even seen a copy of it in the general store. It was expensive, with gold print on the spine and a leather cover. I was surprised Kit had found it in the cottage— I didn't know Henry to be particularly fond of reading. Perhaps it was Abigail's. "I would like to read it. Perhaps I'll ask Henry if I might borrow it."

Kit returned to his reading. Everyone looked up when heavy footsteps descended the wooden steps from the top of the light-house. Henry stood still when he reached the bottom. He looked as if he had added ten years to his face and body since going up to the tower.

"Where's Jeremiah?" he asked.

"I'm here." Jeremiah stood in the doorway to his bedroom.

"It's about time to wind the works," Henry said in a dull voice. He nodded toward the stairs. "And clean the east-facing windows while you're up there. There's soot all over them."

Jeremiah walked past Henry without a word. He trod slowly up the stairs.

"How are you doing, Henry?" I asked.

"I reckon I'll be all right."

"What is Jeremiah doing?" I needed to distract myself from the screaming winds outside. I needed to distract myself, too, from Philemon's relentless pacing, from the oppressive heat, and from the thought of Abigail's body lying close by. Useless conversation filled that need.

"He's winding the apparatus that keeps the light turning. It works on a chain system, like a clock. Has to be wound every two hours."

I nodded. I was about to ask another question, just as rote, when he turned and went into Jeremiah's room. He had no sooner closed the door behind him than the building shuddered and a deafening roar came from the side of the cottage facing the water. In the kitchen, Deborah screamed.

Kit gave a start and dropped his book. "Deborah!" he shouted. "What's all the screaming for?" He stood and strode to the kitchen. I joined him in the doorway.

"I'm sorry. That gave me a fright."

"What have you done now?" Kit asked angrily.

"Nothing," she snapped. "The noise came from outside." She nodded toward the shuttered window.

"My guess is that a wave slammed into the cottage," I said. I stepped between the two of them in case Kit was inclined to scold her for screaming. "From what I saw out there earlier, the water was bound to reach this height. We should expect more waves like that, I reckon."

"We're not very high above the dune," Deborah said. She cast an anxious look from me to her husband. He scoffed.

"Don't worry," I said. "This is a good, sturdy cottage. We'll be safe here while we ride out the storm." I believe I spoke the words to reassure myself as much as Deborah, but I wouldn't admit that to anyone. The foundation of the cottage and the lighthouse rested on little more than sand and faith.

# CHAPTER 8

*K*it and I returned to the parlor. He picked up his book again and I sat as far as I could from everyone, which wasn't nearly far enough. I didn't know how we were all going to pass the rest of the storm together without resorting to incivility borne of boredom and frustration.

I still reeled from the suddenness and cruelty of Abigail's death. I wondered if I should take another look at her body to see if there were any clues I could share with the doctor to help him determine the cause of the poor woman's passing. Such clues might help, too, if there was an inquest. I had already noted the yellow skin and swelling, but there may have been something else I missed. I tried not to think about the pain and anguish etched into Abigail's features, but I couldn't keep at bay the knowledge that she hadn't wanted her husband at her bedside as the hour of death neared.

As much as I tried not to, I returned again and again to the image of Henry and Jeremiah standing in the bedroom doorway, watching from a distance as Abigail breathed her last. Even if Abigail hadn't wanted Henry nearby, their inaction was unthinkable. If I could have been with Evelyn when she died, I would have held her hand. I would have told her I'd miss her every day as long as I lived. Lord in heaven, how I missed her.

But not Henry. He hadn't sent for the doctor when Abigail's illness returned on Friday. Did he even care that she was so sick? How could he watch his own wife suffer like that and do nothing about it? I didn't like the direction my thoughts were beginning to take, but I couldn't ignore the facts as they presented themselves.

Something about Abigail's death wasn't right.

Her appearance was frightful, and it had deteriorated much too quickly to be natural. Why, I had noticed an increase in the swelling of her features even between the time I arrived at the cottage and the time of her death. And her yellow skin was far too dark to have occurred at a natural pace. I was, unfortunately, intimately familiar with jaundice and the ravages of liver disease and people simply did not turn the color of millet and die within four days of becoming ill. Something had hastened the symptoms that led to her death, of that I was sure.

Beyond her appearance, the actions—or rather, the inactions —of her husband and her son were highly troublesome. And I couldn't forget Abigail's own words, beseeching me not to fetch Henry as her life ebbed away. I was certain she had been about to say something to me, perhaps to explain why she didn't want him there, but had never finished her sentence.

Why would Henry not have sent for the doctor? My mind followed the possibilities relentlessly. I could think of no good reason, but there was no shortage of wicked ones. Could it be that he didn't want the doctor to see her? That he didn't want the doctor to know something unsavory was going on inside the cottage until it was too late to save Abigail?

Could it be Henry didn't want Abigail to survive? I couldn't believe that was the case. But even if it were, wouldn't Jeremiah have fetched the doctor instead? Surely he didn't want his mother to die.

And why hadn't Abigail wanted Henry at her bedside? Did she have her wits about her sufficiently to know what was happening to her body? Did she suspect Henry had done something to make her so ill? I wondered if he had administered any medicine that might have made her worse.

One thing was becoming clear to me: Abigail hadn't caused her own death. Someone else had.

I swallowed my burgeoning alarm along with the bile that rose in my throat at the thought of a murder taking place right here in the lighthouse cottage.

Philemon had finally stopped pacing and was seated at the table, picking a scab from his knuckle. I shuddered. He looked up and his deep black eyebrows knit together in a frown. "When can we get out of this God-forsaken place?"

Deborah, who was standing in the doorway to the kitchen, gasped. "Mr. Grebbes, it's sinful to speak so."

"And what's sinful about it? Has God not forsaken this lighthouse and the cottage and the people inside?" Philemon's face twisted into a sneer.

"Of course God has not forsaken us or this cottage or the lighthouse," Deborah replied. "Are we not still alive and well in here? Are we not warm and safe?"

"We're alive for now. Can't say the same for Abigail," Philemon said.

Otto and August looked up from their hands of cards and stared at Philemon.

"What?" Philemon asked. "Do I offend you by speaking the truth?"

Both men avoided Philemon's defiant look.

*He's right*, I thought. Everyone but Abigail was alive, but if the storm continued to worsen and breached the safety of the cottage walls, could we assume everyone else would survive? I doubted so. This was the worst storm I had ever witnessed.

Kit had returned to his book while Philemon and Deborah were speaking. We passed many long minutes in silence.

"Deborah, is there any beverage in the kitchen?" Otto finally called out.

Deborah reappeared in the kitchen doorway. "Yes. Henry and Jeremiah brought some cider in from the storehouse before Kit and I arrived earlier today. I'll pour you some. Would anyone else like cider?"

"Might there be any rum out there?" Otto asked. "I'd rather have rum."

I noticed a glance pass between August and Philemon.

"I'll try to find some," Deborah said. I hoped there was no rum to be had.

Several minutes later she came into the parlor carrying a dark brown glass bottle and several cups. "I found this." She lifted the bottle. "I gather from the odor that it contains rum." She held it away from her as if it contained a lethal poison. She set it on the table before Otto, who uncorked it and passed it under his nose while she distributed cups around the table. I thought briefly about taking the rum from Otto before he could drink any of it, but decided to wait. Perhaps a wee bit of rum would serve to ease the strain in the house.

"Aye. This'll do a man good." Otto poured a large measure of rum into his cup and drank half of it in one swig. Sitting back in his chair, he closed his eyes and sighed.

"I'll have a nip of that," August said.

Otto handed the bottle to his cousin. August poured himself a draught, then one for Philemon.

"George, will you take a drink?" August asked.

"A small one, please." I was on duty, but had to admit a small drink might settle my rattling nerves.

August poured me a measure, then proffered the bottle to Kit.

Kit looked up from his novel. "No, thank you, gentlemen. I'd rather have cider." He flicked a glance toward Deborah, who rose quickly and hastened to the kitchen. She returned a moment later with a mug of cider, which she set down next to Kit. He ignored her and continued reading.

For a long while I listened as the three rescued sailors talked about crops and August's smithy. To my surprise, no one became intoxicated from the rum. Then again, I thought, they had probably only imbibed the amount they were accustomed to drinking. I needed to make sure they didn't drink more than that.

In the kitchen, Deborah prepared supper for everyone in the cottage. I listened to the storm rage outside, wondering if it could possibly intensify. How long could the lighthouse withstand such an onslaught of wind and water?

# CHAPTER 9

*I* was near to starving when Deborah finally announced supper was ready.

She was bustling into the parlor bearing a ceramic tureen of beef soup. She set it down heavily in the middle of the table where Otto, August, and Philemon were still sitting. She hurried back into the kitchen and returned with cups, spoons, bowls, and a large loaf of brown bread.

"I don't know what took you so long," Kit said.

"It's no easy task to work in these conditions," Deborah retorted.

There were two empty chairs at the table. Kit sat in one. I motioned to the last chair. "Deborah, please have a seat."

"Thank you."

Kit raised an eyebrow in her direction as she pulled the chair toward her. Noticing this, she took her hand off the chair and averted her eyes. "I'd rather stand. I'll take food upstairs to Jeremiah in a minute. I'm sure he must be able to eat a scabby horse by now," she said.

I waited my turn to take a ladleful of soup. Steam rose from the bowl and curled around my lips as I inhaled its aroma. The soup was delicious—a hearty mix of large chunks of salt beef, tomatoes, green and yellow squash, potatoes, corn, and onions. The brown bread was hefty and toothsome. As I ate, Henry emerged from Jeremiah's room. His eyes were sunken and surrounded by dark circles. He certainly wore the look of a man who had lost a beloved wife. But could I trust my eyes? Was he putting on a masquerade?

"You all right, Henry?" I asked. "Maybe I should take the next shift. You can show me what to do and then come back down here and get some more sleep."

"I'm fine," came his terse response.

"Does anyone else know how to operate the light?" I asked. "There looks to be a long night ahead of us. It might be helpful if someone other than you and Jeremiah knows how to operate the light in case of emergency." I left unsaid what such an emergency might entail.

"When Jeremiah's shift is over, I'll teach you how to operate the light. No need for anyone else to be going up there," Henry said.

I stood up and thrust my hands into my pockets. Henry frowned at all of us as his gaze swept the room, then he sat and helped himself to soup. His dark glare fell upon Kit, then moved slowly over the faces of Otto, August, and Philemon. I knew he didn't fancy the three sailors in his house, but now I began to wonder if there was something about Kit, too, that bothered him. His countenance when he looked at his guests didn't indicate mere annoyance—it indicated intense dislike. Even hatred.

It couldn't be easy for Henry to have this many people inside his cottage, I thought. Not only was his deceased wife lying mere feet away, but he was also accustomed to living a near-solitary life out here on the edge of the cape with only Abigail and Jeremiah and the endless waters of the sea and the wide Delaware Bay for company. As far as I knew, he did not receive visitors socially. Deborah might call on Abigail occasionally, but not Henry. She and Kit visited once a week to deliver supplies, but I had not seen evidence that Henry and Kit were good friends. No idle or particularly genial talk had passed between them since I had arrived. And I myself did not visit often or for any great length of time. My job duties were satisfied when I ensured myself that the lighthouse keeper and his family were well. There had probably never been so many people in the lighthouse at one time.

After supper Kit returned to his book. I wondered how he could stand reading in such dim light. Henry retreated to Jeremiah's room and the three men who had been plucked from the sea started another game of cards. Deborah delivered a small tray with soup, bread, and cider to Jeremiah and then sequestered herself in the kitchen to eat her own meal in peace.

A scant golden glow from the lighthouse apparatus filtered down to the parlor, but it was feeble. What with the dimness and the warmth and the good food and drink, my eyes started to droop. I moved one of the chairs close to the wall and sat down with a sigh. Leaning against the wall on the back legs of the chair, I closed my eyes, giving in to the exhaustion I felt over every inch of my body. I finally fell asleep to the sounds of the slap of the cards and the storm outside the walls of the cottage.

I WOKE to the sound of Philemon uttering a loud oath.

My arms shot out to my sides as I realized my chair was leaning precariously against the wall. When the chair tilted forward with a *thump* and all four legs were solidly on the floor, I blinked in confusion. I must have dozed more deeply than I thought.

It took me a second or two to remember the storm, the rescue of the two cousins and their boatmate, and our stranding inside the lighthouse cottage. I was on my feet an instant later.

"What's the trouble?" I asked. Looking around, the parlor seemed darker than I remembered.

"Lamp's gone out. Where's another one?" Philemon demanded.

"Where's Henry?" I asked.

Philemon jutted his head in the direction of Jeremiah's bedroom.

"I'm not waking Henry to ask for another lamp so you three can keep playing cards."

"Deborah!" Otto yelled.

"Keep your voice down, man," I said.

Deborah appeared in the kitchen doorway. "What do you want?"

"Where's there another lamp? This one's out of oil."

Deborah was silent for a moment, then she asked in a tentative voice, "Where's the lamp that was in with Abigail?"

I felt every eye turn toward me. I sighed. "I'll fetch it." If another lamp would keep these men quiet, I'd do anything. Anything but wake Henry, that is.

I entered the room slowly, as if I expected Abigail's voice to warn me away, but the room was silent as a grave. Deborah had covered most of the body with a thin cloth. I reached for the lamp that was on the bedside table, still flickering, and turned the flame up. I glanced at Abigail—her grotesque swollen body, visible even under the cloth, and her skin the color of maize. I shuddered to think of what pain she had borne in her final hours.

I recalled going to a farmhouse one evening about a year ago and finding the body of the woman who lived alone there. She was swollen, too, though not like Abigail. I sent for the doctor and when he arrived, he surmised she had died several days earlier. He was able to tell, I remembered, because he said swelling after death doesn't begin for approximately three days.

Abigail had been gaunt the day I saw her in the general store, then become ill again on Friday, according to Henry. The swelling had definitely occurred while she was still alive, and it had occurred rapidly, which I knew wasn't normal.

Henry had some explaining to do. I was trying to give him the time he needed to rest, to come to grips with Abigail's death, and to work in the lighthouse tower, but I could avoid talking to him no longer.

I hurried out to the parlor and placed the lamp on the table, then snatched it back again and headed for Jeremiah's bedroom.

"What do you think yer doing?" Philemon asked. "We need that lamp. Give it back."

"George? Where are you going with the lamp?" It was Kit's imperious voice.

I ignored them, striding to Jeremiah's bedroom door and rapping on it with my knuckles. When Henry didn't respond, I knocked again. He yanked the door open several moments later.

"What do you want? I'm trying to sleep." He glowered at me.

I stepped into the room and closed the door behind me. "I just came from your bedroom, where I got another look at your dead wife, practically swollen beyond all recognition. And you didn't send for the doctor. How can you call yourself a husband, man? Answer me!"

Henry's voice crackled with rage. "She didn't want the doctor. I told you that. Besides, I'm sure she's swollen some since she passed."

"None of that swelling came as a result of her death. It was there before she passed. Every visible part of her is misshapen. Unsightly, even. I've never seen anything like it. And you failed her. Do not ask me to believe that you didn't send for the doctor simply because she didn't want you to. I thought you were a better man than that."

"You believe what you want, but I did as she wished," he hissed.

"When she finally died, in pain and filth and agony just feet from where you stood, did it look or sound to you like she didn't want the help of a doctor?"

Henry made a feeble attempt to draw himself taller. I towered over him. "You listen here, Deputy." He practically spat the words. "What went on between my wife and me is none of your concern. I didn't send for the doctor because she begged me not to and that's all I'm going to say about it. You don't got the right to come in here and pass judgment on me and my family."

"I do when your inaction results in your wife's death."

Henry's eyes widened for a second, but he recovered himself quickly. He glared at me with surprising malice. "I did not cause Abigail's death. Now, are you going to arrest me?"

"I can't arrest you for failing to summon the doctor. I'm sure you know that. But if I could, I would."

"If you're not going to arrest me, then get out of here. I need some sleep."

We stared at each other for many long moments. "Why didn't she want you at her bedside in the moments before her death?" I challenged.

Again, a flicker of shock showed in his eyes. It vanished as quickly as it had appeared. "I don't know what yer talking about." His low, gruff voice was hard to hear.

"She told me not to summon you. Why would she say that?"

"How would I know what she was thinking? She must have been half out of her mind with pain. I'm sure she had no idea what she was saying."

There was no doubt in my mind that Abigail knew exactly what she was saying.

"What did you give her to help ease her pain?"

"I gave her mint and basil to chew on."

"Is that all? Might you have given her something much stronger? Something strong enough to kill her?"

For a moment I thought Henry was going to strike me, but I held my ground. His fists clenched and unclenched at his sides.

"Get out," he finally said in a low voice.

I turned around slowly and took my leave. He closed the door firmly behind me. I had a feeling I had unnerved him enough for the time being.

# CHAPTER 10

*I* didn't have any concrete evidence—yet—that Henry had acted to deliberately cause Abigail's death, but I intended to find it. What I needed was a cool place to think. The heat in the cottage was oppressive. I returned the lamp to the table in the parlor and didn't answer any of the questions the men put to me. Everyone wanted to know what I said to Henry.

I marched up the steps to the lighthouse gallery, where Jeremiah was working to clean the inside of one of the thick glass windows.

"What do you want?" he asked.

Before the storm, he was such a pleasant young man. What happened to him? "I need to clear my head."

"I'm trying to work."

"I won't bother you." My voice was tetchy, but I didn't care. I placed the palm of my hand against one of the windows, then drew it away and placed it on my cheek. The coolness of the glass was like a breath of fresh air. I repeated the movements with my other hand and my other cheek.

"I just cleaned that!" Jeremiah yelled.

"Give me that rag." I thrust out my hand and he shoved his

rag toward me. I drew circles with it on the window I had touched, then tossed it back to him. "I need to talk to you."

The look he turned on me was one of pure distrust. "About what?" His voice was low and hard.

"About your parents."

"I'll not talk to you about them. Get out of here."

"You will, or as soon as the water recedes I'll haul you into the little cell I keep in town. That'll change your mind right quick."

The muscles in Jeremiah's cheek tightened. The seething glare he turned on me was enough to melt the iron in August's smithy.

"Do you know why your father didn't send for the doctor when your mother became ill?"

"Yes."

"Why?"

"Because she told him she would refuse to see the doc."

"Why would she say that?"

Jeremiah shrugged. I stared at him, waiting for an answer. I had a feeling I could remain silent longer than he could. I was right—he finally spoke again as the silence grew long and the air between us became more tense. "That's why he had to go see the doc for himself."

I opened my mouth to ask another question, but paused. "He went to see the doctor?"

"Yes."

"For what?"

"To find out what to do for her."

"And what did the doctor say?"

Jeremiah shrugged. "Told him to give her peppermint and basil to chew."

This was interesting. If Jeremiah was telling the truth, then why hadn't Henry told me he had visited the doctor? Why had he let me assume he hadn't sought medical help at all?

. . .

"ANYTHING ELSE?"

Jeremiah frowned. "I'm about done talking to you."

I tried another line of questioning. "Why would your mother want your father to stay away from her sickbed?"

Jeremiah stood stock still, then leaned right close to my ear. "I don't have to answer any more of your questions and I'm not going to. I won't tell you again to get out of here."

I stared at him as I moved backward toward the stairway. I was still staring at him, not looking where I was going, when I placed my foot at an inartful angle onto the top step. I lost my balance, going straight down on my posterior. Embarrassed, I scanned the floor, hoping to find something to blame for my fall. But there was nothing there, and it was all I could do to ignore Jeremiah's smirk as I descended the rest of the steps.

JEREMIAH CALLED down the stairs a while later. "I need to come down."

Henry emerged from Jeremiah's bedroom. "George, I'm going up to the tower. If you want to know what to do in case there's an emergency, I reckon you should come with me now." His voice was icy—the only cold thing in the cottage.

"Shall we take one more man with us?"

"I'll come up," Kit offered. He set his book aside and stood. He bent his head slightly as if he feared banging it on the ceiling.

Henry hesitated for a moment. I had a feeling he was reluctant to leave Otto, August, and Philemon to their own devices downstairs. "There's no need for you to go up," he said to Kit.

"I think there's no harm in two of us knowing how to operate the light." I hoped my voice conveyed authority. I offered a solution. "Kit can go upstairs first," I suggested. "As soon as Jeremiah gets down here he can keep an eye on these three and I'll join you."

Still, Henry appeared reluctant.

"We don't need looking after," Otto said hotly. I ignored him.

"Be quick about it!" Jeremiah bellowed from the light. Henry frowned.

"All right," he said. "Go on up." He nodded to Kit and indicated the bottom step with a resigned wave of his hand.

Kit nodded once and preceded Henry up the steps. Presently Jeremiah came down to the parlor. He turned a scowl on the men seated at the table and stood against the wall with his arms folded. With his size, I trusted him to deter anyone from committing mischief. Otto, August, and Philemon appeared to have abandoned their card game for the moment and were sitting in sullen silence.

I found Henry and Kit waiting for me at the top. Kit was staring out the windows, though nothing but his reflection was visible in the darkness.

"It is Jeremiah's responsibility to keep the gears wound," Henry began. He showed us how the gears controlled a chandelier of large oil lamps hung from sturdy wires. Each lamp held a long, wide lighted wick. The lamps raised and lowered in time as a series of reflectors turned from east to west and back again. When the lighted wicks were lowered in front of the reflectors, a blinding light shone from the clear glass chimney housing the entire apparatus. It was that light which was responsible for keeping boats large and small safe until they reached the mouth of the Delaware River.

Then he showed us how to load the oil into the lamps being raised and lowered. As Henry spoke, I kept an ear to the frenzied storm on the other side of the glass. Strange to think a pane of glass was all that separated the people in the lighthouse from a storm of such monumental proportions.

After Henry had given us rudimentary instructions, he

repeated the lesson quickly and asked each of us to try filling the oil. I confess I spilled more of it than ended up in the lamp's vessel. Henry pressed his lips together as if trying to avoid criticizing my attempt. Kit was no better than I.

The working of the light was more complicated than I had guessed. I looked at Kit. "You think you can handle this in an emergency?"

Out of the corner of my eye I saw Henry scowling. Kit didn't seem to have noticed.

"I think I could manage it in an emergency," Kit said. "But I hope that won't be necessary. Always better to have a professional at the helm." He slapped Henry lightly on the shoulder.

Henry pulled a face. "All right. Now that you've seen how things work, you should both get downstairs and keep a sharp eye on the other men."

I nodded and descended the steps, followed closely by Kit.

A comical scene greeted us in the parlor. Otto, August, and Philemon sat on one side of the table, looking anywhere but at Jeremiah, who had seated himself on the other side. He was slumped in his chair, his arms still folded in front of him, his brows furrowed as he glared at the three men.

I couldn't help but smile. "Thank you, Jeremiah. I trust these fellows didn't give you any trouble?"

"No."

"Good. I'll take over here if you want to get some rest."

Jeremiah didn't need to be told twice. He stalked to his bedroom without another word. I sat in his chair.

We all sat mutely while the wind and water lashed the outer walls of the cottage. As the silence in the parlor lengthened, my nerves grew more taut. Deborah eventually emerged from the kitchen with a tray holding tin cups and a jug of cider. She set it down in the center of the table.

"I thought you men might hanker for something to drink in

this heat. Mind you don't drink too much. It is for the slaking of thirst only."

"You're worse than my own wife," Philemon growled at her. I considered for a moment the suffering any wife of Philemon might have to endure. Whoever she was, I was sorry for her.

The cottage was stifling. If we could only throw open the shutters for a few minutes, it would cool down. So might the tension that was rising almost imperceptibly throughout the room. Philemon, in particular, was beginning to worry me. The man's gaze snaked between Otto and August almost constantly, as if he were trying to communicate something to them without the aid of the spoken word. I didn't notice Otto or August responding, but it was disquieting nonetheless.

Again and again, Otto looked up to gaze around the room. Suddenly he stood, his eyes glittering. He raked his hands through his straw-like hair. August looked up at him, but said nothing. Philemon ignored him.

With his hands clasped behind his back, Otto began pacing the room like a caged beast. I kept a watchful eye on him. For a man of his build, his presence took up more space than it seemed it should.

"Sit down, man!" Philemon finally roared. The suddenness of the noise made my heart skip a beat.

Otto whirled around and glared at his friend. "You'll not tell me what to do."

Philemon moved to rise from the table, but I put my hand up. "Let him alone," I said.

Kit leaned forward to glance at me. "Would you pass that cider, George?"

"Yer in my light," Philemon growled. "Sit back or get up. I can barely see my own hand in front of my face."

Kit sat back. He reached for a tin cup as I passed the jug of cider. He poured himself a measure, then took a long draught. "Tastes good. It's hot in here."

# CHAPTER 11

*I* wished I had something to do. Kit might have been able to read by the low flame of one oil lamp, but I couldn't. There was obviously nowhere to go, and I didn't care to natter away with any of the people in the cottage.

I was fretting about my horse and about Abe Bradford back in the cell in town, trying not to think about Evelyn, when Henry called down the stairs. "I need Jeremiah up here. The soot needs to be cleaned off the windows again and I need him to repair a barrel stave."

"I'll tell him," Kit knocked on Jeremiah's door and called to him. "Jeremiah, Henry wants you up in the light."

Jeremiah's door flung open with surprising force. He glared at Kit. "I heard him. I'm going."

Kit sat down again and Deborah shook her head. "That poor young man."

"He's full of vinegar. And disrespectful." Kit frowned.

"His mother just passed, Kit. Let him alone."

"Isn't there work you should be doing?" he asked.

Deborah turned on her heel and went into the kitchen.

Light hammering and other noises came from the lighthouse

as we waited ... waited for the storm to end, for daylight to illu-
minate the cottage again, and for the air to cool. Every man
seemed absorbed in his own thoughts. For myself, I struggled to
stop worrying about what was happening back in town, since
there was nothing I could do about it while I remained stuck in
the cottage.

I turned my thoughts again to Henry and Abigail. For
Abigail to insist that he not be called to her bedside and for
Henry to be so distant at the time of her death—perhaps even to
have killed her?—something must have happened between them
to cause a deep rift. I reflected upon the most prudent way to
find out what might have caused such a fissure.

Henry interrupted my musings when he came down from
the light.

"I need you to turn down the lamp wicks in here and extin-
guish the flames. We need to conserve the oil we have in the
house in case it's needed for the lamp in the tower."

Deborah gasped.

"I'm sure it's just a precaution." I used the most soothing
voice I could muster. I looked to Henry for confirmation, but he
ignored me. I hid my concern, but I also wondered whether
there was enough oil in the lighthouse and the cottage to keep
the lamp lit. I dreaded the thought of a ship being tossed about
on the waves, unable to navigate because the light ran out of oil
during the storm. If a ship ran aground, we could have a much
bigger problem on our hands. I dreaded, too, the thought of
having no light with which to see my surroundings and the
people around me.

"Could we perhaps keep two small lamps lit?" Deborah
pleaded. I sensed her anxiety, and I confess I shared it. The last
thing I wanted was a completely dark house in which volatile
men were unable to get along.

Henry sighed. "Two small lamps. Keep the flames low."

He waited while the rest of us extinguished the remaining

lamps. Heavy darkness slowly stole across the room with each small flame that disappeared.

Deborah brought Henry a draught of cider. I requested one, too, since the heat in the cottage was ghastly. Though she grumbled about it, she brought me one. The drink helped to steady my nerves and unclench my muscles. I was surprised Otto and the other men hadn't demanded some.

Henry drained his cup quickly, then came to stand in front of me.

"Deputy, I'd like to see my wife."

I wondered if the measure of Dutch courage bolstered his words. "Certainly."

Henry nodded. He walked past the men staring at him from their seats at the table and went straight to his bedroom door. He opened it slowly and peered inside, but to my surprise, he didn't go any farther into the room.

In the low light from the oil lamp on the table, I would have sworn I saw Otto and August exchange glances, but I couldn't be sure. I moved my chair closer to the table, the better to keep my eye on them. My chair made a scraping sound as I slid it across the floor. Philemon looked up.

"I hate that noise."

"My apologies," I said.

It was difficult not to watch Henry as he gazed into the room where his wife lay, but he didn't stay there for long. I was certain he would go stand at Abigail's side, but he did not. Instead, he sat suddenly in a chair near the bedroom door.

A sour scent wafted on the air once the door was open.

"Are you all right, Henry?" I asked.

"I'll be fine." He leaned forward, his head sagging and his hands clasped between his knees.

"It smells like sick in here," Philemon growled. Otto and August nodded their heads, but said nothing.

Indeed, it did. I was trying to breathe through my mouth,

but the odor was overwhelming. I rose and took up an oil lamp. Holding my breath, I went into the bedroom. Perhaps the scent of illness would lessen if I put a cloth over the chamber pot Abigail had used.

I picked up a small linen towel that lay at the foot of the bed. It was coarse and stiff—just the thing to place over the chamber pot. The chamber pot sat on the floor near the head of the bed. Thin brown liquid filled the pot and lay splattered on the floor around it. I suppressed a gag and bent to place the cloth over the pot. I straightened and shook my head in dismay as I noted again the ochre tinge to Abigail's skin. She had been such a comely woman.

I swallowed hard, thinking of my late wife. Evelyn's skin had gradually become jaundiced before she died. Abigail's was worse—far worse—but looking at the poor woman brought back memories of Evelyn and the suffering she endured prior to her death. And I had seen a man in Cape Island with yellow skin, too. He had died after years of taking too much drink, the doctor told me at the time. That yellow tinge was caused by disease of the liver.

I didn't know Abigail well, that was true. But I knew she never indulged in drink. She had told me so on one of my visits to check on the Brewster family.

Was it true? Did she really avoid drink? I suspected she did. In fact, when I had seen her just a week ago, there had been no yellow tinge to her skin. She was wan, certainly, but the paleness only accentuated the porcelain look of her skin. I recalled thinking how much it reminded me of Evelyn's fair skin.

I shook my head to dislodge thoughts of Evelyn. I could not allow my mind to wander down that path—I had too many concerns right here in the cottage, starting with Abigail's sudden and violently unnatural death and my growing suspicion that her husband may have killed her.

When I returned to the parlor, I closed the bedroom door

behind me. My mind was working feverishly as I tried to organize my thoughts.

What did I know for certain?

First, only a week ago Abigail said she had been ill, but
insisted her health was improving. Her illness had returned,
according to Henry, three days before the storm. She had visited
the privy many times, he said, but had been going less
frequently in the last day or two. Certainly her chamber pot had
been in frequent use, too.

Second, Henry and Jeremiah had been reluctant to enter the
bedroom after Abigail's blood-chilling scream.

Third, Abigail had pleaded with me not to summon Henry to
her deathbed. Alas, she died before telling me why.

Fourth, Jeremiah was an entirely different young man from
the one I knew prior to the storm. True, I hadn't seen him in
several weeks, but he had never had anything but kind words
for me.

And finally, Deborah had been with me in the room when
Abigail took her final tortured breath. I hadn't seen her taking
any kind of malicious action toward her friend.

What else did I know for certain? Not much, I feared. But I
had one advantage: I was a sheriff's deputy. I was the representative of the law in Cape Island. I could ask questions and
demand answers where others couldn't. But did I dare to make
more inquiries in this cottage? It was already an explosive situation—with everyone in close quarters, in the oppressive heat
and dimness, with the never-ending howl of the wind and rain,
a person with unclean thoughts could slip the bonds of self-
control at any moment.

We could all be in danger. All of us, that is, except one. The
one who saw to it that Abigail would not survive the storm.

I sat down near the door. I still held one of the oil lamps in
my hand, so I placed it on small table next to me. The other
lamp was across the room. The atmosphere in the parlor was

tense and strained. I felt as if we were all watching each other, looking for signs of weakness, of frangibility. Could they guess what I was thinking? I tried to relax into the chair.

Philemon rose and walked around the room twice, finally stopping to stand in front of me. "Deputy, you look like you've seen a ghost," he said with a phlegmy cackle.

"I suppose the odor from the bedroom made me a bit bilious."

"You're not the only one. Smells terrible in here," he said.

"Mind your business," Henry said. I had almost forgotten he was still in the room.

I watched Philemon scowl toward Henry, but that seemed to be the ordinary set of his face. Otto and August were looking at each other, but it was impossible to tell if they were attempting to communicate without using words. Kit had picked up his book and was buried in it again mere inches from the other oil lamp. Deborah made her way slowly around the room with a dust cloth, of all things.

"You should sit down and rest," I said. "You needn't be working all the time."

Deborah looked up with a sigh. "I'm trying to keep busy, I suppose. My nerves get the better of me when I have nothing to do. And poor Henry and Jeremiah will have to find someone to do the housework for them now. I might as well make things easier for them if I can."

"Don't feel as though you need to clean for us," Henry said roughly. "We'll manage with Abigail gone."

With this, he left the room without sparing anyone a glance. A moment later he pulled Jeremiah's bedroom door closed behind him.

"Seems like he'd be more tore up over Abigail's passing," August observed.

"Hush, August. That's a shameful thing to say." Deborah stood with her hands on her hips. "What if he heard you?"

"No matter. I'm not afraid to tell him to his face."

Deborah made a *tut tut* sound and turned back to her dusting.

"Well, don't you agree it's strange? Deputy?" August asked.

I had no desire to be lured into such a discussion. "I would say the way Henry grieves the loss of his wife is nobody's business but his own. Think of something else to talk about, August."

"If you say so." August turned to his cousin. "I could use another taste of that rum. I didn't get quite enough last time. You?"

Otto grinned. "Deborah," he said in a loud voice. "Bring in that rum."

*God's teeth,* I thought. *Just what I don't need right now.*

# CHAPTER 12

"There'll be no more swigging of rum tonight," I said.

"'Tisn't illegal, deputy," Otto said. "We'll not be breaking the law by taking a bit of drink."

"Laws about quaffing don't apply under these circumstances," I said.

"Come now, George. I'm not asking to drink the whole lot of it," Otto scoffed.

"I didn't say you were going to drink all of it. You've had enough already and it's my job to maintain order in this cottage. I intend to do it."

Philemon leaned toward Otto and whispered something. Otto let out a laugh that sounded like a bark.

"That'll be enough of that." My voice was stern.

"A man can't talk to another man?" Philemon asked.

I couldn't very well outlaw talking among themselves. I ignored Philemon's question, but dragged my chair a little closer to the center of the parlor.

"I need help up here!"

Jeremiah's voice was loud, breaking the uneasy silence in the cottage. Kit stood, but I motioned for him to be seated. "I'll go see what he needs. You maintain order down here, Kit."

Kit nodded and I hurried upstairs. I felt a twinge of guilt for leaving Kit down there to deal with Otto and his cousin and their friend, but the truth was that I needed a break from their constant sniping and uncouth manners.

"What is it, Jeremiah?"

"Leaks." Jeremiah pointed to two window jambs situated across from each other in the ring of windows circling the light. "I can't fix both at the same time. I need you to patch that one up." He nodded to the farther leak. I craned my neck and spied water dribbling down the wall.

"How do I do that?" I asked.

"There's a storage box back there." Jeremiah gestured toward a small room at the back of the lighthouse gallery. "There's wax in the box. You'll hold a chunk of the wax near the light to warm it up, then before it cools you have to shove it into the crack where the leak's coming from. Get two pieces of wax, because I'll need one. Go fast. These leaks aren't getting any smaller."

I hurried to the back of the gallery and found a wooden box of supplies. It wasn't very big—a man could sit on it and not reach the supper table. I tossed aside a small axe, a hammer, several rags, a small coil of twine, a graphite pencil, a logbook, and a handful of nails before finally locating a small ball of wax at the bottom. I took it back to Jeremiah and held it up. "Is this it?"

"Yes," Jeremiah almost shouted. "I told you to get two."

I returned to the box and raked through the contents again until I could see the bottom. I reached in and felt around, and finally my fingers closed around the cool, rough ball. I raised it in triumph. "I've got it," I called.

Jeremiah grunted and held out his hand for the wax. He and I kneaded and cajoled and shoved the substance into all the visible cracks that were allowing the water to seep into the gallery. The wind and rain continued their relentless battering of the lighthouse and I wondered how a storm could continue for so many hours without any sign of abating.

"I've used up mine." I rubbed my hands on my trousers. "Is there anything else you want me to do while I'm up here?"

"No. Go back downstairs."

Not a word of thanks, not a single indication that Jeremiah appreciated my help at all. I frowned as I turned away from the young man and went downstairs.

The moment I reached the bottom step, I knew something unpleasant had transpired in my absence. Kit and Deborah stepped away from each other and Deborah was rubbing one arm. She turned away and hurried into the kitchen. Otto and August and Philemon whispered among themselves.

"What's happened?" I asked.

"I grabbed Deborah's arm to keep her from slipping on the floor," Kit said. Otto—or perhaps it was one of the other men—snickered. Now, I'm not the smartest man who ever lived, but I knew Kit was lying.

Philemon's devilish grin looked positively spectral in the low flame from the lamp next to him.

"What's so funny, Philemon?" I asked. I tried to keep the weariness out of my voice.

"Can't a man smile?"

"Not like that."

Otto spoke up. "Sheriff, I think y'oughta keep a starp … sharp … eye on that fellow." He swung his arm in a fluid motion to encompass the entire room.

"I'm a deputy, not the sheriff, and what fellow?"

"Kit, o' course." Otto leaned his head way back and laughed, then started coughing.

"Shut your mouth, you sot," Kit grumbled.

What this group needed was a heavy dose of civility. One

thing was sure—the heat in the cottage wasn't helping anyone's temperament. I went into the kitchen.

"Deborah, I think we need to let the fire die down almost completely. If you need it to prepare any food, tell me now. Otherwise I'm going to take the remaining logs off and let it go out."

"That fire's hot, certainly, but it's also giving off some light. I don't think it's wise to do anything that'll make it harder to see in here."

Frankly, I didn't care to hear her opinion, even though part of me agreed with her, but I attempted to respond in a courteous manner.

"I think everyone but Henry and Jeremiah and I will be asleep before long. No sense in having the fire burning overnight. If one of us needs to see something close up, we'll use an oil lamp."

Deborah sighed. "You'll do as you want, regardless of anyone's advice. I don't need to use the fire. If anyone needs food, there's sufficient in here." Her gesture took in all of the kitchen. I shook my head as I left the room. She was not a personable woman.

I smelled rum the moment I stepped into the parlor. I don't know how I had missed it earlier. That would explain Otto's slightly slurred speech. Something glinted under the table in the faint light and I knew someone had stashed a rum bottle under there.

"Otto, where'd the rum come from?" I asked.

Otto grinned. "What rum, Sheriff? I mean, Dep'ty?"

"The rum you and the others had while I was helping Jeremiah upstairs in the light. Kit? Did they drink the rum right under your nose?"

"Kit was busy talking to his wife in the kitchen," August said.

"I only left the room for a few moments," Kit said in a slow, sullen voice.

I sighed, stepping toward the bottle and picking it up. There was nothing in it. They had ingested all of it, and it hadn't taken them long. I cursed myself for not sending Kit up to help Jeremiah while I stayed downstairs.

This evening was about to get even longer.

# CHAPTER 13

*I* took up the tongs from the hearth and used them to remove the remaining logs from the fireplace. I set them on the hearth, where they would eventually stop giving off light and heat, then set the tongs aside.

"What're you doing that for?" Otto asked.

"I should think it's pretty clear what I'm doing. I'm trying to cool it down in here."

"How're we supposed to see anything now?" Philemon complained from his chair by the door.

"You don't need to see anything if you're sleeping," I said. "Now shut your eyes and be quiet. The only people stirring in this place should be Henry and Jeremiah."

"What about you?" August asked.

"I'm staying awake so you and your cousin and your friend over there," I pointed to Philemon, "don't cause anymore mischief around here."

"We ain't causing mischief, Deputy," August said.

"You just do as I tell you."

The air in the room was heavy with sullen silence. Kit had abandoned any attempt to read his book and was sitting with his hands in his lap, his eyes closed. Even in the low light I could see Otto staring at me, and August staring at Otto. Almost as if he was waiting for something to happen. Whatever Deborah was doing in the kitchen, she was doing it soundlessly. She seemed to prefer her solitude in the kitchen to the company of the men in the cottage. I didn't blame her. I would have liked to be in there, too, if she hadn't been in there.

Suddenly Kit stood and disappeared into the kitchen. The other men and I watched as he threaded his way around the furniture in the room. It wasn't long before we could hear heated whispers coming from him and Deborah. I strained my ears to hear what they were talking about, but I couldn't make out any clear words.

The next sound was a loud crash. I leapt to my feet, took up an oil lamp, and with a few strides was standing in the kitchen doorway.

"What're they fighting about?" Otto called. I knew from the sound of chairs scraping the wooden floor behind me that he and his companions were about to make matters worse.

I turned and spoke over my shoulder. "Sit down, all of you."

"We need to know what the fight is about," Philemon said.

"I told you all to sit down." I pointed behind the men and they took their time returning to their chairs. All three pulled their seats close to one another and whispered with their heads together.

I didn't have time to worry about them. I stepped into the kitchen. "Kit, Deborah, what seems to be the trouble? Anything I can help with?"

"No," came Kit's terse reply. In the dim light I saw him cast a menacing look toward his wife.

The look Deborah turned on him was frosty as December.

"I think you two need time to cool down. We can't let tempers flare out of control tonight. There isn't enough room for all this fighting."

Kit glowered at me. "I think you should keep your mind on your own affairs, Deputy. Heaven knows you've got enough to handle with those three worthless curs out there." He jutted his chin toward the parlor.

I gave him my sternest glare and opened my mouth to speak, but was interrupted when Otto came crashing into the kitchen.

"You'll call us 'curs,' will you?" he yelled. He lunged toward Kit. "I'll teach you what a cur can do!"

I leapt between the two men as August rushed into the room and yanked Otto by the shoulder.

"You trying to get yourself killed?" August shouted at his cousin. I was pleased to see that he was trying to stop a fight, not start one as he was wont to do in Cold Spring and Cape Island.

"Take your hands off o' me, August." Otto's tone held a warning.

"Not until you shut your bone trap."

Otto clamped his lips shut and allowed August to drag him back to the parlor. A moment later, though, sounds of a struggle could be heard. August cried out and Otto dashed back into the kitchen.

"At least I'm man enough to provide the seed for my own children. Or my wife ain't barren. One or t'other." Otto turned on his heel and went back to the parlor.

In the shocked silence that followed, I stared at the childless couple. Deborah turned away, her face a mask of shame, while Kit stared after Otto, his hands suddenly limp at his sides. He opened his mouth and moved his lips as if to say something, but shut it a moment later when no sound came out.

"Deborah, Kit, I'm sor—" I began.

"Just get out of here, both of you," Deborah said. She turned away. I couldn't see her face, but I could hear the catch in her voice.

My gaze didn't leave Otto's face as I returned to the parlor and sat down. His hateful words had hit their mark not only on Deborah and Kit, but on me. When my dear Evelyn passed away, she was carrying our only child in her womb. I was usually able to keep the memory at bay, but here, in this hot, airless cottage with a group of men whose skin smelt of sea water and whose breath reeked of rot, the memory rose unbidden in my mind.

Evelyn had been sick for several months. In those days, we made our home in Cape Henlopen, Delaware. Evelyn's doctor, a kindly old man, had tried everything he could think of to cure Evelyn's illness, but nothing worked.

It started with the swelling of her legs and feet. Though it pained her to walk, she carried out her daily duties and chores wearing a wide smile, as always. In the evenings, after the sun set, she would finally sink into a chair to rest. She would often fall asleep in our small parlor, knowing I would wake her to retire to bed.

At first we thought the swelling and pain were the result of the baby she was carrying, but after several months the symptoms did not disappear, as they would usually do for a woman with child. The doctor tried draining some of the blood from Evelyn's legs and feet, but that only caused her more pain. And once he had stitched her skin back together following the bloodletting, the swelling became worse. Foul-smelling liquid seeped through the stitched places, but the odor was of no concern to me—Evelyn's health and the life of the baby were my only priorities.

She moved through her days in a constant state of fatigue. She could not eat much, and the baby was not growing as it should. I tried to hire a woman to help with the daily chores so Evelyn could rest, but she refused any help. It wasn't until her skin and eyes began to yellow that the doctor realized there was something wrong with her liver. He told her she needed to move around more, which of course was nearly impossible with her fatigue and the agonizing swelling of her legs and feet, especially after a long day of doing the work unaided around the house.

It was a fine morning in June when Evelyn passed away. Her health had been declining for several months, but when I left the house early in the morning to take my horse to be reshod, there was no reason to think that day would be any different from the days that went before it. I promised her I would not be long.

As I left the farrier, the doctor hailed me from his house. He handed me a packet of white powder and told me to mix it into Evelyn's tea as soon as I returned home. It would help her swelling, he said. He would be along before the morning was out.

I called out to her when I entered our house, but she didn't answer. The house was silent, so I assumed she had returned to sleep. I didn't want to wake her before it was necessary, so I prepared her tea and added the doctor's white powder before going into the bedroom. I intended to see that she drank all the tea before he arrived.

When I entered the bedroom, though, I knew something had changed. The room felt cold.

I recall dropping the tea on the floor, breaking the cup and scalding my leg. I ran to Evelyn's side, but it was too late. I yelled for her to awaken and promised to fetch the doctor for more white powder. I shook her shoulders to no avail.

I must have shouted for help, because our neighbors, the Carvers, were in Evelyn's room when next I realized what was happening. Mrs. Carver told her husband to take me to the parlor, then fetch the doctor. She cleaned the floor where I had spilled the tea.

I don't know how long I sat in the parlor, begging God to give her back to me, before the doctor arrived with Mr. Carver.

He hastened into the bedroom with a look of shock, but he could not have been more shocked than I.

The baby, of course, died with Evelyn.

"It was the liver disease," the doctor said many minutes later as he sat with me in the parlor. Mrs. Carver had brought us large measures of cider. I drank mine too fast and felt it sloshing around in my stomach as I tried to understand what the doctor was saying.

Truth be told, it didn't matter what he was saying. All that mattered was that Evelyn and the baby were dead and I was going to have to carry on without them.

The last time I saw Evelyn's lovely amber eyes, before I left our house that morning, they gazed at me from the swamp of the damnable pale yellow that had completely covered her body. I couldn't bear to look at her in death. Mrs. Carver and some of the other women in Cape Henlopen prepared her body for burial.

After her funeral, I left Cape Henlopen. Remaining in the house Evelyn and I had shared was too painful. I sold our house and found a boat captain who agreed to take me and my meager belongings across the bay to Cape Island at a reasonable cost.

# CHAPTER 14

*I* departed for Cape Island on a gray day that promised rain. The boat captain I had hired to ferry me across the wide bay waited as two friends helped me load my modest possessions on board. I thanked them, shook their hands, and bid them farewell. I looked forward over the bow of the boat as it carried me toward the New Jersey shore. The lighthouse—the one I was now stranded in with seven other people and one deceased woman—stood sentry where the bay narrowed to become the Delaware River.

Now, three years later, I beheld the lighthouse again, this time from a different perspective. Now I was on the inside and the storm-tossed waters heaved with danger.

I detested Otto for reminding me of Evelyn's death.

I looked around as my eyes adjusted to the darkened room. Otto's head slumped forward onto his chest as he snored. The sound would have been comical if it hadn't been so damnably loud. It was a wonder he could sleep through it. The low flames of the fire reflected in August's eyes as he glanced around the room. Philemon shifted in his seat and muttered an oath.

I gave a start when I saw Kit sitting a few feet to my left. I hadn't even heard him move, lost as I was in memories of Evelyn. He was awake, gazing into the fireplace embers. He seemed not to have noticed me looking at him. Deborah sat on the opposite side of the room, her head resting against the back of her chair. It looked like she was sleeping. I was glad to see husband and wife sitting well apart from each other.

It might be good to know more about them, I thought. I wanted to know if their marriage was a violent one, or merely as unhappy as it seemed to be. I might need to keep a closer eye on Kit after the storm was over. I didn't wish to question them now, since they were being quiet, so I decided to speak to Henry. He was the person most likely to be able to give me the information I sought. I moved to Jeremiah's door and listened. I heard rustling, so I knew Henry was awake. I knocked on the bedroom door.

He opened it a few moments later.

"Mind if I speak to you privately?"

Henry regarded me for a moment, then beckoned me to follow him with a sideways nod of his head. I glanced around to see if anyone was watching us. Kit and August seemed to be following my movements with their eyes, though it was hard to be sure in the dimness. I followed Henry into the bedroom and he closed the door behind me.

"What do you want?" he asked. "I'm not talking about Abigail."

"What can you tell me about Kit and Deborah?"

Henry hesitated a moment before speaking. "Why are you asking?"

"I don't care for the way Kit treats her."

"I wouldn't know anything about that." He averted his eyes and I knew he was lying.

"Are you and Kit good friends?"

"No. He and Deborah just bring us some of the supplies we need for the light."

"They only come around once a week?"

"Yes. But Deborah comes by herself on occasion, too."

"Have you ever witnessed any violence between them?"

Henry's eyes narrowed. "And what would you do if I have?"

We both knew there was little I could do in such a situation. A man had every right to discipline his wife as long as it didn't disturb the neighbors. But that didn't make it right.

"I'd like to know."

"Well, I haven't. I mind my own business, Deputy."

"Can you tell me—"

"I'm done answering questions. You need to get out of here."

"I'll do as you ask for now, but only because I don't want to be absent from the parlor for long. But we will speak again, I can promise you that," I said. I left him and returned to the main room. In my brief absence, Otto and Deborah had awakened. I could hear mutterings from different parts of the room. The darkness was almost complete—only a low scarlet glow from the fireplace offered any illumination. The heat had lessened, but I and everyone else had practically been deprived of our sense of sight.

Looking back, I don't know which was worse, the heat or the darkness.

"That you, George?"

It was Kit's voice. I frowned in the darkness.

"It's me, yes."

"What were you and Henry talking about?"

"That's between me and Henry."

I could hear a low chuckle and knew immediately Philemon was the source. I heard him rise from his chair and move toward me and Kit. "There's nothing funny about this situation." I hoped that would silence him, but I should have known better.

"Let him alone. George and Henry want to share their secrets like the lasses." Philemon laughed mirthlessly.

"Philemon, you need to shut your bone box and sit yourself down," I said hotly.

"Are you going to make me sit down?"

"If I have to." I couldn't see clearly through the gloom, but I heard the legs of a chair scraping against the floor and the heavy sound of him sitting.

A ponderous shroud of uneasy silence descended on the keeper's cottage. With all the oil from the lamps being conserved, there was not enough light to read, to play cards, to note someone's expression as he spoke.

So long was the silence in the room that I caught my breath in surprise when someone spoke. It was Otto, and below his voice I thought I could hear the quiet tinkling sound of glass being set carefully on the floor. God's teeth, he or someone else had gotten hold of more rum, probably while I was in the bedroom talking to Henry.

"You've all heard of Neptune's Curse, haven't you?" Otto asked.

I sensed a subtle shift in the room. Was it a feeling of fear? Apprehension? I felt, rather than saw, heads turn toward the sound of Otto's voice.

"Sounds like a yarn to me," Kit said with a scoff.

"Oh, it's not a yarn," Otto said.

"Your rum is talking." Deborah's voice held an edge of apprehension.

"I've had no rum."

A coarse laugh shot across the room. It was impossible to tell who it was from.

"Tell us about Neptune's Curse," Philemon said. I could practically hear a malicious grin spread across his face.

"Very well, then." Otto lowered his voice and I grimaced

when I found myself leaning closer to hear what he was about to say.

"Of course you know who Neptune is. The Roman god of the sea. He—"

"I'll not listen to this blasphemy." Deborah's skirts made a rustling sound as she walked past me. She bumped into a chair or two before I heard her shoes in the kitchen. It didn't sound like she moved very far from the doorway, though.

"According to Neptune's Curse, the sea rises up to claim its due in the face of unforgivable sin committed by someone who lives near the sea. Or someone whose livelihood depends on the sea." He paused, as if to let the effects of his words seep into the ears of his listeners. I suspected the listeners included Deborah.

August took up the tale. "It's said Neptune punishes sinners by conjuring storms that lash the land and sea for days on end. Storms such like mortals have never witnessed. Storms like the one raging around us even now."

"The question is, who has committed such sin that Neptune has become enraged? What has that person done?" Otto asked.

Kit scoffed. "That is a fanciful tale that God-fearing folks know better than to believe. You'll not get anyone else in this house to give credence to your ridiculous notions."

"Are you sure of that?" Otto asked.

"Of course I'm sure."

"I believe it," Philemon said.

"I believe it, too," August said.

"The very thought of it is lunacy." It was Deborah's voice from the kitchen. "The storm may be punishment for sins, but it comes straight from God, not Neptune. I don't doubt you'll all be sorry if you continue to believe in the tale you're telling. It's shameful." While she spoke, I heard again the now-familiar clink of a bottle against the floor.

# CHAPTER 15

"*I* thought you weren't listening to such blasphemy," Otto said with a harsh chuckle.

"I cannot go far enough from you to avoid hearing your stories," Deborah retorted, though I had a feeling she hadn't even tried.

"Tell us the truth, madam," Otto said. "You wanted to hear about the curse."

"Stop this immediately." It was Kit, in a low, threatening voice. "You'll not talk to my wife in such a manner."

"You'll not talk to my wife in such a manner," Otto repeated in a falsetto. Philemon laughed, but in a manner that sounded more menacing than merry.

"Otto, give me that bottle," I demanded.

"What bottle?" he asked, his voice full of innocence.

"The one under the table."

"We drank all of it," he said.

I hoped he was telling the truth and that he didn't have a second bottle under there. I had no desire to go crawling under the table to retrieve the bottle myself.

My eyes had become accustomed to the scant amount of

light in the cottage and I could make out objects and people around me. Deborah stood silently in the kitchen doorway. Every time someone spoke, her head turned in the person's direction. Kit's person was even larger and more imposing in the darkness. As usual, the two cousins and their friend sat huddled at the table in the center of the room. I turned when I heard Jeremiah's bedroom door open.

"Can't a man get any sleep in his own house?" Henry asked in a surly voice. "Bad enough we have this storm to deal with, but now I can't get a minute's rest with all the nattering out here. Keep quiet, now, all of you."

He slammed the bedroom door. For a moment, all I could hear was the shrieking of the wind, which seemed never to end. I squeezed my eyes shut.

Before I knew what was happening, Otto was on his feet. He held an oil lamp in one hand and a bottle in the other. In the low light, droplets of liquid, probably rum, glittered in his beard.

He lurched toward Jeremiah's bedroom and pushed the door open.

"Otto!" I barked. "Get back in here."

Henry was standing in the doorway now. "Yer a sot if ever I saw one, Otto Schuhmacher. Yer mother would be ashamed of you. Now go sit down and sober up."

Otto clumsily swung the bottle at Henry, but Henry put up his hands and stopped the assault. August and I were clambering over each other to reach Otto.

August reached him first and placed his hand on Otto's arm, but Otto shook him off. "Leave me alone, ya pigeon-livered snake," he snarled.

"Henry's right. You've had enough drink." August grasped Otto's arm again and tried forcing him to sit.

But Otto, remarkably, managed to remain standing. He spoke to August. "I ain't about to let that Henry Brewster tell me what to do—that squat calf of a man." He held the rum bottle aloft, then brought it to his lips and drank deeply before August could wrest the bottle from his grasp. I groaned inwardly. So there had been a second bottle of rum under the table, after all.

"Squat calf, eh?" Henry asked. "I may not be a bean vine like you, but I'm the one who saw to it that you and your horse-faced companions aren't lying at the bottom of the sea right now!"

I had been trying to keep my mind off my horse. Henry was doing me no favors.

"Shut your maw." Otto glared at Henry with fierce animosity.

I reached out quickly and took the oil lamp from Otto before he could drop it and set the place ablaze. Then I grabbed his arm. "Otto, you've had enough. I would advise you to sit down right now." I locked my eyes on his.

"I won't be takin' orders from you. Why don't you go back to Delaware where you belong?" He scowled.

"You will take orders from me, Otto, because I am the sheriff's representative whether you want me here or not."

Otto looked away. August shook his head and spoke. "Apologies, Deputy. He won't be any more trouble." He gave his cousin a hard look and shoved Otto roughly toward the table. Henry slammed the bedroom door and Otto slumped into his chair.

Philemon laughed aloud. It was a raw, braying noise.

"What's so funny?" Otto slurred.

"You are. You're a toper and you're laying it bare before friend and foe alike." He laughed again.

"And what do you mean by that?" Otto struggled to stand again, curling his knuckles into a ball.

Philemon became serious. "I mean you drink too much. Now sit down before I make you sit down. And don't be raising your fist at me."

I watched the scene unfold before me with a sense of dismay. I hesitated to get between Otto and Philemon. If I didn't think I'd be stuck in this hotbox with these men for the foreseeable hours, I would have separated them and bade them be silent until Otto had sobered up. But for now, I would merely observe them. If Otto became more unruly, I would have to find a way to secure him safely from the others until I could take him back to town.

"Deputy." It was Deborah's voice. I glanced toward her, almost hidden around the corner beyond the kitchen doorway. I joined her, keeping one eye on the men.

"Yes, Deborah? What is it?"

"Isn't there something you could do to restrain Otto? I'm afraid he'll go mad and take out his anger on Henry."

"If I see that he's becoming more disorderly, I will do just that."

"There's hate between those two going back to that incident years back," she said. "I don't want to be a witness to Henry Brewster being attacked by that coyote of a man."

"I'm not going to let Otto attack Henry," I said. Then it dawned on me what Deborah had said. I lowered my voice and gestured for her to move a bit further into the kitchen. "What incident from years back?"

"You don't know the story?"

"What story?"

Deborah opened her mouth to speak, but Kit interrupted us. "George, you'd better get out here. Otto's finishing off the rum."

Otto's silhouette was lowering the bottle from his mouth when I went back into the parlor. We had all endured more than our share of Otto's troublemaking and I needed to do something about it before he was out of control.

"Otto, put that bottle down," I demanded, striding toward him as quickly as the darkness allowed.

His next movement was so fast I barely had time to duck. The sound of an object hurtling through the air warned me and I dropped one knee to the floor just in time. The rum bottle missed me, but hit August.

August let out a howl that chilled my blood, then slumped sideways in his chair. Otto lumbered unsteadily to his feet and leaned over his cousin as Deborah screamed.

"Get out of the way, Otto." I stood behind August, placing my hands under his arms to support him. "Kit, grab his arms." Kit didn't stop to ask whose arms I meant—he took hold of Otto's arms in a vise-like grip.

Henry wrenched the bedroom door open and stormed into the parlor. "What the devil goes on out here?"

I didn't bother to answer, as August was slumping down farther. "Deborah, get me water and a cloth," I said tersely. I lowered him to the floor. Deborah's footsteps receded into the kitchen, and she was back just a few moments later with the items I had requested.

While Otto struggled against Kit's strength, Deborah and I tended to August. He had a long, deep gash above his left ear and his blood was quickly seeping into my clothes and puddling under his head.

"August," I said loudly. "Wake up." There was no response. I was vaguely aware of Henry and Philemon standing behind me, watching the scene unfold as if it were a play on a stage. "Get back and give us some room," I ordered them. Both men took a step backward. "Someone light a lamp and bring it here."

Henry reached for an oil lamp and lit the wick using a piece of kindling he stuck into the fireplace embers. He handed me the lamp. Deborah dipped the cloth into the water and applied it to August's wound. Philemon stood still as I peered at August's head to see the wound more closely.

As I did so, he let out a low moan.

# CHAPTER 16

"He's alive. August? Can you hear me?" I asked.
He responded with another moan and a small movement of his hand.

Deborah reached for the cloth again and dabbed his head with it. As she did so, he moved his face slightly away from her and squinted as if he were trying to keep his eyes closed. The pain must have been awful. He mumbled something. Deborah and I leaned closer to hear him as sounds continued coming from his mouth, but we couldn't decipher his words.

I looked up at Henry and nodded toward Jeremiah's bedroom. "Can you help me get him into the bedroom?"

Henry's eyes widened. "On the bed?"

"Yes."

"He'll not be getting blood all over Jeremiah's bed."

I exhaled loudly in exasperation. "There's no other place to put him, Henry."

"What about the other bed?"

A stunned silence fell over the room. Even Otto and Kit stopped their tussling. The wind and rain whistled outside. The walls shuddered.

"The other bed?"

"Yes."

I could not believe what I was hearing. "The one where Abigail is now?"

"Yes."

"I don't know if we should be moving her body," I said doubtfully. "It isn't respectful."

"I still need to sleep on the bed in Jeremiah's bedroom and he'll sleep on it when I spell him upstairs. Abigail is gone. She doesn't care where she's put. Her bed is already covered in filth, so blood won't make any difference."

Shocking though it was to hear Henry speak so of Abigail's body, his words made sense. Better to let the living get the rest they needed to ride out the storm than to refuse to move the dead.

"Do you really think this is a good idea?" Kit asked. "I don't think we should move Abigail's body."

"We're not leaving my cousin on the floor." Otto spoke as if he had nothing to do with the injury August had sustained.

"Enough. We're moving Abigail's body," I said. I spoke to Henry. "Deborah and I will stay here with August while you and Philemon go into the bedroom and move Abigail as close to the side of the bed as you can. Then you can help me get August in there."

"I'll move her myself," Henry said. He looked at Philemon. "You're not going in there."

Philemon shrugged. "Do what suits you."

Henry disappeared into the bedroom he had shared with Abigail. It wasn't long before we heard thuds and shuffling coming from the bedroom, and after several minutes Henry returned to the parlor, breathing heavily. "All right. I put her on the floor."

Kit was still holding Otto by one arm. They looked on as I took hold of August under his arms and Henry took his feet.

Together we dragged him into the bedroom. When it became clear we would need one more person to help us lift August onto the bed, I asked Kit to leave Otto and join us since Henry forbade Philemon from going into the bedroom.

With his help, we were able to lift August in one swift movement. We tried to avoid the areas of the bed that Abigail had soiled, but were not able to do so completely.

August groaned angrily as we arranged him on the bed. He seemed to realize where we were placing him, but we ignored his mumbled protests. He needed to rest someplace other than the floor, and Henry had denied him access to the only other bed in the cottage.

When I returned to the parlor I took the seat nearest the lamp. Otto seemed finally subdued as he sat at the table, his hands folded in front of him.

Deborah took a look at my clothing and made a clucking sound with her teeth. "You'll need to change out of those clothes, Deputy. There's blood all over you."

I had known it, of course, but it wasn't until I looked down that I realized how much blood August had lost. It was a wonder he had any left in his body.

"You can change in Jeremiah's room," Henry said. "He'll have extra clothes in the bureau."

I nodded my thanks as Henry made his way up to the lighthouse tower. I picked my way carefully through the dimness to Jeremiah's door. I would owe him a pair of trousers and a shirt when the storm was over—the clothes I had been wearing belonged to him and I doubted Deborah was going to be able to wash all the blood out of them.

"Bring the clothes when you come out and I'll launder them," Deborah said.

I closed the door behind me and the darkness in the bedroom was complete. I almost returned to the parlor for a lamp, but I preferred leaving it out there so Kit could keep an eye on Otto. I recalled Jeremiah's bureau being on the far side of the room, so I felt my way over to it, taking care not to bump into the bedstead or the chair.

If Jeremiah was anything like me, he kept his underthings and other miscellany in the top drawer, his shirts in the middle drawer, and his trousers in the bottom drawer. I withdrew the first article of clothing from the bottom, then felt it up and down to determine that it was, in fact, a pair of trousers. From the middle drawer I took out what I hoped was a shirt and placed that on the floor with the trousers.

Peeling off my shirt, I could feel my chest sticky with August's blood. I used the shirt as a rag to clean up as best I could, then dropped it on the floor where I knew it wouldn't touch Jeremiah's clean clothes. Then I did the same thing with my trousers, which were mostly bloodied on the thighs and knees. Somehow even my stockings were wet with blood. I quickly stuffed my arms and legs into Jeremiah's clothes, then reached for my soiled things on the floor, gathering them into a bundle.

I felt around the floor for my stockings and found one of them around the side of Jeremiah's bureau. I must have kicked it accidentally when I was changing my clothes. I bent to retrieve the stocking, and when I pulled it toward me, something came with it. Was it a piece of paper? Jeremiah might be looking for it —I could give it to him when he came downstairs. I stuffed it in my pocket and went back into the parlor, where I handed Deborah the bloodied clothes.

# CHAPTER 17

*D*eborah looked at the pile of garments with dismay. "I'll try to get the stains out of these things, Deputy, but without sufficient light …" She shook her head.

I followed her as she retreated into the kitchen with one of the lamps. She turned with a gasp when I cleared my throat.

"I didn't hear you behind me, for heaven's sake. What do you want?" she asked.

I spoke in a low voice, close to her ear. "A little bit ago you mentioned there was a story. About Otto. Can you acquaint me with it? I need as much information about him as I can get, especially given his behavior."

Deborah didn't say anything for a long moment. I thought she had changed her mind about sharing whatever information she had, but she finally spoke after casting an eye toward the parlor.

"There's been bad blood between the Schuhmachers and the Brewsters for years." Her voice was practically a whisper, so I had to lean closer to hear her over the sounds of the storm. "I suppose being rescued by the likes of Henry Brewster was quite a blow to Otto."

"What's the source of the conflict?"

"Are you sure you haven't heard the story?"

"I'm sure."

She paused before speaking. "Now, I don't want you to think I'm telling tales."

"Of course not. I asked you to tell me what you know."

"It goes back many years. I probably shouldn't be gossiping about him. Especially now that we're all stuck in here."

I suppressed a sigh. "You'd be doing me a great favor, Deborah. I need to know what the problems are between the men, like you said, especially now that we're all stuck in here. I'd like to be able to anticipate troubles before they arise."

"You haven't done very well so far."

I couldn't see her face very well in the dimness, but from the sound of her voice, I knew it was pinched and disapproving. I declined to respond to the insult, but stood waiting for her to speak. She sighed. "Very well, I'll tell you what I know." She glanced toward the doorway to the parlor as if to make sure no one could overhear.

She leaned closer to me and spoke in a barely audible tone. "I don't know the whole story, but I know the trouble between Otto and the Brewsters started when Otto's brother, Karl, killed Abigail's brother, Horatio."

I blinked. I'd never heard an inkling of any such thing.

She continued. "Everyone knew it was Karl who killed Horatio, of course, so Karl had no choice but to flee. He never returned."

"And have you any idea what caused the trouble between Otto's brother and Abigail's brother?"

"I don't know what prompted the fatal attack on Horatio, but I've heard tell that he wronged Karl first. I'm only telling you what I've heard. Like I said, I'm no teller of tales. Before God, I am not telling you this is the honest truth. I don't—"

"Deborah? What's going on in here?"

The booming voice belonged to Kit. He walked slowly through the kitchen and came to a stop at my side. He held the other oil lamp in one hand. He stood for a moment in silence, then his eyes narrowed as he addressed both of us. "Anything I should know about?"

"Just asking Deborah a few questions about a matter of local history."

"And what matter would that be?" Kit seemed suddenly wary of my presence. He positioned himself between Deborah and me, as might a jealous dog.

"Nothing of great import," I said. I took care to keep my tone light and friendly. I leaned in as if I were going to share a confidence with Kit. "I was hoping Deborah could tell me about the trouble between Otto and the Brewsters."

Kit glowered at Deborah. "What have I told you about repeating ill-intentioned gossip?"

I expected her to cower under Kit's gaze. But on the contrary, she stood up straighter. It was as if she mustered the ability to stand up to him in this cottage—perhaps because of all the other men around. Her voice became almost a hiss. "I have made it perfectly clear to the deputy that I do not go around spreading gossip. I told him I have heard there was some trouble between Otto and the Brewsters and that it started when Karl Schuhmacher killed Abigail's brother, Horatio. I did not tell him I personally witnessed anything." Her eyes narrowed, almost like she was inviting a challenge, but Kit did not respond.

"When was Abigail's brother killed?" I asked.

Kit spoke up. "It must be nearly twenty years ago now. Jeremiah was very young when it happened." Deborah nodded.

"And people are certain Karl Schuhmacher killed him?" I directed my question to Kit.

"I do not know. It is not my place to ask or discuss the matter." He shot Deborah a dark look. "Nor is it yours."

She smirked and turned her back to us, then took up a washtub from the floor and busied herself away from us in a corner of the room.

"Is there anything else you can tell me about Otto and the Brewsters?" I asked Kit.

"I don't know anything more than what Deborah told you. I cannot make it clear enough, Deputy, that this is all idle gossip and gossip is a low form of entertainment."

"I do not wish to entertain myself, Kit." I feared my exasperation was beginning to show. "There is a certain amount of tension in this cottage that doesn't seem to come from the heat or the storm alone. It is my job to know what might cause trouble and what I can safely ignore. If there has been serious conflict in the past between Otto and the man who runs the light, I need to know about it. I have a responsibility to keep everyone safe. Knowing about secrets between the men in here is important for me to do my job."

I jerked my head toward the kitchen doorway when another voice muscled its way into the kitchen from darkness of the parlor.

"What's going on in there? Should the rest of us join you?"

It was Philemon. Kit and I exchanged glances as Kit moved toward the doorway. I followed him and nearly ran into him when he stopped short. The man was solid as a wall.

"Apologies," I muttered.

Kit spoke in a quiet voice. "The next time you wish to speak to Deborah, you will tell me so I can come along." He turned and walked into the parlor.

I could feel my face flame from his reprimand. I didn't care for the way he spoke to his wife or, indeed, anyone else. I would never have treated Evelyn in such a way. I had trusted and respected her more than that.

"I'm going to check on August," I announced when I went back into the parlor. My voice sounded loud. Philemon rose to go with me, but I stopped him. "Sit down. I'm going myself. You can see him when I give you permission or when Henry decides to let you into the room."

I could hear the sneer in Philemon's voice when he replied. "I don't take kindly to being told what to do, Deputy."

The man's audacity was astonishing. "I don't care what you take kindly to and what you take unkindly to, Philemon. Stay put while I check on August. Kit, watch him." It could have been worse—Otto could have joined his voice to Philemon's demand, but mercifully he remained quiet. Perhaps the man finally felt something akin to remorse for the injury he had caused.

I took the lamp, leaving the parlor in even deeper darkness. The bedroom door creaked slightly as I opened it and peered into the gloom, holding the lamp aloft. I could make out August's form lying on the bed. I closed the door and walked toward him.

"August? Can you hear me?"

He made an almost inaudible sound. "You all right, August? That was quite a lump you took."

A groan.

"Can I get you anything?"

Another groan.

"Mind if I have a look at that gash on your head?"

August shifted slightly, then croaked, "Otto? That you?"

"No, it's Deputy Moore."

"I want to talk to Otto."

"In a minute, August. First I need to look at your wound." I set the lamp on the small table next to the bed and leaned over August. Even in the dim light I could see how pale he was. No wonder. He had lost a lot of blood. I leaned closer and he winced and turned his head away from me.

"I need to see the wound. If it's still bleeding we need to get more rags to clean it up again."

He let out a growl and I took a step backward. "All right,

August. All right. I won't come any closer or look at your head. Would you like me to get you some water so you can clean it yourself?"

"No."

"Can I get you some cider?"

"Hmh."

I took that to mean "yes," so I carried the lamp to the kitchen, leaving the bedroom door open behind me. Deborah was wringing out the bloodied clothes.

"I'm getting August a drink," I told her by way of explaining my presence. I poured a ladleful of cider into a cup and took it back into the bedroom.

Again I closed the door and walked slowly toward the bed. Before I could say anything, August started to mumble. "Otto, mind no one finds out about the boat."

What boat? What about it? Was he talking about the boat that had broken apart in the storm?

# CHAPTER 18

*I* wasn't about to tell August that he had me confused with his cousin. His thinking was obviously addled. I glanced over my shoulder to make sure I had closed the door securely, then turned back to August.

"The boat?" I tried making my voice deeper and meaner, the way Otto's voice sounded.

August moaned.

"What'll they find out?"

August was mumbling so I couldn't be sure of what he said, but it sounded like "Philemon."

"What about him?"

August uttered only senseless sounds after that, and no matter what I asked, he revealed nothing more—nothing about Philemon, nothing about the boat. Nothing at all. A shiver of tension crept up my arms. I wished the storm would blow itself out so Philemon could be on his way, wherever he was headed.

I set the cup of cider on the table beside August, then left the room quietly.

"How is he?" Deborah asked. She was sitting in the parlor,

near the remains of the fire. Kit sat against the wall across the room.

"He's in a bad way, I'm afraid. I can't determine if that gash on his head is still bleeding because he won't let me near to look at it. I tried to get him to let me clean it off with wet rags, but he pulled away. We need to get a bandage on that wound."

"Would it help if I tried?" Deborah asked.

I shook my head. "I reckon not. He's pretty ornery about it."

"Can I go in and see him?" Otto's voice betrayed concern. He was already half out of his chair.

I didn't answer right away. After all, this was the man whose actions had resulted in August's injury. But then again, he had behaved since it happened and he did sound contrite. "I shouldn't allow it because you caused his injury, but you might be able to get him to agree to clean himself off. Or at least let someone else do it. Go on in. Leave the door open."

Otto nodded once as he made his way into the bedroom. I watched in silence as he pulled the door until it was only slightly ajar. If Philemon hadn't been in the room, I would have stood outside the door to hear what the cousins were saying to each other. But I didn't dare, especially now that I had learned there was something Philemon wasn't telling the rest of us.

I strained to hear what, if anything, Otto and August were saying. I wondered if Otto would be able to pull August out of his confusion and get the man to make some sense. I couldn't hear anything above the constant howling wind and driving rain, except for a low murmur that I assumed belonged to Otto.

Presently Otto came out shaking his head. "He ain't making a sound in there other than angry moaning. I can't get him to talk at all. But that gash is pretty deep."

"Do you think he'd let you clean the wound with a rag?" I asked.

"If I did that, he'd bite my finger clean off."

"He didn't say anything?"

"I told you already, Deputy. I couldn't get him to talk at all. You think I'm telling tales?"

"No, no. Just making sure. I wish we could get the doctor out here, but I'm afraid no one is coming anywhere near this cottage until the storm blows out to sea."

"Do you think he's going to be all right?" Deborah's voice sounded fretful.

"He'll be fine," Kit said. "If I know August, that hard head of his will serve him well." He chuckled.

"Ain't funny, Kit." Otto's voice held a warning. The effects of the rum seemed to be waning.

Kit glared at him. Philemon chuckled and I frowned when I saw him nudge Otto. The strain in the cottage was drawing ever tighter. I watched Philemon warily. "You hail from Philadelphia, don't you?" he asked Kit.

"Yes. Why?"

"You're quite a swell," Philemon said. "I wager you think you're better'n everyone else hereabouts."

"Then you would be making a foolish wager." Kit scoffed.

Philemon pushed himself away from the table. "Foolish, am I?" His voice was rising.

"You heard what I said."

Philemon advanced around the table toward Kit. "You and your books and your fancy language. You're a flapdoodle if I've ever seen one."

Kit stood up at this most carnal and despicable insult. He clenched his fists. "Would you care for me to show you how much of a man I am?"

I stepped quickly between Kit and Philemon, noting how Kit loomed over Philemon's shorter and more rotund figure "That'll be enough, gentlemen. Philemon, you'll keep your insults to yourself. And Kit, I'll not stand for fisticuffs. There is a lady present and the last thing we need is for a petty argument to come to blows when we're all cooped up in here with no option to leave before the storm dies down. Now sit, both of you."

I moved to the center of the room as Kit and Philemon sat in chairs as far from each other as possible. "Deborah, I could do with some cider. Is there enough left in the kitchen?"

"There's plenty."

"Could I trouble you to get some for me?"

She sighed. "If I must. Would anyone else like cider?"

Kit and Philemon said they would have some. Otto remained quiet. I had a feeling he was worrying about his cousin.

"He'll be fine, Otto," I said.

"I hope so. His wife is a downright fussock and my own wife'll skin me alive if she becomes my responsibility."

I was astonished at his callousness, though I probably shouldn't have been. Deborah, who was making her way to the kitchen, turned and gasped. "Otto Schuhmacher! Bite your tongue. Martha is no fussock. She may tend toward plumpness, but it's not good to be too lean, either. She has lovely dimples and an agreeable voice. That should count for something."

"Be off with ye, woman," Otto said.

Deborah turned abruptly and hastened into the kitchen. If I expected Kit to object to Otto's rudeness toward Deborah, my expectations went unmet.

Presently she returned with several cups and a pitcher of cider. She set them on the table with a thud and moved immediately toward the fireplace, where she sat with her back to the rest of us. Kit moved cautiously toward the table in the darkness.

I drank the cider slowly, savoring its earthy tang. I was lost in my thoughts, turning our circumstances over in my mind, and didn't notice until it was too late that the pitcher was empty. For once Philemon had taken only a small amount and

Otto's cup sat on the table, untouched. Kit had consumed almost the entire pitcher.

He gulped a mouthful of air and eructed loudly. The sound was wet. I could smell his foul breath as he exhaled in my direction, and I turned my head to one side to avoid the odor.

"I'm tired. I'm going to rest." On the tabletop, Kit dropped his head abruptly onto his crossed arms. Deborah inhaled as if to say something, but remained silent. I wondered if she had been about to chastise him for sleeping at the table. Whatever she had been about to say, it was likely she avoided a dressing down by her husband when she decided to keep her thoughts to herself.

"I need someone to help me up here," came Henry's voice from the top of the stairs. "Someone tall enough to reach the lamp workings. One of the chains is about to break."

That sounded ominous. Without all the chains, the light would cease to turn and flash properly. Anyone unlucky enough to be on the sea in the storm, if they were still alive, would surely not survive without a beacon to guide him away from the shore.

I moved to the bottom of the stairs. "Shall I wake Jeremiah?"

"You'd better. I'll need two men to fix the chain. Send Kit, too. I need the tallest men for this job."

I looked behind me into the darkened room where shadows from the fireplace embers dipped and danced on the walls in grotesque arcs. I wondered briefly if I should go in Kit's stead. I was only a couple inches shorter than he. After practically a pitcher's worth of cider, did he have his wits about him sufficiently to get up the stairs and assist Henry?

Kit hadn't fallen asleep yet, so he staggered to his feet and made his way toward the steps, bumping a chair here and a table there.

"Kit, maybe I should try to help Henry instead," I said. "I'm not sure you're steady enough to get up the stairs."

Even in the gloom, I could sense the disdainful look he

turned on me. He scoffed. "You may be tall, George, but you're not as tall as I am. Besides, Henry requested me. I'm going up. It is the least I can do in exchange for the excellent drink he has provided for us." He laughed, then grasped the railing and began his slow climb up the steps. I watched his shadowy form from the bottom step, making sure he didn't stumble and come toppling down.

I turned back to face the others in the parlor. It was probably best that I remained downstairs, since I wasn't sure Otto and Philemon could be trusted to maintain civility toward Deborah. I knocked on Jeremiah's door and he answered gruffly.

"What?"

"Your father needs you upstairs. The chain's about to break."

Jeremiah uttered a loud oath. A moment later, he left his room and tromped up the stairs.

The rest of us sat in silence, listening to the wind shriek and feeling the cottage shudder with each terrible gust. Several minutes passed before we heard Kit's voice.

"God's teeth, Henry! If neither Jeremiah nor I can reach it, no one can. I'll get something to stand on downstairs and bring it back up."

Only seconds later, there was a scream and the sickening thud of someone plunging down the stairs.

# CHAPTER 19

*I* grabbed an oil lamp, turned it up, and in three strides was at the bottom of the steps.

"Kit? You all right?" Henry's voice came from the top of the stairway. Quick footsteps descended.

At his words, Deborah gasped. "Kit? Is Kit hurt?" She followed me up the steps. "Is he all right, Deputy?"

I had reached Kit and stared at him in shock and dismay. Kit was not all right. His body lay across several steps, his head cocked at an unnatural angle. His vibrant blue eyes were wide open. I knew they observed nothing.

Behind me, Deborah clattered up the steps. I shifted so she wouldn't be able to see his upper body. Suddenly the sound of her agonized scream overpowered the noise from the storm.

"Get her back downstairs," I ordered. I didn't care who came up to fetch her, but I wasn't about to let her see Kit's head and neck. I didn't know if she realized yet that he hadn't survived the fall.

Jeremiah followed his father down from the tower, but Henry instructed him to go back upstairs to work on the chain.

"I need help moving Kit," I said grimly.

"Is he alive, Deputy?" Deborah's voice quivered.

I didn't answer her—I couldn't bear to. Not yet. I harbored a wild, irrational hope that there might be a slight chance he was still alive. His head was situated several steps above where I stood and his arms were flung above his head, so I couldn't reach his neck or wrist to feel for a pulse. We needed to get him down the stairs immediately if there was a chance we could administer aid.

"Otto, Philemon, help me."

Henry stood on the step above Kit's head, staring at him. "Is he alive?"

"I don't think so." I spoke in a low voice. "Check his pulse. I can't reach his wrists."

Henry placed his hand on Kit's neck. After several moments he shook his head.

"I'll take his head and shoulders," said Henry. "You all get below him and we'll carry him down that way."

Otto and Philemon took their places directly behind me. I pressed my body against the wall as best I could so the two men could reach Kit's legs and feet. Henry was positioning himself at the head. Once we were able to move Kit, I would station myself in his middle and support his back. I extinguished the lamp so I could leave it on the stairs and use both hands to help. This was going to be no easy task with a man of his size.

"On three," I said. "One ... two ... three." The men snorted and huffed with exertion as they struggled to lift Kit's body from the steps. Inch by inch, we moved him down. I had hoped we could carry him, but the best we could manage was to slide him down clumsily from one step to the next. At least Henry had hold of his head.

Finally we had him at the bottom of the stairs. We stood panting, resting a moment before taking him into the bedroom. I had intentionally blocked Deborah's view of Kit with my own body. Before taking him into the bedroom, I put two fingers against his neck for several seconds. I confirmed Henry's finding—no pulse.

"Let me through, Deputy. I want to see him."

"As soon as we get him settled, Deborah," I promised. "All right, men. Let's get him into the bedroom now. It'll be easier to carry him now that he's off the stairs."

Otto and Philemon were still at Kit's feet. I was alongside, supporting his back. Henry continued to support Kit's head and shoulders. We were against the parlor wall, so Deborah couldn't get around to the other side of her husband. She moved behind me, trying to see him. The light from the fire was very dim, so I hoped she would not be able to discern him clearly even if she could see around my back.

Our progress was still slow, but we managed better than we had on the steps. Once we were near the door to the bedroom where August still lay, Otto reached out with one hand and pushed it open. "Where do you want him, George?" he asked.

"We can put him on the floor for now."

"The floor?" Deborah cried out. "No. You'll put him on the bed where he belongs."

I couldn't see the faces of any of the other men, but I had a feeling they were looking at me for guidance.

"Very well, let's put him on the bed. Philemon, can you hold his legs while Otto moves August? We'll need more room on the bed."

"The bed is soiled," Deborah said, her voice rising. "You can't put him there."

"Deborah, we need to place him somewhere. We have to keep Jeremiah's room available for the lighthouse keepers to rest between spells upstairs. If we don't put Kit on the floor, the bed is our only other choice. Unfortunately, August is not able to get out of the bed because of his injury, so we have to make do in the best way we can."

She squeezed through the bedroom door and now stood

opposite me, helping support Kit's back. She must have been frantic with worry, but she worked as hard as any of us men to position Kit on the bed. As soon as we had laid him out, she reached for his throat. She held her fingers there for a full minute before letting out a chilling, animal-like howl.

I moved to put my hand on her arm, but she shrank away. "Don't! No one touch me! Leave me alone." She knelt by the side of the bed, sobbing. Otto, Philemon, Henry, and I backed quietly out of the room. August moaned from his side of the bed, then fell silent.

Back in the parlor, I pulled the door closed behind me. I retrieved the oil lamp from the stairs and joined everyone in the parlor, standing in an awkward circle staring at the floor.

Philemon was the first to speak. "That makes two deaths in this house since the storm started. And one man near death."

"What should we say to that?" Otto asked.

"Nothing. But you have to agree it's mighty strange." Philemon let out an unpleasant noise. "The odor in here is rank."

"I need to get back upstairs if we're to repair that chain," Henry said in a rough voice. Kit's death had no doubt affected him. He departed.

Above the sound from the wind and rain, Deborah's sobs continued in the bedroom.

Otto spoke in a low voice. "Everyone knows Kit raised his hand to her all the time. I don't know why she's carrying on like she is."

"No one else'll have her," Philemon said.

I wanted to disagree, to scold him, but he was probably right. I went to the door and opened it a small crack. The cries came from the floor next to Kit, and though it was dark, I could picture Deborah curled into a small ball near his side of the bed.

"Deborah? May I come in?"

She made a noise that sounded like assent, so I stepped further into the room and closed the door quietly behind me.

"I'm sorry, Deborah. I believe he was gone before we reached him on the steps."

Her shoulders shook and she gulped loudly. I could hear her skirts rustling. Her voice was a bit closer, and I knew she had raised herself off the floor.

"Can I bring you something to drink? Or to eat?" I asked. "You need to keep up your strength."

"For what?" She wailed afresh. "Keep up my strength for what? For a dead husband?"

"To get through the storm safely," I said in a quiet voice. "Come along with me. I'll get you something to drink while you sit by the fire."

"I'm too hot to sit by the fire."

"You can sit anywhere you'd like. But let's get you something to drink. You can come back in here afterward, if you'd like."

I waited. Presently she rose and walked slowly toward me. I opened the door and in the sliver of dim light that spilled in from the parlor, she sought my arm and grasped it.

# CHAPTER 20

*A*fter Deborah had taken a drink from the cup of cider I handed her, she returned to the bedroom where, I presumed, she took up her vigil again on the floor next to Kit's side of the bed. I went in twice over the next thirty minutes to check on her and to make sure August was still breathing. Her crying had slowed; August seemed to be asleep.

Back in the parlor, Otto and Philemon were blessedly quiet. Kit's death had taken the vinegar out of them. I could just make out both of them, sitting at the table and staring sullenly into the darkness.

My nerves were unsettled. I was the representative of authority in this cottage, and as long as I was stuck there, it was my job to ensure the safety of everyone inside. I had to admit to myself that I had done my job very poorly, considering there had now been two deaths in the cottage since the beginning of the storm and August lay close to death.

I knew I couldn't have done anything to prevent Abigail's death, but the same couldn't be said of Kit. I knew he had taken too much drink too quickly, and yet I allowed him to go up to the lighthouse gallery to assist Henry in fixing the chain. Did that make me culpable for his fall down the stairs?

The answer was yes. He wouldn't have fallen down the steps to his death if I hadn't permitted him to go up. I didn't know how I was going to live with myself after the storm was over.

And now that Kit was gone, would I be responsible for Deborah's well-being? She and I had managed to maintain a certain level of civility between us, but the truth was that I didn't care for her and I was quite sure she did not care for me. I could tell from the tone of her voice when she spoke to me. The thought of spending the rest of my life ensuring her welfare was not something I relished. A wave of guilt washed over me for thinking such thoughts.

I sat in the chair closest to Jeremiah's bedroom. I was feeling flushed, and I needed to be away from the heat. The only sound was the incessant storm, which had not abated. I took a deep breath and let it out slowly. I leaned forward, my elbows on my knees and my head in my hands. I closed my eyes and tried to take deep breaths. It wouldn't do to lose control of myself here in front of Otto and Philemon.

There was no question this storm would be easier to tolerate without their presence and that of Otto's cousin, August. They had done nothing to assuage the hardships we were all experiencing. To the contrary, they had made things considerably more difficult.

And the more I thought about them, the more uneasy I became. I had never deemed Otto or August particularly principled, and now in the company of their friend, I felt strongly that none of them were trustworthy. First, August had plainly thought he was talking to his cousin Otto when he mumbled warnings about the boat and about Philemon. It was clear they were hiding something.

Second, had they really been fishing out there in the bay? I recalled looking out the window after the wagon woke me early that morning—I had noticed then how much the wind had worsened overnight. Even I knew better than to take a boat out in such a gale. Were Otto, August, and Philemon really so foolish as to attempt to fish in this weather?

I could no longer sit still. I rose and paced the length of the room. Back and forth, back and forth. I trod as quietly as I could, lest I disturb Otto and Philemon. Hopefully they had finally fallen asleep.

I thrust my hands into my trouser pockets and my fingers brushed the coarse paper I had gathered up from Jeremiah's bedroom floor with my bloodied clothing. I had forgotten to give it to Jeremiah. I pulled it out and tried smoothing it.

I hadn't intended to read the note, but the sad fact was that I was nosy. Between my curiosity and my boredom, I knew I would not be able to resist peeking at it. I had little hope it would contain any information that would help explain anything that had happened since the storm's onset, but might it hold the key to explaining why such a pleasant young man had become rude and ill-tempered since I had seen him last?

I moved quietly to the chair next to the oil lamp, hoping no one was watching me. I hadn't noticed any movement, so it was safe to say the men were asleep. Or they were ignoring me. Leaning close to the lamp's chimney, I squinted to see the words written on the paper, which I now noticed was torn and soiled. The ink on the paper was smudged, so I could not read the entire message. I was able to make out a date, though—26 August 1821. Only eight days ago.

... *must meet with you to warn you about something I have discovered. You will find it of great interest, I am sure. I will be behind the ... on the first day of September ...*

The bottom portion of the note was torn off. I quickly forgot about the problems I had encountered since arriving at the lighthouse many hours previously. This paper fragment was more intriguing. Who had written the message? Who was it meant for? Who had read it? What was the warning it mentioned? Question after question ran through my mind. There was no indication whether the author of the message was a male or female. The slanted handwriting could belong to anyone.

It was possible, of course, that the message had nothing to do with anyone in the lighthouse keeper's family, but since I had found it on the floor of Jeremiah's bedroom, that possibility seemed remote. It was also possible it was an entirely innocent missive, but because it mentioned a warning and did not specify the subject of that warning, I felt suspicion growing within me. A warning about what? A vision of Abigail's swollen, yellow face surfaced before my eyes. Someone was responsible for her death—of that I had no doubt. Was her premature passing somehow related to the warning in the letter?

I reread the message, then folded it and returned it to my trouser pocket. I glanced over toward the other men in the room. If they were awake and wondered what I was reading, they did not make it obvious. They were not the sorts to hesitate when they wanted to ask or say something, so I presumed they hadn't noticed me.

I had more questions than answers. Now in addition to trying to learn what happened to Abigail, I wanted to know more about the letter. I had a strong hunch that the warning referred to in the note had a connection of some kind to the events that had unfolded since I arrived at the lighthouse. I needed to find out more about the other people in the cottage with me without arousing their suspicions. I had seen from the actions of Otto and Philemon that they could be quick to anger, and even dangerous, and it wouldn't do to make an already tense situation worse. And Deborah, especially, might be in too fragile a state to face further calamity.

Otto shifted in his chair.

"Can't you sit still?" Philemon growled.

"Mind yourself," Otto's tone held a warning.

The door to the sick room opened and Deborah stepped into the parlor. The flame from the oil lamp brightened and danced in the slight draft created by the door moving on its hinge, then settled into its natural state again when Deborah closed the door behind her. I noticed in the momentary light that Otto was facing away from Philemon. Deborah sat heavily in the chair next to me.

"I'm very sorry about Kit," I said.

"Thank you, Deputy. I apologize if I offended you with my harsh words earlier."

"You didn't offend me. I'm no stranger to the death of a spouse." I was staring straight ahead into the blackness of the room, but I could feel Deborah's head turn toward me.

"You aren't?" she asked quietly.

"That's correct." I already regretted my statement, because Deborah would no doubt want to know what I was talking about and I did not wish to discuss my wife's death. I hoped my tone conveyed my desire to put an end to any questions. But it did not.

"What happened, if I might ask?"

Should I tell her everything? How my wife had died in agony? Should I tell her there were many times I was barely able to get myself to work because I was overwhelmed with grief? Should I tell her I couldn't sleep at night? That I missed Evelyn every hour?

I could not bring myself to discuss those things. I did not want to frighten her with tales of the path she could find herself on now that Kit was gone. And it would be even worse for her, a woman, with a farm and livestock to raise. Besides, I had no wish to let Otto and Philemon know of my private musings.

"My wife died."

That short explanation served to stop Deborah from asking any further questions. I did not mean to say the words so tersely, but I could not help it.

# CHAPTER 21

*D*eborah stood and, using her hands to guide her, went into the kitchen. She bumped into furniture with her legs as she moved. She emerged a short time later and set something on the table with a dull thud.

"I've brought potatoes," she announced in a tired voice. "They're not hot, but they're cooked. I made them this morning. We should all eat something. I'll take some up to Henry and Jeremiah."

"I'll do that. You rest. You must be tired," I said.

"Thank you, Deputy. I am quite spent."

Otto and Philemon were already seated at the table. They helped themselves to potatoes—the sounds they made gnawing and chewing were grotesque. I picked up a lamp and used it to light my path to the table, then took two potatoes and left the lamp where it was while I made my way clumsily up to the tower.

I found Henry rummaging in the box where I had found the balls of wax earlier. Jeremiah was wiping down one of the large panes of glass that separated us from the storm. I thought for a moment of the peril of anyone who might be out on the water in this weather. The light shining from the lighthouse apparatus was dimmer because the chain still hadn't been fixed and the reflectors weren't working properly.

"I brought some food. Deborah cooked potatoes this morning."

I must have startled Jeremiah, because he spun around with a look of surprise. Henry emerged from the small storage room and joined us.

Each man took a potato. "Thank you," they said in unison.

"How do things look from up here?" I asked.

"Storm's not slowing down yet," Henry said.

"I can't see nothing out any of the windows." Jeremiah chewed thoughtfully on his meager meal.

"It makes an awful noise up here," I said. "Worse than downstairs."

Jeremiah nodded, still staring out the window into the storm. I stood between him and Henry, my eyes narrowing as I tried to peer beyond my reflection and into the dark, slashing rain. Only a few moments had passed before I realized the movement and sound of the storm almost had the power to put me into a trance. It was easy to see how I startled Jeremiah when I came upstairs.

"Hard to believe the storm isn't letting up yet after all these hours," I mused.

"It'll work itself out to sea before too long," Henry said.

I hoped he was right. He had been watching storms from this lighthouse for over twenty years, so I trusted what he said. The question was how many hours we could all endure each other in this lighthouse and the cottage without fresh air and sufficient light.

I left father and son to their work. When I returned to the parlor, it took my eyes some time before I could make out shapes and figures in the dimness. I eased myself into the chair next to the lamp.

"I believe I'll try to rest." Deborah's voice came from the floor.

"Are you all right there on the floor?"

"Yes. I've piled two quilts over here. That should be sufficient. There are plenty of quilts left for you and the others to use if you want to sleep, too."

"Thank you." I waited for Otto and Philemon to say something, but I heard only the wind. I wondered that Deborah did not try to sleep on the floor next to Kit in the bedroom, but her next words responded to my unspoken thoughts.

"I would sleep on the floor next to my husband, but it would be inappropriate for me to go to sleep in the bedroom with August in there."

"I understand."

I sat at the table and helped myself to a potato. I bit into it and found it very dry. I wished I had a big mug of cider to drink, but I didn't want to disturb Deborah by trying to find my way around the kitchen. I chewed the potato slowly while I thought about the two other men in the room, neither of whom had made a sound since I came down from the light. My thoughts hearkened back to their rescue.

I doubted more and more that they had been fishing. Not only had the weather been too stormy earlier in the day for rational people to be on the water, but the three men hadn't even agreed on what they were trying to catch when I asked them. Each one had named a different species of fish.

How best to ask them what they had been doing in the bay when their boat broke apart? I wanted to avoid testing their short tempers as long as I could in this furnace of a cottage, but I also wanted answers. And I felt it unwise to confront them simultaneously.

Philemon reached for another potato. "Much as I hate these potatoes, I'm still hungry."

"They're there for the eating," I replied in a low voice, for I hoped Deborah might already be asleep. "I don't want another one."

"Why are we whispering?"

"So Deborah is able to get some sleep. She must be exhausted after all she's been through tonight."

"That were a bad sight, Kit being dead."

"Shh. You don't want her to hear you."

"And if she does? Would it change anything?"

"Philemon, I must ask you to have some regard for the woman."

Philemon scoffed. "It won't change anything if she hears us."

There was no convincing him of the need to speak quietly, so I said nothing. Perhaps that would get him to keep his mouth closed. Did the man ever have anything useful to say?

I stiffened when I heard a loud cry issuing from the bedroom where August lay. A chair scraped against the floor in the parlor and I knew Otto had stood quickly. We reached the bedroom door at the same time. Otto burst into the room.

"August?"

The man on the bed answered his cousin with a low groan and Otto stepped toward him. "What do you need?"

There was no answer save for August's labored breathing. I moved forward to stand next to Otto. "August, it's Deputy Moore. Can I bring you a bit of potato? The potatoes aren't hot, but they're cooked and soft."

August lay motionless. I could barely make out his form in the darkness, and I was sure Otto couldn't see him, either. If he had moved, we would have heard his body shift against the bedclothes.

"He needs to see a doctor," Otto said in a low voice.

"I'm afraid there's no way of getting August to the doctor. And even if we could somehow get word to the doctor that he's needed here, he would never be able to get out here in this storm."

"There must—"

Otto's words were cut off by a terrific crash of shattering glass and a shout from the lighthouse gallery.

"Someone help!"

We ran clumsily into the parlor, now in complete darkness. Not even a feeble glow shone from the top of the lighthouse steps.

The light had gone out.

# CHAPTER 22

*I* felt my way to the bottom of the stairs, with Otto following closely behind me.

I turned around when I heard Deborah's voice. "Deputy, what's happening? George?"

"The light's gone out. Stay down here. We're going to see if we can help fix it somehow."

"Can I help?" she asked.

"Stay down here," I repeated. "Philemon, stay with her." I experienced a moment of hesitation over leaving Deborah and Philemon together downstairs, but it could not be helped. The light was the most important concern at that moment.

Henry and Jeremiah were yelling to each other upstairs over the tumult of the raging storm. By the time I reached the gallery, with Otto still at my heels, the wooden floor was already slick with rain and drops of oil that had spilled over the years. Broken glass crunched beneath our feet.

"Someone clean up all this glass," Henry yelled. "There's a broom in the storage room." I didn't know who he was talking to, so I took it upon myself to do the job. I groped along the wall until I reached the storage room. With my hands in front of me,

I cast around for the broom until my fingers closed on its rough handle. I gripped it tightly, turned around, and made my way back into the gallery.

I swept the floor as best I could, but I know I missed places. Each time I felt glass crunch under my feet, I swept that spot. I tried to corral all the glass into a pile where no one was standing. It was a nearly impossible task in the dark.

As I swept, Henry told Otto where to find rags to start mopping up the mess from the floor. Otto bungled around, walking first into Jeremiah and then into me, in his attempt to locate the rags. Finally he found them and announced loudly that the rest of us needed to mind where we walked because he was trying to clean the floor.

At least he was helping, though it was practically impossible to see where he was.

Finally, Henry and Jeremiah wrestled a number of large pieces of wood from the storage area to the perimeter of the gallery. They nailed the wood to the framework around the windows and gradually, the sound from the wind decreased and the amount of rain streaming horizontally into the gallery ebbed. We all heaved a sigh of relief when the final nail was hammered into place. I could hear Henry and Jeremiah slump against the makeshift window coverings as the hammer slipped to the floor.

"You two all right? Henry? Jeremiah?" I asked.

"I'm all right." Henry's voice sounded tired.

Jeremiah mumbled his assent.

"Nobody asked, but I'm all right, too," Otto whined. I ignored him.

I reached for the staircase railing and gingerly tested the steps. I feared any oil on the bottoms of my shoes would cause me to slip. Slowly I went downstairs, followed by Otto, who muttered at every step.

"God's teeth, man, what are you gabbling on about?" I finally asked. I actually preferred the sound of the storm to his voice.

"Henry Brewster should have been more prepared for this storm," he said angrily. "I shouldn't have to risk my own skin to mop up his mess."

I couldn't see Otto, but I whirled around. "Enough of that. Henry hasn't put you out into the storm, has he? He didn't refuse August a place to lie down after he sustained the injury you caused, did he? Give the man some resp—"

"Deputy? Is that you?" Deborah's strangled voice reached out of the darkness at the bottom of the stairs.

"Yes."

"You'd better come down here. It's August."

My stomach twisted. I quickened my step, but Otto pushed his way past me in an instant.

"Let me go first," he demanded.

"Otto …" I warned.

He hurried down the stairs, cursing as he slipped several times.

"Otto, wait," I called.

But it was no use. I hadn't even reached the bottom of the stairs before I heard Otto's roar of rage coming from the bedroom. I knocked over a small table in my haste to reach him.

"What happened?" I asked. Philemon echoed my words and reached the bedroom door at the same time as I.

"He's gone. August is dead." Otto let out a cry of despair. "We left him alone to die while we were on a fool's errand." His voice was thick with anger. "He is my aunt's only son. What am I going to tell her?"

I placed my fingers on August's neck and felt for a pulse. When I didn't feel anything, I tried his wrists. I finally had to admit it was time to give up. "I'm sorry, Otto. He has no pulse."

"I know." Otto was quieter now. Deborah had brought a lamp into the room and in the flickering lamplight, I saw his eyes rise to meet mine. "That makes three dead since the storm started. It's Neptune's Curse."

For the first time, I wondered if it were truly possible that a curse plagued the lighthouse and its occupants. Then I shook my head vigorously. Such a thought was nonsense.

An involuntary shiver snaked down my arms. I couldn't stem the sense of foreboding that threatened to consume me. I gritted my teeth, trying to avoid its grasp, and responded. "I don't believe it was any such thing. The causes of death have been completely unrelated. It's merely an uncanny run of misfortune, I would say." I didn't want to share with him my conviction Abigail's death had been caused by someone in the lighthouse. My mind brimmed with images of her lifeless face.

Kit's fall down the stairs had been an accident, albeit one I should have prevented. And as for August ... I didn't say aloud what was going through my mind. It was not the time, as long as we were all prisoners in this cottage. In a drunken frenzy Otto had all but killed his cousin himself when he swung that glass rum bottle. Perhaps that hadn't been his intent, but that was the foreseeable result. I had encountered several such situations since becoming deputy sheriff, but those victims survived with prompt treatment from a physician.

Otto knelt near his cousin, his head hanging. I grasped him by the arm and helped him to stand, then we both moved into the parlor. He sat down heavily in the now-dark room. I took both oil lamps and carried them upstairs—Henry and Jeremiah needed them more than we did downstairs—then returned to the parlor.

I have never been afraid in the dark. Darkness is when the most dastardly deeds occur, but it is also a time of quiet. Of rest. When darkness falls, good people find comfort in their homes and families.

This darkness was different. This darkness held a sense of malice. I was not afraid, but I was on my guard. I was keenly aware of the need to remain cautious and vigilant for the remainder of the storm.

If the circumstances had been ordinary, I would have placed Otto under arrest and taken him to the cell where he couldn't harm anyone else. I was quite sure he was no longer feeling the effects of too much drink, but I didn't know whether I could trust him to behave rationally now that his cousin had died. Again, the specter of Abe Bradford, sleeping off his drink in the cell in town, rose before my eyes. I wondered if he was still alive. I hoped he was. I couldn't bear to think about my horse, stuck out-of-doors in the paddock, wide-eyed and terrified as the storm screamed around her.

I bade my thoughts return to the lighthouse before I drove myself mad with worry over Aces and Abe. This situation required careful consideration. The darkness was complete, so any attempt to arrest Otto might imperil him or me, not to mention the others in the building. I had a hunch he would not take to arrest without argument. Furthermore, at the moment I had only Philemon for assistance, and I wasn't sure I could trust him. And finally, of course, there was a woman present—a woman whose husband had just died. I could not in good conscience cause further harm to her fragile state.

I would need to keep close watch on Otto for the duration of the storm. It was my job to ensure he harmed no one else.

# CHAPTER 23

*O*tto, Philemon, Deborah, and I sat in silence in the parlor for some time. Occasionally we could hear Henry and Jeremiah raise their voices to each other in the lighthouse gallery upstairs. Each time I heard one of them speak, I expected to look up and see light filtering dimly from the top of the stairs.

But no light, however weak, shone down the steps. And as the minutes elapsed, even the sound of Henry's and Jeremiah's voices gradually stilled. Finally heavy footsteps descended and came into the parlor.

"Henry?" I asked.

"Yes, it's me. Light's not working. The rain and wind that got inside caused too much damage. We can only keep trying." Henry's voice sounded defeated, exhausted.

"The storm has to lessen sooner or later."

"I'm surprised it's lasted more'n a few hours."

"Do you know what time it is now?" I asked.

"About half-past four. Dawn isn't too far off."

The thought of dawn, with the possibility of the light it might bring, was heartening. It wouldn't help much inside the cottage where the windows were still covered by shutters, but if one ventured up into the gallery, one might glimpse a bit of gray where now there was only black.

"Jeremiah's upstairs minding the equipment. He'll tinker with it for a while. I'm going to rest for a bit, then I'll go up again."

I cleared my throat. "Henry, August has passed."

There was a long pause. "That makes three," he said in a quiet voice. "I'm sorry for the man's mother and wife, who depend on him."

"Who's next?" It was Otto's voice, coming from across the room.

I thought it bold of him to ask such a question, given his proximate role in August's death.

"I've come to believe this house *is* cursed," Deborah said.

"Now, Deborah, we've just endured a great deal of hardship tonight. There's no curse. When the storm lifts we'll get answers to everything that's happened here." I hoped she would let the matter rest.

"Enough of that talk, Deborah." It was Henry's voice.

"Do you disagree, Henry?" she asked. She sounded a little stronger than she had earlier. "Can you stand there and tell me you don't believe in Neptune's Curse after all that has happened?" Henry didn't answer. Deborah went into the bedroom where the bodies lay and closed the door firmly behind her.

Henry moved toward Jeremiah's bedroom, but then turned to me.

"Is there any food left in the kitchen?" he whispered. "That potato wasn't nearly enough."

I knew how hungry he had to be to suggest going into the kitchen. "There's probably some soup left," I said.

He made his way out of the parlor, carefully avoiding any

furniture, and a moment later I could hear him setting a bowl onto the table. Several minutes later he came out.

"Did you find something?" I asked.

"The mushroom soup is good, even if it's not hot any longer. Did you have any earlier?"

"No."

"Now that I've eaten, it'll be easier for me to fall asleep," Henry said.

"Godspeed."

Silence fell once more among those in the parlor. I leaned my head against the wall behind my chair, listening to the wind and rain and wondering what Jeremiah was doing up in the light. I was sure he was as exasperated as Henry about the situation.

It wasn't long before I heard snoring coming from Otto's direction. I waited, and presently the soft notes of Philemon's snores joined Otto's louder ones. Both men had fallen asleep at last. I wanted to know more about Otto, and this was my chance. I wished someone in the lighthouse besides Otto had known Philemon before the storm, so I could gather information about him, too.

As quietly as I could, I eased myself out of the chair. Walking very slowly to avoid bumping into any furniture, I groped my way to the bottom of the stairs that led up to the tower. Softly, I climbed the spiral steps to the lighthouse gallery.

In the low light of the oil lamp that sat on a table next to him, Jeremiah stood with his back to me. He held a cup to his lips. I didn't want to startle him as I had done earlier, so I gave a light cough. He turned around, but when he saw me he turned away again.

"What do you want?" he asked. It was hard to hear him over the sound of the wind.

"I thought I'd come up to see if there's anything you need."

Jeremiah grimaced. "I don't need nothing. And if I do, I'll wait until my father comes back up."

I nodded, thinking. There had to be a way to get the young man to talk to me. I wandered close to the ring of boarded-up gallery windows, my hands in my trouser pockets. I felt the paper in there, with its strange message, but this wasn't the time to ask about that. What I needed at the moment was answers about Otto and his brother, Karl.

"When this storm is over I'm sure you and your father will be glad to be rid of all of us."

He made a sound of agreement.

"I, for one, will be gratified to leave. I worry that there's been damage all around Cape Island. Until the storm blows out to sea I can't go anywhere to inspect the harm that's been done."

"Hmh," he answered pensively.

I wondered what thoughts were going through his head. Perhaps he was thinking about how he and his father were going to maintain the light and the keeper's cottage without a woman's help. I wondered if he was distraught over his mother's death. He didn't seem to be, but men often concealed their true feelings.

"Even though the light has gone out for the time being, there's plenty you and your father have done today to keep us all safe and I'd like to thank you for that. You even saved three lives out on the water." I watched Jeremiah's reaction out of the corner of my eye, knowing as I did of the ill feelings between the Brewsters and the Schuhmacher families.

Jeremiah's face twitched. It seemed I had finally said something that might elicit a response.

"We should have let 'em drown."

"But surely you and your father would get trouble from the lighthouse officials if that had happened?"

"Not if they thought we tried our best to save 'em."

"Do you dislike Otto and August that much?"

"I do."

"Is it because they refused to offer condolences after your mother died?"

My question, though intended to prompt some response from the young man, was enough to spur him to throw his cup on the floor. I raised my eyebrows in surprise, but didn't move. "Don't talk about my mother again."

I continued talking. "You all right, Jeremiah? I don't blame you for being angry."

The flame in the oil lamp flickered and Jeremiah's glare narrowed. "This is none of your concern, Deputy."

"I think it might be. There's been a lot of trouble in this place since the storm started and I have a hunch those men downstairs are to blame for much of it. I'd like you to tell me more about Otto, if you're willing."

Jeremiah didn't answer for a long time. I began to wonder if he would speak to me at all. I was about to repeat my request when he reached down, picked up the cup he had thrown, and sat on a barrel near the lamp.

"I hated Otto and August long before their boat ever broke apart in the storm."

"Why's that?"

Jeremiah tilted his head toward the stairs. "Do you reckon anyone is listening?" he asked.

"Everyone was asleep when I came up here. That's why I chose now to come up and talk to you."

Jeremiah gestured for me to come closer. "A long time ago Otto had a brother, Karl Schuhmacher, who lived in Cape Island. My mother's brother lived here, too. His name was Horatio. Karl killed him."

# CHAPTER 24

"What happened between Karl and your Uncle Horatio?"

We were interrupted by a footfall on the steps. We turned to see Henry standing at the top of the stairs.

"Henry, aren't you able to rest?" I asked. "I'm sure you could use some sleep."

"Can't sleep. I'll take over up here," he said gruffly.

Jeremiah didn't say anything, but nodded once and pushed past me toward the stairway.

"Be quiet, Jeremiah. Everyone's asleep down there," Henry warned. Jeremiah looked over his shoulder and glanced archly at his father before hastening down the stairs. Was there something significant in that glance, or was exhaustion making me question things that weren't there?

"You can go downstairs, too," Henry told me.

"I think I'll stay up here for a few minutes, if you don't mind."

Henry cast a wary glance at me. "Why?"

"I'd like to talk to you."

A curtain of suspicion descended over Henry's face. "'Bout

what?" He turned around and took a step toward the storage room.

"What can you tell me about Abigail's brother?" I asked.

He stopped mid-step and jerked around to face me. "Horatio?"

"Is there another brother?"

"No."

"Then yes, Horatio."

For a moment I thought he might not answer, but finally he moved toward the storage room again. I followed him.

In the small room, Henry sat on an upturned barrel. "Horatio was Abigail's younger brother."

"Was?" I knew the answer, of course, but wanted Henry to tell me the entire story in his own words.

"Yes. He died eighteen years ago."

"Were they close?"

"As close as a brother and sister ever were. They were the two youngest in a large family from Philadelphia. A wealthy, influential family. Their siblings were much older than they were, practically adults by the time Abigail and Horatio were born, so my wife and her brother were always together. They were the best of friends." Henry paused before continuing.

"Horatio had a fiery temper. He did certain things in Philadelphia that angered people. But because of the position of the family, he was never punished."

"What sorts of things?"

"Bad things."

I wondered if it mattered—perhaps the only important things were those that took place in Cape Island. "Very well. Go on."

"Horatio angered the wrong people, powerful people in Philadelphia. They plotted revenge against him. They tried to kill him."

"But they didn't succeed?"

"That's right," Henry said. "He caught wind of the plot and fled, leaving his family behind."

"And Abigail?"

"She fled with him. She was afraid for him and didn't want to always wonder what had become of him. She and her parents did not get on well, so she didn't mind leaving them behind."

"So Abigail fled Philadelphia with her younger brother. What happened then?"

"They came here."

"To Cape Island?"

"Yes."

"But there are wealthy and influential families from Philadelphia who spent time in Cape Island in the summer months. Weren't Abigail and Horatio concerned they would be recognized?"

"No. Abigail and Horatio didn't frequent the same places as those folks. They didn't worry about anyone recognizing them."

I waited for Henry to continue, but he paused for a long time. Finally he spoke again. "They hadn't even traveled as far as Cape Island the day I met them."

"How did you meet them?"

"They had spent two nights in Stites Point at an inn. They paid the innkeeper's son to drive them to Cape Island, but one of the wagon wheels broke just south of Cape May Court House. I was in Cape May Court House that day tending to a legal affair and I happened by them on my way back home. At that time, I farmed a few miles from here. I offered to drive Abigail and Horatio the rest of the way to Cape Island. They came with me and I let them stay in my home for a time in exchange for doing work in the house and on the farm." He paused, as if recalling distant memories.

"Horatio did an honest man's work for me every day. One day two men from Philadelphia arrived in Cape Island looking for him. Someone in town told the fellows about a newcomer—

a dandy—working on my farm and they came to see me. They were bad characters—I could tell right away. I had an idea they weren't looking to make friends with Horatio, so I told them Horatio had been there but he'd left and I didn't know where he'd gone."

Henry paused again, and I didn't say anything. I wanted him to keep talking.

"O' course, Horatio and Abigail were thankful I had gotten rid of the men from Philadelphia. I never saw them back here again. Abigail and Horatio stayed on and continued working for me after that, but it wasn't long until Horatio started trouble around here. Same problems, different people—and those people sought revenge. By then I had become the lighthouse keeper, so I hid him again, here in this cottage."

"But surely people in this area knew he was nearby."

"I married Abigail just before I became the lighthouse keeper, and if anyone asked, we told them Horatio left when we were married and we didn't know where he went. Jeremiah was born and it was easy for people to believe Horatio didn't live with us. It worked for almost two years. We were careful to keep him out of sight of people. Not many folks come out as far as the lighthouse, so he could be out-of-doors without anyone seeing him."

"What happened then?"

"He couldn't hide here forever. He tired of behaving and went back to his old ways. People just thought he'd finally come back to town. I suppose they figured I was letting him stay here, when really he'd been here all along. Horatio made men angry, stole their wives. He met his end with Karl."

"You mean Horatio died at the hands of Karl?"

"Yessir. Karl Schuhmacher killed him."

"How did Horatio wrong Karl? It must have been grave, since Karl killed him over it."

"I suppose there ain't no harm in telling you now. Horatio

stole into Karl's house one night when Karl was in the village. He and Karl's young wife had a stitch and she was with child as a result. When Karl found out, he tried to kill her. Took a couple weeks before she died."

"So Karl was responsible for his wife's death, too? And his unborn child's?" My mind swam with horror.

Henry nodded. "Horatio learned what had become of her and he attacked Karl. Wasn't long before Karl struck back, and he killed Horatio. The Brewsters and the Schuhmachers have hated each other ever since." He stood and nodded toward the staircase. "You'd best be getting downstairs now."

"Can you tell me—"

"I already talked enough. I got to fix this light. Go downstairs."

"But—"

Henry clenched his jaw. "I said, I already told you enough."

I had a feeling I would have to wait to ask any further questions. I nodded and left him alone in the tower.

# CHAPTER 25

$O$tto and Philemon were still snoring when I reached the parlor. I sat away from them and closed my eyes. My mind was turning over the information I had learned from Henry and Jeremiah, however sparse it was. I knew only a bit more than I had before talking to them.

First, Abigail and her brother, Horatio, were "as close as a brother and sister ever were." So close, in fact, that when Horatio found himself in trouble in Philadelphia and decided to flee the city, Abigail left her comfortable life behind to follow him. After they met Henry, he offered to give them a place to stay in return for doing house and farm work. But that wasn't all he did—he hid Horatio when the man was in danger. Abigail must have been very grateful for that. She stayed in Cape Island, working for Henry, then married him. And when he became lighthouse keeper, he continued hiding Horatio, even after the birth of his only child, Jeremiah.

Second, Horatio had had relations with Karl's wife. This was intriguing, but I was unsure what it meant.

But in addition to those bits of information, I thought I might have stumbled onto something else, too. The instant

Henry told me that Karl killed Horatio, he refused to entertain any further questions from me. There had to be a reason. Was he keeping something from me? Had something happened after Horatio's death that he wanted to keep private?

My thoughts turned to Abigail and Henry. Something about their marriage gave me pause. In my thirty years, I had seen plenty of instances where a comely woman had wed a tree stump of a man. It was always strange, seeing couples like that, and I would find myself wondering if the wife could have married better. Or what the man had done to woo her successfully.

It was especially puzzling in the case of Abigail and Henry Brewster. Every time I met Abigail, I was struck by her poise and intelligence. She spoke differently from many of the other women in Cape Island. Where they would often speak with plain words and sentences, Abigail always spoke with refinement. Even as she suffered in pain before she died, I recalled the gentility of her words. It was easy to believe she had been reared in a city, surrounded by wealth and art and music and books. And she was beautiful, there could be no arguing that. Every time I saw her, her dewy skin was fresh and unblemished, her hair falling in rings to frame her face. She never looked like a lighthouse keeper's wife, whom one would expect to be wiry and weathered.

But Henry ... Henry was the opposite of his wife. He was short and stocky, with a head of unruly hair and calloused, tough skin. Where Abigail tended to speak softly, Henry's words came out with an abrasive rasp that could be grating on the nerves. In three years of visiting his family in the lighthouse, I had never seen him with a book.

MY EYES FLEW open at the sound of Otto's voice.

"Woman, fetch me some cider."

"Get your own cider, you no-good jolterhead."

I smiled to myself in the dark. It was good to see Deborah standing up to Otto's impertinence.

I could hear Otto's chair scrape against the floor, then his footsteps advancing slowly. I stood and walked closer to stop him from going near Deborah. "Go back to your seat, Otto."

"Mind your business, George," he growled. His rotten breath mingled with the odor of perspiration and uncleanliness.

"Why don't you do as Deborah told you and get your own cider?"

"Why should I, when there's a woman here who can fetch it for me?"

Philemon spoke up in a snarl. "If everyone doesn't shut their mouths right now, I'm going to—"

"That's enough, Philemon. Go back to sleep." I could hear him shifting his body. A few minutes later, he was snoring softly again.

Deborah rose and went into the bedroom where Kit's body lay. I turned to Otto. "I would think you'd pay her some mind. Her husband just died."

"Some would say that was a stroke of luck."

"Have you no respect?"

"Don't see as that's any of your business."

I determined to ignore his impertinence. Since Philemon was asleep and Deborah had left the room, it was as good a time as any for me to ask Otto my questions. I needed him to cooperate and it wouldn't help if I scolded him for being rude to Deborah. "I'll be back," I said. I went to the kitchen, returning a few moments later with two cups and a pitcher of cider. I sat at the table and told him to sit, too. I poured a cup of cider and slid it toward him.

"What's this for?" His voice betrayed his suspicion.

"I thought you might be thirsty." I wasn't sure it was wise

offering him more drink, but at least it wasn't rum. Hopefully it would loosen his tongue and prompt enough congeniality to give me the information I sought.

"How long have you lived on the cape?" I asked. I concentrated on keeping my tone conversational.

He took a gulp of cider, then smacked his lips. "Since I were a boy."

"And you moved here with August?"

"Him and his family, and my kinfolk."

"Who's in his family?"

"It was him and his four sisters, his mother, and his father. His mother lives with him because his father's dead now these past six years. Sisters all moved away when they married. He's got a wife, too."

"And what about your family?"

Otto didn't answer right away. Finally he asked, "Why do you want to know?"

"We are merely two men having a conversation. I like to know the people in my jurisdiction."

"Funny you never bothered to know us before now."

"As I said, I'm just making conversation." I took a sip of cider and could hear Otto following suit.

"I came here with my mother and father. My father's dead, too."

"Any sisters? Brothers?"

"Why d'ye want to know about my sisters, George?" Otto let out a phlegmy laugh. "Lookin' for a woman o' yer own?"

I didn't answer, but waited for Otto to keep talking. The question was revolting, and my mind immediately flooded with thoughts of Evelyn—her porcelain skin, her pink lips, her intelligent brown eyes, and her favorite scent, lilac. It took all my strength not to knock Otto right to the floor.

"My two sisters stayed behind in Pennsylvania with my aunt. They were both engaged to be married and didn't want to leave."

"Brothers?" I repeated.

"No brothers." He lifted his cup and drank.

"What about Karl?"

He set his cup down and I sensed his body become still. "What about him? How do you know about him?"

"Oh, word gets around. Tell me about him."

"Karl was attacked by Abigail Brewster's brother, Horatio. He nearly killed Karl." Otto's voice was rough and angry.

"And then what happened?"

"What do you think happened? Karl couldn't let the attack go unanswered, could he? Wouldn't be a man if he just let Horatio just get away with it."

"So he killed Horatio?"

Otto paused. "I'll tell you this much: Horatio died. I don't know what killed him."

"Where is Karl now?"

"He left after Horatio died. But I ain't saying there's a connection between Horatio's death and Karl disappearing." I could hear him scratching either his beard or his head. No matter which, it was a sound that made me shudder in disgust.

"And Karl's wife?"

"What about her? She were nothing but a hoyden."

"Did he kill her?"

"I'm done answering your fool questions."

His answer told me all I needed to know. I had a hunch any further questions about Karl and Horatio would be futile. Anyhow, I wanted answers on another topic.

"And Philemon?"

Otto paused, probably because I changed the subject so abruptly. "What about him?"

"How do you know him?"

"Are you playin' a game, Deputy?"

"No. Why do you ask?"

"Why all the questions? What business is it of yours?"

"I'm interested, that's all. Here, have a bit more cider." I filled his cup halfway.

"Philemon and August and I are in business together, if you must know." He took a gulp.

"What kind of business?"

"We build boats."

"Boats?"

"Didn't I speak clear enough for you, George?" He slid the cup slowly to and fro on the tabletop.

"I didn't realize you had a business other than farming."

"There's plenty you don't know about me."

"Like what?"

"You're chasing my patience away, George. And I don't think you want to be talking to me when you've chased it gone." He took a drink, then set his cup down hard.

"If that's a threat, it doesn't work with me, Otto. As long as you and I are sitting here, we're going to talk. Tell me about this boat-building business." Otto didn't say anything for a moment, then I heard him leaning back in his chair.

"We all have a talent for building things, so we started building boats. We have some customers who like what we have to offer."

"Did you build the boat you were riding in earlier today?"

Otto fell silent and I could practically hear him seething.

"We did." He spoke in such a low voice I had trouble hearing him.

"I would say you didn't use your talent for that particular boat."

"You mind what I said about losing my patience, Deputy."

# CHAPTER 26

$\mathcal{I}$ decided to let Otto stew before asking him any
further questions.

Now I was ready and eager to talk to Philemon. Thanks to
August's mumbled words earlier, I knew there was something I
wasn't being told about Philemon and about the boat that had
sunk in the storm. I intended to find out what it was. I couldn't
talk to him right away, though, because I didn't want Otto to
hear us. I waited for what felt like hours, until I heard snoring
coming from Otto's corner of the room, then made my way
across the parlor, walking close to the chair where I knew
Philemon to be sitting. I deliberately used my feet to find the
furniture in the dark, hoping to wake him up. And it worked,
because just a moment after my foot struck a chair leg, causing
me to wince in pain, Philemon awoke with a snort.

"Who's there? What do you want?"

"I apologize. I'm a bit restless, and I must have bumped into
your chair. Hope I didn't wake you." I spoke in a quiet voice so
as not to wake Otto.

"You certainly did wake me. I'm trying to get some sleep, and
you come along and kick my chair."

I continued to speak quietly in the hope he would do the same. "Like I said, I'm sorry for that. I haven't been able to sleep at all, so I know how you're feeling."

"You do not. Were you in a sinking boat less than twenty-four hours ago? No. But I was. I need my sleep so when this goldarned storm is over I can get back to work."

I picked up a stool that was nearby on the floor and settled onto it next to him. "Speaking of work, what exactly do you do?"

"I farm a piece of land."

"Anything else?"

"Why are you asking?" He shifted loudly in his chair.

"Far as I know, there's no law against asking a man if he does anything besides farming."

"I want to get back to sleep."

"You can, just as soon as you and I talk for a bit."

"Fine. I'll tell you whatever you want to know as long as I can get some sleep. Otto and August have a business building boats. I help them sometimes."

"What kinds of boats do you build?"

"Fishing boats," he answered tersely.

"Like the one that capsized earlier?"

"Yes." He paused, but spoke again before I could ask him another question. "I know what you're trying to do, and it won't work, George."

"What do you think I'm trying to do?"

"You're up to something. You're trying to weasel something out of me." I imagined a malicious grin spreading across his face.

"Why would you assume that, unless there's something there to weasel?"

Philemon chuckled, a menacing sound that sent a shiver slithering down my spine. "I got nothing to hide."

"I didn't say you did."

"Then go sit yourself down somewhere far from me and let

me get back to sleep." He growled softly and I could hear him turning away from me in his chair. I hadn't learned much, but Philemon had his hackles up and there was a reason for it.

It would be dawn before long, and surely the new day would bring an end to the storm. Otto and Philemon were becoming agitated. I wanted the storm to end quickly for the sake of the people of Cape Island, but ironically for myself, I wanted the storm to last just a bit longer—I was convinced something was amiss in the house besides Abigail's death, and the longer Otto and Philemon were unable to leave, the longer I would have to figure out what they were hiding.

I had to keep myself busy because I was going to go daft in this cottage if I had to sit idle while the storm blew itself out. There were some things I could try to accomplish. I hadn't forgotten the note I had found under Jeremiah's bureau. Perhaps it was time to find out more about the warning it contained or the significance it held.

I put my hand in my trouser pocket and felt the paper again. Maybe the note was unimportant, completely unrelated to anything I might need to investigate, but I had a feeling it was significant. It didn't hold many clues about the writer or the recipient, but there were a couple things I might be able to learn or deduce from it.

First, I had found the paper in Jeremiah's room. That suggested it may have been meant for him. But perhaps not—perhaps it was meant for someone else and Jeremiah found it. I had seen his bedroom earlier in the day with the aid of an oil lamp. It was sparse and clean. There was no rubbish or other items on the floor, which told me someone had looked at the note after the rescue of the sailors, when we had to change into dry clothing borrowed from Jeremiah.

Could Jeremiah have authored the note himself?

Possibly, but if the note had been meant for Jeremiah or if he had written it himself, why would it be crumpled on the floor next to his bureau? Why wouldn't he have destroyed it or placed it in a safe place? I assumed, for the time being, that the note had been meant for someone else and Jeremiah found it.

One thing seemed clear. It appeared the writer of the note did not wish to share certain information in the body of the note—instead, the person requested a face-to-face meeting. And the writer wanted to warn the recipient about something. Certainly it was secret information, and that led me to suspect it suggested the possibility of danger. Was the recipient of the note in some kind of danger? I closed my eyes and rubbed the bridge of my nose. It was exasperating to know so little about the note. Besides that, something was bothering me, something I knew I should remember, but I couldn't figure out what it was. It seemed just out of my reach. If I weren't so tired, I thought, I wouldn't have forgotten it in the first place.

I tried thinking of something else. That often worked when I couldn't bring a thought to mind. I shook my head to clear it of confusion and weariness and tried to make sense of things other than the note for a time.

Otto, his cousin, and Philemon came to mind first. What did I know about them? The most important thing was that Otto's brother was strongly suspected of killing Abigail's brother years ago. Following that incident, he had disappeared, never to be heard from again. In addition, Otto, August, and Philemon were in the boat-building business together, besides their other jobs of farming and blacksmithing. Philemon said he helped Otto and August with their business, but could I trust him? What reason would he have to lie about such a thing? I didn't care that the men built boats, so there was no reason to lie to me about it. Perhaps the men didn't simply build boats, but were engaged in some other behavior they didn't want me to know about. One thing I did know: I had seen boats survive great storms, and their boat was not one of them. Was it possible they were simply ashamed of the craftsmanship their boats displayed? But that wouldn't explain why August cautioned me about Philemon, thinking I was Otto.

Thoughts of August's death followed naturally from my musings about his puzzling words. I still worried that the act of arresting Otto would result in violent bedlam, so I would wait until we got out of the lighthouse. August's death had not been intentional, but nonetheless had clearly been caused by Otto. He certainly should have known that hurling a bottle in a confined space was likely to wound someone, or worse. I was well aware that Otto had meant for that bottle to hit me. It looked like the Schuhmacher family would not only be planning a burial after the storm, but a visit to their kin in jail, too.

Then there was Kit's death. I dared not dwell for too long on his fatal tumble down the stairs and my own sorry decision to allow him to go to the lighthouse gallery after he had consumed too much cider. He was a hale and healthy man and he was leaving behind a wife who, if I didn't help her or she didn't remarry soon, would have to farm their land herself in order to survive. I wondered what the sheriff would say when he learned Kit would have been alive if it weren't for my poor decision. Would I even have a job once he found out?

Thankfully Jeremiah came out of his bedroom, putting a temporary end to my fretting. He trudged heavily up the stairs. He could not have gotten very much sleep, I thought. The life of a lighthouse keeper's family was not an easy one, I had come to realize, and I had a new-found respect for anyone who under-took the job.

It wasn't long before Henry came downstairs. "George?" he asked.

"I'm over here."

"Is there any cider left?"

"Yes. It's on the table." I went into the kitchen and returned with a cup.

He filled his cup and took a noisy slurp. "I hope this'll work to settle my stomach."

"You sick?" I asked. The last thing we needed was for the lighthouse keeper to fall ill.

"Not too bad yet." Henry took another swig of cider. "I think the storm might finally be letting up."

"That is good news. How long do you think it'll be before we can leave?"

"It's still too dangerous to even think about leaving, and I imagine it'll be that way for a couple more hours, at least."

*Good*, I thought. *That leaves me some time to do my job.*

# CHAPTER 27

*H*enry set his cup down and yawned. Without another word, he walked away, straight into Jeremiah's bedroom. As he closed the door behind him, Deborah emerged from the bedroom where Kit's body lay. She went to stand before the fireplace. I sat at the table alone, listening to the wind outside and straining my ears to hear any stirring from Otto or Philemon. I could hear nothing but snoring.

My mind was working like a plow mule. I still had questions about Henry and Abigail, and I needed to organize my thoughts as they pertained to Otto, August, and Philemon. Who best to ask about Henry and Abigail? I could have made inquiries of Henry before he went to Jeremiah's room, but I had a feeling neither he nor Jeremiah would likely be receptive to providing the information I needed.

I could ask Deborah. She was now lying on a quilt in front of the fireplace. I was loath to put the poor widow through anymore, but I was beginning to fear the storm would blow itself out to sea completely before I could get my questions answered.

I walked as stealthily as I could to where she lay, bent close to her, and whispered her name.

"What? Who is it? You gave me a start."

"Shh," I said quietly. "It's me, George. I need to ask you some questions and I don't want to wake the others."

"What sorts of questions?" Her voice held a note of wariness. "I don't want to talk about Kit."

"No, no. I won't ask you about Kit. I have other questions." I sat on the floor next to her so we could converse in whispers. She sat up slowly, gathering the quilt around her. "I need you to tell me what you know about Henry and Abigail."

"What could I possibly tell you about them?"

"How long have you known them?"

"Years. Since Kit and I were married. A few years before Jeremiah was born."

"Did they seem to enjoy one another's company? Did they argue?"

"Why, mercy me, I don't really know how to answer that."

"Shh," I said.

She lowered her voice. "I s'pose they got on all right. O' course, I didn't see them together very often because Henry was always busy up in the light or doing something out-of-doors. And when he wasn't doing those things, he was sleeping."

"Did Abigail seem happy?"

I sensed Deborah's shrug as the fabric of her dress rustled. "Who among us are? Cooking and cleaning and doing the wash and growing and harvesting the food. Abigail had a young one to care for, too. The chores never end. We're awake from before sunup to after sundown. I would say Abigail was as happy about her life as any woman is."

"Did they argue?" I asked again.

"I heard them argue now and again."

"About what?"

"I'm afraid I don't recall the exact circumstances."

Someone across the room shifted in his chair and I paused, listening. If whoever moved was waking up, I would have to stop querying Deborah. For several moments I said nothing, but then I heard the snores again. I turned toward her. "Please try to remember the circumstances."

She hesitated. "It isn't right to speak ill of the dead."

"You mean Abigail?"

"Abigail, yes." Her voice was so soft I had to strain to hear it.

"I need you to tell me about it," I said.

Deborah sighed. "When her brother died, she couldn't be consoled. She cried all the time. I had to come over and help with Jeremiah, and I did the cleaning and the washing and the cooking, too. Henry paid me, of course, and the money came in handy. Abigail didn't get out of bed for the first month after Horatio's death, then when she was finally able to rouse herself, she would disappear for hours at a time. Sometimes she walked the dunes, which I know because I could see her from the cottage, but sometimes she would disappear and no one knew where she had gone. Many was the time I thought she had left and would never come back."

"What did Henry do during all this time?"

"His job. He had a lighthouse to run and so that's what he did. He couldn't go off chasing Abigail every time she got the whim to leave."

"Couldn't he see her from the lighthouse? It's high enough to see everything around this area."

"He said he couldn't. Besides, there are plenty of places she could go that he wouldn't be able to see her. The woods, for instance. There were lots of places in the woods where she could go."

"And how would you know to come to the cottage to help Henry?"

"I would come to the lighthouse around mid-morning most

days during that time to see if they needed any help. I knew she was suffering."

"How did you do your own and Abigail's work after Horatio died?"

"It was hard, but I managed. Those were long days."

"And when did you hear or see Abigail and Henry arguing?"

"Every time she came back to the cottage and I was there. He would tell her in that coarse voice of his that she couldn't just leave every time the whim suited her, Horatio or no Horatio."

"And what did she say?"

"That he had no idea what it was like to lose a brother. But eventually she started doing for herself again."

"Was Henry pleased when she got back to her responsibilities?"

"I imagine so. He never said. He must have been, since that's what he'd been asking her to do."

"You and Abigail have been friends for many years, correct?"

"Yes. We're the only two women who live out this way."

"And I suppose she confided in you on occasion?"

Deborah answered me slowly. "Friends do that, yes."

"Is there anything she might have told you that would lead you to believe her marriage to Henry was not a good one?"

She didn't answer.

"Deborah?"

Finally she sighed. "I might as well tell you." She lowered her voice. I felt a prick of unease. She leaned closer to me and said very quietly, "Abigail told me that she and Henry ... that she and Henry never had relations again after Horatio died."

My mouth hung open for a moment. "And Horatio died eighteen years ago?"

"Yes."

"Are you saying Henry and Abigail didn't have marital relations for eighteen years?"

"Shh," Deborah warned.

I lowered my voice again. "Is that what you're saying?"

"Yes, it is."

"Did Abigail tell you why?"

"No, but I think it was because as long as Horatio was alive, there was a possibility Henry could protect him from harm. At least she thought he could. In the end, Henry wasn't able to protect him from Karl Schuhmacher. When Horatio died, there was no reason for her to rely on Henry to protect him any longer."

"And therefore there was no reason for her to continue having relations with him?"

"I believe that's right." She took a deep breath and let it out in a quiver. "I shouldn't have told you any of this."

"I appreciate your candor. May I ask you another question?"

"I think I've said enough, Deputy." She shifted her body away from me.

# CHAPTER 28

*I*f what Deborah said was true, it meant Abigail married Henry because of her desire to protect her brother. Or even out of gratitude for sheltering him when he was sought by those who would have their revenge on him.

And they had really stopped having marital relations almost two decades ago? It seemed almost impossible, but if it were the case, that could explain a great deal. It might explain why Abigail did not want Henry near her at the time of her death—perhaps she found his presence disagreeable. Deborah said they got on all right, but she said herself that she rarely saw them together. So how could she know for certain whether they got on all right?

There was another thing that might be explained by the things Deborah had revealed. It might explain why Henry wouldn't want Abigail in the house anymore. Upon her death, he would be free to wed another woman, one who might be a proper wife to him.

Leaning my head back against the wall, I closed my eyes to think. Could I trust Deborah's judgment about Henry and Abigail's marriage? She probably knew as much about them as anyone else, but if she was only hearing from Abigail, she was only getting one side of the story. I didn't want to accuse Henry of harming his wife without hearing his side of the matter. I dreaded broaching the subject with him. The man would no doubt be ashamed to discuss his marriage, especially if everything Deborah said was correct.

Reluctantly, I stood and stepped quietly to Jeremiah's bedroom. I knocked on the door as softly as I could so as not to wake anyone in the parlor, then turned the doorknob and walked in.

"Who's there?" Henry asked.

"George."

"God's teeth, get out of here. I need some rest. And my stomach is roiling."

I hesitated. I didn't want to be near him if he was ill. But I forged ahead since I didn't know how long I would have to ask him questions. "I'll only keep you a minute or two, Henry. I have a couple things I'd like you to clear up."

"What things?"

"Things about Abigail and Horatio."

"I already said all I'm going to say about them."

"I won't keep you long." When he didn't respond, I proceeded with my inquiries. "I suppose Abigail was grateful to you for hiding Horatio all that time, wasn't she?"

Henry didn't answer right away, and I supposed he was weighing whether he should or whether he could force me to leave the room. He finally answered, "Of course she was."

"How did Abigail respond to her brother's death?"

"She couldn't be consoled, that's how. Isn't that how most folk would respond to the death of a brother?"

"But surely in time she got back to her duties around the cottage and the lighthouse, correct?"

"In time, yes."

"Is there anything in particular about Abigail that changed after Horatio's death?"

"Anything in partic'lar? I don't understand what you're asking."

I gritted my teeth. I couldn't think of a tactful way to say it, so I was going to have to be frank with him. "Well, for example ..." I faltered. "For example, sometimes a husband and wife don't ... after a particularly awful event they don't ... have relations." There. I said it.

Henry was silent for a long time. I hesitated to speak. Finally he released a deep sigh. "I s'pose it doesn't matter, now that Abigail's gone." He paused. "As I said, Abigail and I were already married when Horatio was killed. Jeremiah was a young 'un. I knew how close Abigail was with her brother—they were kin, after all." He paused and I wished I could see his face. "I should have done more to protect Horatio, hide him. I should have—could have—found somewhere safe to send him, but I didn't. Abigail blamed me for that. I suppose she was right."

"It wasn't your responsibility to protect Horatio."

"I know that. The truth is, I was tired of hiding him. It meant the world to Abigail and I wanted to please her, but I just wanted Horatio to go away so we could go on as man and wife." Henry paused. "Problem was, I knew why Abigail married me. She did it because she felt beholden to me after I protected Horatio. She felt duty-bound. I figured that if Horatio would go away, she might realize that I could make her a good husband."

For a man who hadn't wanted to talk to me, Henry was being surprisingly loquacious. I felt suddenly very sorry for him.

"Abigail and Horatio were unlike two any creatures I ever knew. They looked alike, talked alike, and thought alike. It sometimes seemed like they were the same person." He cleared his throat.

"When Jeremiah was born, I thought he might be the thing

we needed to fix ourselves and be a family. But even though we both loved Jeremiah, Abigail couldn't love anyone as much as Horatio. And when he died, she nearly did, too. She started keeping to herself. She would cry for entire days. She refused to see to her wifely duties anymore as far as they concerned me. She cooked and cleaned and did the washing, but we slept far apart every night. Same bed, but it seemed like different rooms."

"And how long did that go on?"

"It went on until yesterday. When she died."

So Deborah had been correct. Abigail had married Henry out of her need to protect her brother and hadn't performed her womanly responsibilities with Henry since Horatio died.

Henry continued. "It's true. I ain't proud of it, but I couldn't force her to do something she didn't want. I loved her until the end."

"Are you telling me the truth, Henry?"

"O' course I am. Why would I lie about that?"

"I'm merely asking." I stood and walked to the bedroom door. "I want to believe you. I truly do. But something killed your wife, and I will find out what happened. If you did anything to hasten it along, I will not hesitate to arrest you."

# CHAPTER 29

There were no more questions I could ask right now about Henry and Abigail without causing a ruckus, so I left Jeremiah's bedroom and turned my attention back to Otto and his unfortunate crew. If Henry was correct and the storm seemed to be abating, I needed to work quickly to find out more about the men. I could conduct an investigation after we returned to Cape Island, of course, but I didn't know where Philemon was from or where he would go. I didn't know if I would ever be able to find him again. It would be far easier to investigate while we were all together in the cottage.

My thoughts came back again and again to the men's boat business. There was clearly something about it they didn't want me to know, and I could only assume it was because they were doing something against the law. Something I would have to address as the sheriff's deputy, whether by levying a fine or making an arrest. It would, of course, depend on what they were doing.

For that matter, was there really a boat business at all? The boat they had been in earlier broke apart in the waves. It was a small boat, to be sure, but if they couldn't build a small seaworthy boat, could they be relied upon to build a larger seaworthy boat if a customer needed one? Besides that, I had never heard talk about Otto or August being involved in such a business.

I wondered who their customers were, or if they were even telling the truth about having customers.

Given the information I had so far, the most logical explanation I could formulate was that they were smuggling. Their customers were likely the people willing to pay higher prices for things they couldn't obtain legally. I knew, of course, that smuggling had been a profitable business pursuit until 1814, during the years America was at war with Britain. Men would sneak goods up to New York City by way of the Delaware Bay and the New Jersey coast. But trade agreements were again in place between America and other nations. The need for smuggling was almost nonexistent.

Therefore, I was forced to conclude the Schuhmacher family was not in the business of smuggling goods.

So what, precisely, was their business?

It was time to talk to Otto again.

By this time I knew my way around the parlor of the cottage quite well and could get to Otto in the dark without tripping over furniture or walking into walls. When I reached him I found him sound asleep in a chair. I nudged his foot with mine.

"Otto, wake up."

He did, but with a snarl that told me he did not welcome another conversation with me.

"Who's there?"

"It's me, George."

"What d'ye want this time?"

A snort could be heard from a few feet away and Philemon spoke up.

"Can't a man get a few minutes' rest in this place?"

"I'm not talking to you, Philemon. Go back to sleep," I said.

"Can't with you rattling on," he grumbled.

I ignored him and sat down next to Otto.

"What d'ye want?" he repeated.

"I want to know more about this boat-building business of yours."

"Why?"

"Maybe I want to buy a boat."

"You can't afford a boat." Derision dripped from Otto's voice.

"Let's say I've come into some money."

"If it'll get you to leave me alone, I'll go along with you."

"How big are the boats you build?"

"All sizes."

"Like a three-master?"

"One-master sloops, mostly."

"Not 'all sizes,' then. In fact, they're quite small."

"I suppose."

"Who buys your boats?"

Philemon coughed loudly. I waited for him to stop before proceeding.

"People in the business of sailing short distances."

"People like who?"

Otto scratched at a callous on the palm of his hand. "I ain't got to tell you who our customers are."

"Why not?"

"Because that's private. You want to know who buys our boats, you go figure it out yourself."

"What do the buyers need them for?"

"I told you. Sailing short distances."

"Do they race 'em across the bay? Where do they sail the boats? Come now, Otto, answer the question."

"How am I supposed to know that? I only build the boats and sell 'em. I don't go sailing with the people who buy 'em."

"You were sailing in one yesterday afternoon."

"We were testing it out."

"It failed the test, I imagine."

Otto harrumphed. "I'm done talking. Get away from me."

Finally Philemon's voice roared into our conversation. I had expected it—I figured he was listening to my discussion with Otto. "Good God, man! Haven't you asked enough fool questions? Otto told you about the boats. Now be quiet and let a man get some rest."

I obliged him, but only because I was beginning to form an idea about what Otto and his compatriots might be up to. I needed time to think, to get some of the details clear in my own head. I returned to my chair and closed my eyes. For once, images of Evelyn and Cape Henlopen were replaced by images of boats and storm-tossed waters.

As I sat there, the wind's keening became quieter. If I was to prove myself as worthy of my badge and worthy of the trust the people of Cape Island placed in me, I needed to make haste and figure out what was going on in this cottage. First, though, I needed to go up to the gallery. I needed to know how much the storm had lessened and determine how much damage there might be.

At the top of the stairs, Jeremiah was tinkering with something behind the light apparatus. I was heartened to see the sky turning a lighter gray and the rain teeming a bit less. I could even see out one of the unbroken windows. I stared in the direction of Cape Island and was shocked by what I saw—or rather, by what I didn't see.

# CHAPTER 30

Water covered every visible inch of Cape Island. Where there was land before the storm, there was water now. I couldn't tell its depth, but one thing was clear: no one was leaving the lighthouse yet, despite the rain and wind letting up. There was no way out without a boat, and the boat that Henry kept tied to a post down on the ground was nowhere to be seen. Underwater, I figured. Waves crashed relentlessly against the cottage.

My thoughts hopped from the water to Abe Bradford and Aces. A sense of unease snaked through the hollow pit of my stomach. I needed to get out of here and check on them. Again, a feeling of guilt assailed me when I admitted to myself that I worried more about my horse than the man I had left in the cell.

"Everything's flooded," I said to Jeremiah. "It's like the days of Noah out there."

He came to stand next to me, gazing out the window. "No one's leaving here yet." The young man's voice was frustrated, but resigned.

"We'll get out of here as soon as we can. Looks like we'll need a boat, though."

"Boat's underwater." Jeremiah pointed to where the boat had been tied. He shrugged. "Unless she's just gone out to sea."

"Let's get this place cleaned up and back in order. By that time maybe the water will have receded."

"It's low tide out there, Deputy. That water's staying for a while."

I hadn't realized that. I didn't pay much mind to the tides, since my work was on land. I was aware of the tides, of course, but they didn't affect my day-to-day tasks and affairs. I ran my hand through my hair, which was stiff and thick with salt from the waters of the bay. "I'll tell the others. Do you have enough light up here for me to take the oil lamp downstairs?"

Jeremiah nodded and I descended the steps slowly. In the cottage everyone was starting to stir.

"That you, Deputy? You've brought a lamp." It was Deborah.

"Yes. The storm's let up a bit, so there's enough light upstairs for Jeremiah to do his work. Maybe he and Henry'll get the light working again soon." I set the lamp on the table in the center of the room and could make out the shapes of Philemon stretching and Otto picking something out of his nose.

"Storm's over?" Philemon asked.

"Not quite, but it's blowing itself out to sea. Finally."

"Good. Then we can get out of here," Otto muttered.

"Not so fast," I said. "Cape Island's completely flooded. We can't get out of here without a boat and the boat's underwater."

Otto and Philemon groaned loudly while Deborah gave a shuddering sigh. "Deputy, we have to leave. There are three dead bodies in this house!" Her voice rose quickly and she struggled into a standing position from where she had slept.

"I know." I hoped my voice sounded soothing, but the truth was, I was a bit nervous about being in the same house as three dead bodies for an indefinite amount of time, too. "We're going to do the best we can to figure out how to get out of here."

"I don't see that we have any choice but to wait until the waters recede," Deborah said.

"We'll think of something." I tried to lighten the atmosphere. "After all, Henry and Jeremiah don't want us here forever, do they?" I chuckled.

"That's right, we don't." I turned in surprise at the voice from behind me. Henry had emerged from Jeremiah's room and was standing just outside the doorway.

"The good news is, the storm's dying down," I said. "So things are looking better than they were yesterday afternoon."

"Did I hear you say the boat's underwater?" he asked.

I nodded. Now that the lamp provided a bit of light, I didn't have to answer every question with words when a gesture would do.

"I guess I shouldn't be surprised," he said.

"I got to get back to my farm," Otto said. Philemon bobbed his head in agreement.

"We all have things we need to get back to." I flicked an annoyed glance at the two men. "But we'll just have to wait until we can get out of here safely."

"We could swim for it," Otto suggested.

"I can't let you do that," I said. "Too dangerous. Who knows what the currents might be doing out there?"

"I'm willing to take a chance."

"I'm not," Philemon said. We all turned to look at him.

"Why not?" Otto asked.

"I can't swim. If I could, I wouldn't a' needed rescuing yesterday."

"God's teeth, man. You can't swim?" Otto leapt from his chair.

"Leave me alone, you goldarned ape."

Otto shook his head and scoffed. "What are ye, a girl?" he asked Philemon.

"Enough, both of you. You'll get back to your farms soon

enough. Right now we need to decide what to do with the bodies in the bedroom."

Deborah fixed me with a look of horror. "What are we supposed to do with them? Let them out the door to float away?"

"Of course not. I thought we might be able to open the windows in the bedroom and chop through the shutters. At least that would allow some air into the room."

"Hold on there a minute." Henry stood with his hands on his hips. He looked comical with his short stature, but I dared not smile. "I won't have you chopping up pieces of this house."

"It would just be temporary. We'd help you build new shutters and put them up." I looked around for confirmation. Both Otto and Philemon looked away. "Well, at least I'll help you."

"I wouldn't want them back here, anyhow." Henry jutted his chin toward the two men. Otto sneered at him.

"That's fine. They don't have to come back," I said. "But can we open a window in the bedroom? If there was a way to get outside to open the shutter the proper way, we'd do it. But the water's come right up to the cottage and we can't risk it."

"All right." Henry shook his head in dismay. "I'll get the axe."

# CHAPTER 31

We waited several minutes for Henry to return from the lighthouse tower with the axe, then I followed him into the bedroom. At the window, he pushed up the sash with some difficulty—"the wood's swollen from the rain," he muttered—and ran his hand over the inside face of the shutter.

"I don't have time to be building shutters and putting them up again," he said over his shoulder.

"I told you I'd help build a new one and put it up," I said with some annoyance. Did the man want the three bodies putrefying in the bedroom instead?

He lifted the axe. His thick, stocky arms were strong. It took him several minutes to hack the shutter away from the window, but he was working carefully and grasping pieces of shutter before they could fall into the water. He stacked the pieces on the floor next to him. When he was finished, I joined him at the window.

Earlier, when I looked out the windows of the lighthouse tower, I could see everything. Even with all the flooding and damage, it was exhilarating to be able to see so far. But downstairs, in the bedroom, the feeling was quite the opposite. I felt hemmed in, more so than I had felt all night with the darkness and the heat pressing upon me. Henry and I stood quietly, watching the waves lap at the cottage walls not far below us. Everywhere I looked, all I saw was water. Water where the land should have been. A milky gray light filtered into the room.

"I don't know how you're going to get out of here," Henry said. "It'll be some time before this water recedes enough to walk away."

"Could we build a raft with the pieces of wood from the shutter?" I knew as I asked the question that it sounded desperate and ridiculous. Henry stared at me as if I were a madman.

"You'll need a lot more wood than that to build a raft, Deputy." His voice was tinged with sarcasm.

"I reckon you're right. Let's go." I led the way back toward the parlor.

"Should we close the door?" he asked.

I looked into the parlor where, with help from the light issuing from the bedroom, I could see Otto and Philemon hunkering in the center of the room. Deborah sat next to the fireplace. Some light from outdoors might diffuse the tension. The darkness had been oppressive for so many hours. "I'll ask the others."

In the parlor, all eyes turned toward Henry and me.

"It's like we said. The water's up to the cottage walls and rising. We're going to have to wait a little longer before we can get out of here. The question right now is, would you like me to leave the bedroom door open to allow some light from outdoors into the room?" I asked.

Deborah's head snapped up. "No."

Otto and Philemon, predictably, had a different response. "Keep it open," they said in unison.

"But the bodies," Deborah protested.

"What's your vote?" I asked Henry.

He was silent for a moment, then nodded. "Open for now."

I didn't need to cast my vote, which would have been to keep the door open. "Deborah, I'm afraid we have to go with the majority rule here. We can close the door later if it becomes necessary." I didn't say what would necessitate closing the door again, but I think everyone realized we would close it if the odor of sickness from the room became overpowering or if the bodies began to molder.

"Very well." She stared into the fireplace.

"How about some food?" Otto asked, staring at Deborah.

She turned to him with a withering look. "I'll see what I can find in the kitchen." She left, and I figured she was probably grateful to leave the presence of all us men.

"Deborah," I called after her, "why don't we open the shutter in there, too? It'll be easier for you to work in the kitchen with some light from outside." I glanced at Henry as I made the suggestion. He might have other thoughts about hewing down a second shutter.

He shook his head and scoffed, but said, "If we have to." We dismantled it after I promised to help him rebuild the shutter for the kitchen window.

"That's much better," Deborah said when we were finished.

Henry and I joined the other men in the parlor. Henry strode to the bottom of the stairs. "Jeremiah," he called.

"What?"

"You want food? Deborah's fixing something."

"Bring it up," Jeremiah shouted.

We sat in silence while we waited for something to eat. The wind was still audible, but more comforting sounds came from the kitchen. Deborah was moving about, clinking cups and utensils. She brought in a tray of cider and set it on the table. "I'll bring in bread and honey," she said, returning to the kitchen.

Food never tasted so good as it did that morning. Deborah

brought a jar of honey to the table, along with two loaves of bread and a crock of butter. With the gray light from the window, she was able to find the tinderbox and managed to boil water for coffee, too. The tasks of preparing food and drink for breakfast seemed to revive her. I was glad to see her lift out of her sadness, if only for a short time.

Henry ate nothing himself, but took several pieces of bread up to the gallery for Jeremiah. Neither man came back downstairs for a long while. Thudding, tapping, and other loud noises filtered down to the parlor, and I hoped they were able to make the light functional before evening fell. While Deborah was clearing away the plates and cups from breakfast, I went into the kitchen to see if there was any discernible difference in the water level outside the cottage.

There was. It was getting higher.

"How does it look, Deputy?" Deborah asked.

"Not good."

She joined me and gasped when she saw how high the water had risen against the wall of the cottage. It was only a foot or so below the bottom of the kitchen window. I was beginning to think flooding might be a bigger problem than the storm itself.

"What are we going to do?" she asked in a small voice.

"Not much we can do right now. Water's too high. We could try to swim, of course, but that'll be long and strenuous. And dangerous. Besides that, Philemon can't swim. We may have to build something that'll hold us all until we can get to water shallow enough to walk."

"How would we ever do that?"

"We'd have to make some kind of raft using the wood from the shutters we've taken down, and likely all the other wood we can find. Who knows how long this water will take to drain back into the bay?"

"I'm not leaving Kit."

"We don't have to discuss it now, but you may have no

choice. It's going to be hard enough to get the living persons out of here, let alone the ones who passed overnight."

"I don't care if I never leave. I'm not leaving without him."

The only thing I could do was repeat myself, so I returned to the parlor. Otto was picking his fingernails while Philemon sat back in his chair, staring at the ceiling. I had a feeling boredom was going to be more of a problem today than it had been yesterday. We could only play cards for so long, and neither of the men seemed to be interested in books. Yes indeed, I was getting worried.

I was surprised to see Jeremiah and Henry come downstairs a little while later. "How is everything up there?" I asked.

"Making progress. I don't know how long it'll take, but we're trying to get the gallery cleaned up," Henry said. Jeremiah retreated to his bedroom and closed the door behind him.

"Is there anything I can do to help?"

"No. Jeremiah and me have a plan."

"Henry, can I speak to you in the kitchen?" I asked. He followed me wordlessly while Otto and Philemon stared after us. Deborah was still cleaning up from breakfast, so I asked her to give Henry and me some privacy to talk.

"I'm sure you've seen how high the water is," I began.

He nodded. "Getting higher. You might have to get everyone out of here if the cottage starts to flood."

"I broached the subject with Deborah and she said she's not leaving Kit's body behind. Would you be able to leave Abigail's body behind if we had to?"

"If I had no choice, I could do that. I'd talk to Jeremiah and make him understand. You might have trouble on your hands if Otto refuses to leave his cousin, though."

I nodded. I hoped it wouldn't come to that, but we had to be prepared.

"As daft as it is, we'd have to build that raft you mentioned," Henry said.

"I know. And unless you have more wood in here some-where, we'll have to use more shutters."

"There ain't many more shutters. One in Jeremiah's room, two in the tower stairway."

"We may be forced to use furniture."

Henry frowned. "If we don't have any other choice."

"Hopefully we'll have enough wood from the shutters."

"Deputy, I don't want those men in my house any longer than they have to be. You need to get them out of here. Jeremiah and I will stay here. We have a job to do. But the others can't stay."

"What about Deborah?"

"She can't stay, either."

I raised my eyebrows. I had assumed Henry and Jeremiah would welcome the presence of a woman who could cook for them and help clean up the mess that would undoubtedly reveal itself once the waters receded. And now that I thought about it, perhaps they could hire Deborah to work for them. She could do the cooking and cleaning and other work around the house and property that Abigail had done. She wouldn't be forced to survive by working her farm. I could concern myself with that later, though. At the moment, getting out of the cottage was the most important consideration.

"What about food? And fresh water?" I asked.

"You can send someone out here with a supply boat. We'll pay for everything they bring. My job is to keep that light running and I failed last night. I don't intend to fail again, so I'll be working as hard as I can to repair it. Otherwise I'll lose my job."

"But surely the Treasury Department wouldn't dismiss you because of storm damage."

"They'll say we should have been better prepared."

There was nothing I could say to that. In fact, Otto had said much the same thing earlier. But would anything have changed if Henry and Jeremiah had been better prepared? What could they possibly have done to weather the storm with less damage? The force of this storm was something no one could have foreseen or prepared for.

"All right, Henry. Let's keep an eye on the water level and see what happens. I'll get Otto and Philemon started on building a raft with the wood from the shutters. They build boats—they ought to be able to build a raft that can carry them, me, and Deborah."

Henry turned and left the room. I heard his boots clumping up the stairs to the gallery. All eyes in the parlor turned to me. Deborah spoke first.

"Well, Deputy? What were you and Henry discussing?"

"We were talking about how to get out of here."

# CHAPTER 32

*O*tto and Philemon exchanged glances. No doubt they couldn't wait to leave the cottage.

"What do you propose?" Deborah asked. The men leaned forward as if to hear me better.

"First, we take down Jeremiah's bedroom shutters and those in the stairway leading up to the gallery. Henry and I can do that. Then we're going to use the wood from all the shutters and build a raft. Otto and Philemon, you'll be doing that."

Philemon scowled. "A raft that's going to fit all of us?" He counted on his fingers and muttered the names of everyone in the building, including the three who had died during the night. "Nine of us on a raft? It'll never work."

I chose my words carefully before replying. "We only need a raft big enough for four people."

Deborah's eyes widened and she leapt from her chair. "I told you I'm not leaving Kit." Spittle flew from the corner of her mouth.

"We ain't leaving August." Otto held up a finger and pointed to himself and Philemon. Philemon nodded vehemently, his eyes like slits.

"We only need to leave them here temporarily," I explained. "Henry and Jeremiah are going to stay here and try to fix the lamp. They need to get it working as quickly as possible. They'll watch over things here and nothing will happen to August or Kit or Abigail before I or someone else can come back with a boat to retrieve them."

"What if you're wrong? What if something happens to Kit?" Deborah asked. Her hands trembled as she spoke. "Deputy, I need to speak to you in the kitchen."

I followed her from the parlor after cautioning Otto and Philemon to stay where they were. In the kitchen, she turned to face me. "Can't we just take Kit with us on the raft? It's only one more person. I need to make sure he receives a proper burial."

"Of course you do. But don't you think Otto and Philemon feel the same way about August? And don't you think Henry feels the same way about Abigail?"

She scoffed. "I doubt it."

"Why? Henry and Abigail were husband and wife, just like you and Kit, and Otto and August are blood kin. And Philemon is his friend."

Her lips were a thin white line as she stared at me without answering. "I already told you that Henry and Abigail were husband and wife in name only."

"Nonetheless, they were married for over twenty years. So can you explain why you are the only one who cares about a burial for your loved one?"

She hung her head as she braced herself against the wooden counter. Her voice was very soft. "Henry has Jeremiah. Otto has his wife. Even Philemon has a wife, unlucky though she may be. Do you not see? I am alone. I am all alone. I've never been able to have a child. Now my husband is gone. I have no other family. The least I can do is bury him." Tears fell from her eyes and splashed onto the counter.

I did not know what to say to that. She was right and it was not going to be easy for her with no husband, no children, and no other family. Even if I could eventually convince Henry to hire her to do the things around the house that he and Jeremiah couldn't do, right now he didn't want her to stay.

I returned to the parlor so that Deborah might have some privacy in the kitchen. I was beginning to worry about her. She had held up quite well so far, but the thought of leaving Kit here in the cottage while she joined us in reaching dry land might be too much for her to contemplate. Of course we would return for the bodies once everyone was safely deposited on firm ground, but it would take time and there would likely be other, more life-threatening problems for me to handle in Cape Island.

In the parlor, Otto and Philemon still hadn't moved. "What are you waiting for?" I asked crossly. "I told you to get started on a raft."

They exchanged glances. Otto spoke first. "I ain't going in that room with them bodies to get the wood you and Henry hewed from the shutter."

"Me, neither." Philemon added his useless voice to Otto's.

"Very well. I'll get the wood myself and bring it out to you. You can start building it right here." I strode to the bedroom where the bodies lay and stooped to gather several pieces of the sodden wood. I deposited it on the floor of the parlor and headed back in for more. I allowed my eyes to stray to the bed and the floor, where the bodies lay.

A shudder ran through me at the sight of them, and that was quickly followed by a tremor of guilt. I had failed each of these people. Kit's death troubled me the most, since I might have been able to prevent it, but it was the sight of Abigail's body that I knew would haunt me. Whereas Kit had died quickly and probably felt little pain—and August slid in and out of consciousness and did not cry out much in discomfort—Abigail had suffered unimaginably before her death. What had the poor woman done to deserve such a horrible end? I thought briefly of Neptune's Curse.

But I knew Neptune's Curse was a story, a fabrication from the mind of a half-drunken man stuck in a small cottage with oppressive heat and little light. Everyone knew it was blasphemy, as Deborah had said, but one had to confess it was an unsettling tale.

As I was reaching for the final pieces of wood to give to them, Deborah appeared in the doorway. She stepped into the room and closed the door behind her. I straightened up.

"What is it?" I asked.

She gazed at me with dead eyes. "I'm sorry, George. But I have thought about it and I cannot and will not leave Kit."

I suppressed the urge to ignore her. I opened my mouth to speak when the door opened again. Henry was standing there. The look in Deborah's eyes changed from flat to … fearful? I would have sworn she was afraid of something.

"What are you doing in here?" Henry asked. He slid a suspicious glance from me to Deborah and back to me.

"Deborah just came in to talk to me," I said. "Do you need my help for something?"

"No. I came down to tell you it'll be a while before I can help you with the shutters in the stairway. There are a few things I need to do in the light first."

"That's all right. Come get me when you're ready."

Henry nodded once and reached for the door handle, but froze at Deborah's next words.

"George, you need to ask Henry how he felt about his wife in the days before she died."

"I've already asked him." His response was none of Deborah's concern.

"Are you sure he told you the truth?" Deborah opened her mouth as if to say something else, but closed it and swept out of the room.

Henry's eyes met mine.

"What is she talking about?" I asked.

"I haven't any idea. "She's gone daft."

I raised my eyebrows. "Has she?"

Henry closed the door, as Deborah had left it open when she departed. He sighed. "I told you the truth. But there's more you should know." He took a deep breath and frowned. "I'm going to talk about this one time, d'you hear? One time. And once I'm done talking I'm not going to talk about Abigail anymore."

*We'll see about that*, I thought. Aloud I asked, "What more should I know?"

"I didn't want her to die. I loved her, like I said. I only did what she wanted me to do. She was sick and getting sicker." He hesitated and swallowed hard. "She wanted to die, George." He shook his head. "She wanted to die."

I couldn't say anything. I felt everything beginning to slow down around me with such a revelation.

Henry continued. "All she wanted was to be with her brother. The kindest thing I could do for her was to let her die."

"But her condition ..." My voice failed me.

"Don't say it. Don't you think I saw her, too? Don't you think I wanted her to get well?"

In my work I frequently see people on their worst days. Their most anxious days. The days they are filled with fear. One can never predict how a person is going to behave under great mental or physical strain.

Henry surprised me, though I tried not to show it. I expected him to shout, to threaten, to curse. I expected him to erupt in anger. But what I saw was the opposite. One tear rolled down his unshaven, filthy cheek. He blinked rapidly, as if to stem the flow of other tears that might follow. Then he thrust his arm across his face to wipe away any sign of weakness. He sniffed once, a wet, thick sound.

I wished I didn't have to witness it. I wished he'd stayed

angry with me. I would be embarrassed in such a situation, and he was very likely much more embarrassed than even I would have been. He was a hard man, used to the elements of wind and sea and sand. His very bearing spoke of strength and stubbornness. To be seen allowing a tear to escape his eye must have humiliated him.

I turned toward the window to give him a moment to compose himself. When I faced him again, he was leaning against the door, his head in his hands.

"You all right?" I put my hand on his shoulder.

He nodded, not looking up. "I didn't want her to die. But I knew she didn't want to live anymore. She loved Jeremiah, and I fancy she even loved me in her own way, but her greatest love was for Horatio. When he died she gave up wanting to be alive any longer. She lived for many more years, but now that Jeremiah's grown and he knows how to operate the lighthouse when I'm too old to do it, she wanted to go. She wanted to join her brother. So when she started getting sick, I think she saw it as the quickest way to be with him." Henry swallowed and exhaled a long breath.

"Did you do anything to hasten her death? Give her a dose of something?"

He shook his head vehemently. "No. No. Believe me when I tell you I begged her to see the doctor. The doctor'll tell you that I went to him several times, asking what I could do to help her, to make her well. She told me that if I brought the doctor to the cottage, she would refuse to see him."

Jeremiah had said Henry saw the doctor to ask for guidance, but I hadn't known Abigail said she would refuse to see him if he visited her. I was beginning to get a different picture of what transpired before the storm arrived. That is, as long as I could trust what Henry was saying. It certainly appeared to me that he was telling the truth. Deborah had hinted that Henry's feelings toward Abigail had changed shortly before she died. Was he afraid for her? Was he sad? He certainly must have felt despair and hopelessness.

Henry wiped his filthy sleeve across his face and stood. "I told you I won't talk about this again, and I meant what I said. I'll be down when I'm ready to take down those shutters." He left the room without a backward glance and disappeared up the stairs.

I deposited the wood from the bedroom shutter on the floor next to Otto and Philemon and for once, they kept their foolish tongues quiet.

# CHAPTER 33

$\mathcal{A}$s long as Henry couldn't help with the shutters yet, there was something I needed to do. I took up an oil lamp and tapped on Jeremiah's bedroom door. A noise issued forth from inside, so I invited myself in and closed the door behind me.

Jeremiah was pushing himself up from what looked like a kneeling position in front of his bureau. The action immediately caught my attention.

"You looking for something, Jeremiah?"

"I didn't say you could come in here."

"I didn't ask your permission." I gestured toward the straight-backed chair against the wall. "Sit down." Jeremiah brushed the palms of his hands on his trousers and did as I instructed. Not without a scowl, though.

"I need to get back to work. You can't keep me from my work."

"I won't keep you long. I just have a few questions."

"What questions?" He looked at me with undisguised suspicion.

"What were you looking for when I came into the room?"

The stony look he turned on me held a challenge. "None of your concern."

"I think it might be. Tell me what it was."

"Nothing."

"I know you're lying to me, Jeremiah. You might better think again before continuing down this path."

"I got nothing to think about. I thought I dropped a button." He looked at his lap.

"If it was a button, why wouldn't you just tell me that?"

"Because, like I said, it's none of your concern."

He was lying, of course. And I had a pretty good idea what he was looking for. I reached into my pocket and slowly withdrew the crumpled piece of paper I had found earlier under his bureau. I held it up. He moved as if to lunge toward me, but I held the paper out of his reach and stepped back calmly. He sat back down immediately.

"Is this what you were looking for?" I asked.

"No."

"Then why did you react so strongly just now when you saw it?"

"I thought it was something else."

"How could you think it was something else if you don't know what this is?"

He opened his mouth as if to say something, then closed it again. I didn't mind—we both knew I held the paper he was looking for. With a burst of movement Jeremiah stood and the backs of his knees sent the chair crashing into the wall. His fists opened and closed several times as he stared at me, then he strode toward the door, opened it, and slammed it behind him with the force of a thunderclap.

～

I HAD CERTAINLY PROVOKED JEREMIAH, though I still didn't know what the note was about, who wrote it, or who it was meant for. It hadn't necessarily been for Jeremiah's eyes—he could have found the letter and thrown it under his bureau when someone came into the room. It could have been meant for him, of course, but why hide it under the bureau if it belonged to him?

One thing was sure—there was something about that note Jeremiah didn't want me to know about. It was essential for me to ascertain what it was.

Should I ask Henry? He was the only family member left to talk to. And if I were going to talk to him before Jeremiah could reach the lighthouse gallery and warn him that I had the letter, I needed to do it quickly.

I sped up the stairs, nearly overtaking Jeremiah in my haste. "Now what?" He scowled at me when I reached the tower.

"I need to speak to your father. Privately, please."

"Now listen, Deputy," Henry began. "Jeremiah and I have work to do. You take yourself downstairs and wait there until we're ready to talk to you."

"I fear the work will have to wait another few minutes. Jeremiah, please leave us. I'll come downstairs to get you when we're done."

Jeremiah and his father exchanged glances. Jeremiah turned around after emitting a low grumbling sound in my direction. He took his time descending the steps, stomping on each one for good measure. Yes, I had clearly upset him.

Now to figure out what had him so agitated.

Henry looked at me with frowning expectation. "Well? What do you want? You're bound to see me dismissed from my job, aren't you?"

"My only interest at present is figuring out what is going on around here. Now, I know you said Abigail wanted to die, but I don't believe she made herself sick. I believe someone made her sick."

My stern look matched his frown as I pulled the paper from my pocket. I watched his reaction closely. Was that surprise I saw in his eyes for just a moment? Was it fear? Was it something else?

"Do you know what this paper is?" I asked.

As his son had done, Henry shook his head.

"I don't believe you, Henry. I think you know what this is and what's more, I think you and Jeremiah are trying to keep me from learning about it. Is that true?"

Henry stared at me wordlessly.

"Sit down," I ordered.

He did not. "Unless you're going to arrest me, Deputy, I suggest you go downstairs and send my son up here to help me."

We stared at each other for several long minutes. He was correct—he did not have to submit to my questioning. I had no reason to arrest him, not yet, so I could not easily compel him to say anything. But something had shifted: I had made an effort to keep my questioning cordial to this point. The tone of our discourse had changed. We were now on opposite sides of a problem, that of determining the contents of the letter I had found under Jeremiah's bureau. Was he protecting his son? Was he protecting himself? Were father and son sharing a secret?

"I will find what I'm looking for, I can assure you of that," I said. "You would be wise not to force me to set myself against you and Jeremiah. But if that is your choice, then so be it."

I made my way down the staircase. As I descended, a gust of wind buffeted the lighthouse stack, causing the structure to shudder. I grabbed the railing and stood on one step waiting for the shaking to stop. At the bottom of the steps I called to Jeremiah who, unsurprisingly, had retreated to his bedroom.

"Jeremiah! Your father wants you upstairs."

It was likely the tone of my voice that indicated to Otto, Philemon, and Deborah that I was highly vexed. They stared at me in obvious surprise, but I cared not. I sat in the chair I had vacated earlier.

I stared at the raft Otto and Philemon had started. A rectangle of wood sat on the floor. Several pieces of the bedroom shutter were lashed together with rope. "We're going to need more rope and more wood soon if anyone's expecting to leave here on this." Philemon nodded, his large hands on his knees.

"You and Philemon go up the stairs and start hewing the shutters away from the windows. Then do the same in Jeremiah's room."

Henry and I were supposed to do that, I knew, but he was busy with the frenzied efforts to repair the light. Besides that, he needed time to cool down and I needed time to think.

# CHAPTER 34

*I* was surprised at how quickly Otto and Philemon were able to dismantle the shutter and bring the wooden boards down to the parlor. But, I reminded myself, they're supposedly boat builders. If there was one thing they should know how to do, it was working with wood.

They now had a large pile of wood to use for the raft. They discussed the best way to continue building it while I ascended the steps and gazed for a long time out one of the stairway windows. It was going to be hard work to get everyone out of this lighthouse, and it was unclear when I or someone else might be able to return for the bodies.

I searched the horizon for any signs of movement or people. It was frustrating, being trapped in this lighthouse. I was in charge of the safety of all the people in and around Cape Island, and I couldn't get to them. I had no way to communicate with them.

To the northwest, I caught a movement from the corner of my eye. I focused closely on the area where I thought I saw something. My eyes watered as I stared and I had to blink several times to clear my vision. There it was—I saw the movement again. I squinted to see.

A group of three negroes was paddling a small raft over the flooded plain, through thickets of trees toward the mouth of the river. They were too far away for me to recognize them, but one of them wore a red shirt. I immediately thought of Titus Fuller, whom I had seen the day before. Two of the people sat taller than the third. Perhaps two men and a woman? They looked young and strong from where I stood, but I was a long way off. There was a small pile of something next to each person, perhaps satchels or even valises. It looked to me as though they were headed on a trip. I wondered at the timing of their journey. Surely they could wait until it was safer to travel.

I watched as they made quick progress with the help of the stiff wind still driving off the bay. As a man of the law, I was required to uphold the statutes of New Jersey, including the 1804 law that would keep Titus and his brother and sister enslaved until they were twenty-five (for the two young men) and twenty-one (for their sister). But as a human being, I was appalled that ownership of a fellow human being would be permitted under any law.

I hoped the three people on the raft were leaving for a safer place and I was momentarily thankful to be trapped in the lighthouse where I could do nothing to hinder their escape, if in fact that's what I was witnessing.

I wished them Godspeed.

I turned and went downstairs, in part so I could plead innocence if asked at some future date whether I knew anything about three negroes who escaped their servitude.

In the parlor, Deborah was fussing. "These two are making a mess faster than I can clean it up." She gestured widely to include Otto and Philemon.

I smiled as benevolently as I could. This was no time to be worried about rubbish in the parlor. We could concern ourselves with cleaning the cottage when this ordeal was over and the light was working again.

"Deborah, they're doing what's necessary to quickly build the raft that will carry all of us to dry land and safety. Don't fret about it."

I thought again about old Abe Bradford stuck in the cell in Cape Island, and Aces left in the paddock to fend for herself, and my stomach gave a lurch. I wondered how they had fared through the storm. Not for the first time, I hoped Daniel or someone else had thought to free them from their respective enclosures. I was anxious to return to my home to satisfy myself with their well-being.

A few moments later, Otto and Philemon were still working diligently on the raft. I was pacing in the parlor, organizing the thoughts in my head and very likely irking the men, when a terrific crash and a scream rang out from the kitchen. At the sound, Philemon startled and dropped the pile of wood he was holding. He cursed loudly.

I was the first one to reach the kitchen, where Deborah was sitting on the floor, holding her leg. The iron kettle, which normally would have been on top of the stove, was on its side next to her.

"What happened?" I ran toward Deborah.

"It fell." She nodded toward the kettle and her breath hitched.

In the watery light coming from the kitchen window, I could see Deborah's leg was swelling and already turning purple. More concerning, though, was the tip of shin bone poking through the skin.

I had no idea what to do. It was a gruesome sight. Deborah's eyes were squeezed closed and her breath was coming in short bursts. "The pain is terrible," she moaned.

"It's all right, Deborah. We're going to help you."

Otto and Philemon were still standing behind me. I glanced over my shoulder. "Otto, I need you to—"

The floor shifted with a terrific lurch.

Deborah screamed again. "What was that?"

Otto and Philemon exchanged glances of surprise.

I ran to the kitchen window and looked down. I could touch surface of the water now. I glanced as far to the left as I could and noted the water level against the side of the lighthouse—it was only a little bit higher than it had been earlier.

That meant one thing: the cottage was pulling away from the lighthouse tower. We were sinking.

"Both of you, help me with her." I positioned myself by Deborah's legs while Otto and Philemon stood by her head.

"We're moving her into the parlor." I spoke tersely. There was no time to waste.

"What's happening?" Deborah cried.

"The cottage has shifted under the force of the water," I said through clenched teeth. We needed to move quickly in case it happened again.

"What?" Her voice bordered on hysteria, and I didn't doubt her fear was made worse by pain. I looked at her leg again. We were going to have to carry her somehow, since I didn't know if she would be able to walk at all.

Otto held Deborah under her arms and I held her uninjured leg. Her injured leg dragged on the floor until I instructed Philemon to lift it carefully. We moved slowly and clumsily as she hollered from the pain. When we were finally able to set her on a chair near the fireplace, she leaned her head back with a shuddering inhale. "It hurts so much!" Tears coursed down her cheeks.

"Deborah, we'll keep you as comfortable as possible until the raft is finished." I hoped Henry had a supply of laudanum in the cottage, because Deborah was in sore need of it. "Otto, Philemon, how much longer do you think it will be?"

"We're going to need four barrels, one for each corner of the raft. They can be small, but we need them for stability," Otto said.

"Very well. I'll go up to the light and ask Henry if he has any small barrels up there we can use. Perhaps he can tell me where I can find the laudanum, too." I also needed to apprise him of the worsening situation in the cottage.

I hurried up the steps, pausing on each landing to catch my breath. By the time I reached the top, I was perspiring and panting. "Henry," I gasped, "we have an urgent problem."

Henry and Jeremiah were leaning over the counter, looking closely at something that looked like it had come out of the light mechanism. Henry raised his head and gave me an inscrutable look. Jeremiah didn't look at me at all. I was quite sure they were still angry about the questions I'd asked them earlier regarding the perplexing note. No matter—their anger would eventually fade. And if it didn't, so be it.

"We already know. The foundation of the cottage. It's nothin' but sand and rocks—we never had to worry about the water coming up as far as the foundation before, but now it's here. We can't waste time by going up and down the stairs. You'll need to hurry the men along making the raft in case the cottage is overwhelmed with water. You all must get out of here as soon as you can."

"Otto and Philemon need four small barrels to construct the raft. Are there any up here we can use?"

"Look over there." Henry pointed with his chin toward the west-facing side of the gallery. "There are some empty ones."

"We need laudanum, too."

"What for?"

"Deborah's hurt. Her leg is certainly broken. She's in a great deal of pain."

Jeremiah looked up, his look of surprise matching his father's. "How did that happen?"

"The kettle in the kitchen fell on it. I didn't see it happen."

"We heard her screaming and figured it was because of the cottage sinking. The woman is nothing but a nuisance," Henry muttered. "I wish she and Kit had never come here."

It seemed an unkind remark, considering Kit's death and all Deborah had done for Henry's family, but I had neither the time nor the inclination to ask him to reflect on his words. I hurried to the place in the gallery Henry had indicated. There were several small barrels on the floor.

"Are these filled with oil?" I called.

"No. They're empty. Take 'em."

One barrel at a time, I carried the cumbersome things to the top of the stairway. "And the laudanum?" I called over my shoulder.

"In the top drawer of my bureau." I could hear Henry's voice quite easily—further proof that the wind and rain had greatly lessened.

I thought quickly about the best and fastest way to get the barrels down the steps. I didn't dare roll them, lest they break apart. I decided to carry one at a time to the first landing, then repeat the process all the way down to the parlor. I almost failed at my mission before even getting started—I tripped over a nail sticking out of the doorway at the top of the stairs and dropped my first barrel. It tumbled down the steps and landed with a loud thud on the first landing. I held my breath, hoping it wouldn't continue bouncing all the way down the stairs. Thankfully, it did not. I hurriedly carried the other three barrels down to the landing. After several long and exhausting minutes of exertion, I had deposited all the barrels in the parlor. Otto and Philemon mumbled their thanks, not looking up from their pressing task.

Deborah still moaned and gasped in pain, so my next task was to find the laudanum.

I wished I could avoid altogether the sight of the bodies in the bedroom, but I couldn't. There was little change in them. An errant fly buzzed around Abigail's face. I stepped toward her quickly and shooed it away, but it returned after only a moment. Any other insects in the cottage would arrive very soon, I was sure. We needed to get the living out of the lighthouse and the cottage before the bodies could putrefy much more.

I crossed the room to Henry's bureau in two steps and pulled the top drawer open. I swept aside a set of underclothes. The laudanum was there, as Henry had said it would be. But there was something else, too.

Something I knew was going to be crucial to figuring out what had transpired in this structure long before the storm arrived.

# CHAPTER 35

Under Henry's garments lay a crumpled piece of paper —paper that looked like the one I had found in Jeremiah's room.

I snatched it up and shoved it into my pocket before anyone could come into the room.

When I stepped out of the bedroom holding the bottle of laudanum, I was not surprised to see Henry bounding down the stairs from the gallery. Judging by the look of panic in his eyes, I knew in an instant what was going through his mind—he had forgotten the note in his bureau.

He had been lying to me.

I made a hasty decision to pretend I hadn't seen it, at least until I could read its contents.

When he saw the bottle in my hand, he stopped short. "You found the medicine." His eyes bored into mine, seeking confirmation of what he doubtlessly feared.

I ignored him and proceeded to attend to Deborah. After administering a large dose of medicine, I held on to the bottle.

I kept my voice light when I spoke to him. "I found it right where you said it would be. Thank you, Henry. Deborah will be feeling the effects of it very soon and it should relieve some of her pain for now."

He reached for the bottle. "I'll put it away for you."

I held it away from him and slipped it into my shirt pocket. "I'm sure I'll be giving her a second dose, so I'll keep it for now. No need to spend any more time than necessary in that room. It won't be long before those bodies begin to emit a quite unpleasant odor."

I could see the war going on behind Henry's eyes. He couldn't discern from my actions or my words whether I had found the note. After several seconds during which I watched his eyes dart around, no doubt calculating whether he should insist upon taking the bottle, he opted to return to the light-house gallery. After he was out of sight on the circular stairway, I stole into Jeremiah's room and closed the door quietly behind me. Standing next to the shutterless window, I withdrew the missing top portion of the note from my trouser pocket and matched the ragged edges together.

The writing was hard to make out, seeing as how the paper had obviously been crumpled into a ball and then smoothed over again. By whose hand? With luck, I would know soon.

I squinted in the dim gray light over my shoulder and was able to make out a few words. They were in the same hand-writing as the note I had found in Jeremiah's room.

*Henry, do not tell Kit about this. Once we have spoken, you may decide to speak to Jeremiah. I ...*

So the letter was meant for Henry. Then why did Jeremiah have part of it crumpled underneath his bureau?

I pulled the other part of the note out of my trouser pocket and scrutinized the writing.

*... must meet with you to warn you about something I have discov-ered. You will find it of great interest, I am sure. I will be behind the ... on the first day of September ...*

As with the bottom part of the note, which was missing a signature, there was no clue from the handwriting whether the writer was male or female. However, the words themselves gave me a clue. It wasn't Kit, since the writer wanted to conceal the information from him. It wasn't Jeremiah, since he was mentioned in the note. It very likely wasn't Abigail, because she would simply have spoken of her discovery to her husband.

Who would most likely wish to hide something from Kit?

If I were a betting man, my money would be on his wife.

Deborah.

Unfortunately, I now had more questions than answers. And my next steps would require careful deliberation. How was I to broach the subject of the note with Henry? He might be a small man, but I had seen evidence of his anger and defiance, as well as his physical strength, since arriving at the lighthouse fewer than twenty-four hours earlier.

And how to broach the subject with Deborah? Had she imparted sensitive information to Henry that she wouldn't wish to share with me?

My next questions were about Jeremiah, the young man who spent his life in this lighthouse and cottage with his mother and father. The young man who had been previously kind and engaging and was suddenly surly and angry. How did he come to have part of the note in his possession? The condition of the paper, rent into several pieces, was telling. It hinted at a mildly violent act. Had Jeremiah torn the paper? Henry? Someone else? Where did Jeremiah find it? I was quite sure now that he hadn't found it in his bedroom. And why did he feel the need to hide it?

And finally, whatever information the writer had to impart, it had to be kept from Kit.

Why?

I didn't know yet, but one thing was sure—I couldn't ask Kit about it. Because he was dead.

WHAT I NEEDED MORE than anything was time to sort out the
information I had. It was almost humorous—time had been
slow and abundant during the storm, but now, just as I was
making discoveries and beginning to stitch my thoughts
together, time was moving faster and growing shorter. We had
to get the living out of the cottage soon, in case the building
sank further under the force of the water. And we had to get the
dead out, too, before they started to decay. Or before we lost
them to the sea.

What did I know so far?

First, I had three dead bodies. Someone had killed Abigail,
that much was certain. People's bodies simply didn't turn the
color of millet and swell up suddenly, causing death over a
matter of a few days. Every time I had seen or heard of a case of
liver disease, from which Abigail seemed to be suffering, it
progressed slowly. And while Abigail may have been willing to
die so she could join her long-dead brother, I did not believe she
somehow caused her own death.

We all knew how August had died—from wounds sustained
when his cousin slashed him on the head with a broken bottle.
Otto would be punished for that.

And there was Kit, a hale and hearty man who died from a
brutal fall down the stairs of the lighthouse. For the first time, I
felt a twinge of unease about his death. There was a secret the
writer of the note wanted to keep from him. Was it possible his
death, like Abigail's, had not been an accident? I struggled to
remember if both Henry and Jeremiah had been up in the light
with Kit at the time of his death.

Second, there was an underlying current of unease among
the men in the cottage and lighthouse. I knew now of the
trouble between Henry's brother-in-law, Horatio, and the

Schuhmacher family. But I suspected there was more to the story than I was being told, and I wanted to know what it was.

Third, the strange letter to Henry was very likely authored by Deborah. The letter mentioned something "interesting" and pled with Henry not to tell Kit about it. I knew nothing of the subject matter of the letter. I looked over at Deborah, wondering if I could ask her about it, but she was asleep, no doubt from the strength of the laudanum. She was in no condition to answer my questions—even if I woke her, she would probably be so disoriented and confused that she would have no idea what I was talking about.

An alarmed shout rang from the top of the lighthouse steps. "George!"

I ran to the base of the stairs and started climbing. "What is it?" I was out of breath even before reaching the halfway point of the stairway. When I got to the top, my chest was heaving with the exertion from going so fast.

"What is it?" I bent over to catch my breath, my hands on my knees.

"Look." Henry pointed toward the roof of the cottage.

I straightened up and had to squint because of the salt and grime on the outside of the glass pane, but then I saw it.

A gaping chasm where the cottage should have been attached to the lighthouse.

I knew from looking out the kitchen window earlier that the cottage was tipping toward the water faster than the lighthouse, but seeing the growing crevasse between the tower and the cottage flooded me with dread.

I raised my eyes to find Henry and Jeremiah staring at me.

"We've got to get everyone out," Henry said. "That cottage is going to end up in the water as sure as I'm standing here."

"How long do you think we've got?" I asked.

Henry shook his head and ran his fingers through his beard.

"Can't say. Could be hours, could be minutes. That water isn't getting any lower."

"The raft isn't ready yet."

"Then you'd better get them fellows working harder, unless you want to swim."

"I would swim, but Philemon can't swim and there's no way Deborah can swim in her condition. She's asleep from the laudanum. And when she wakes up, the pain from her leg is going to be so bad she won't be able to kick in the water."

Henry scanned the horizon before answering.

"The only thing we can do is get that raft built in a hurry. Tell them nothing fancy, just wood and rope and barrels."

"I'll go down and help them. Another set of hands can't hurt." I paused. "Henry, what do you reckon is going to happen to the lighthouse if the cottage detaches completely? Is it going to crumble, too?"

Henry exhaled and puffed out his cheeks. "I don't know. What I can tell you is this: now that the water is getting under the foundation of the lighthouse, it may go the way of the cottage. Jeremiah and I are duty-bound to stay here and try to fix the light as long as we can. We can't leave on the first raft out of here. Besides, I'm sure there won't be enough room."

He was right. "Then it sounds like Deborah, Otto, Philemon, and I are leaving as soon as the raft is built. If we can get out of here soon enough, I'll bring it back before nightfall to get you two and the three bodies downstairs. If not, I'll come back at daybreak."

If the lighthouse was still standing at daybreak.

"What if the staircase buckles as the cottage pulls away? You two will be trapped up here," I said.

"I wouldn't worry about that. If we see that's about to happen, we'll get downstairs fast. Jeremiah and I can only leave if the light is fixed or if we are in danger of losing our own lives by staying. I hope to fix it by tonight, but if I can't, then I have to start again in the morning. And here's another thing we'll have to think about—if Jeremiah and I do have to leave on a raft, can it support the weight of six people, three living and three dead?"

I hoped so.

# CHAPTER 36

After speaking to Henry and Jeremiah, I hurried back down to the parlor. I had considered talking to Henry about the letter while I was in the tower, but immediate circumstances became more important.

There would be time for questions about the letter later, and I would confront Henry when the time was appropriate.

Otto and Philemon couldn't have heard what I was saying to Henry and Jeremiah up in the gallery, but they seemed to sense my urgency. When I joined them in the parlor, they were working without speaking to each other unless necessary. I was pleased with the progress they had made.

"Otto, Philemon, the situation is getting worse quickly. What can I do to help?"

Otto pointed to a saw lying on the floor near him and a pile of planks which had once formed the cottage shutters. "Cut each of those in two and bring them here. We need them to make the bottom of the raft stable."

I did as I was told, looking over my shoulder occasionally to see if Deborah showed signs of awakening from her laudanum-induced sleep. She lay motionless, but I could hear her occa-

sional quiet whimpers. I deposited my stack of timbers behind
Otto, who returned to his work. Nearby Philemon was lashing
the four small oil barrels to planks using rope and nails. They
would serve as floats for the raft. I helped him by steadying the
planks as he wrestled each oil barrel into its proper place.

We were nearing the completion of the work when a low
moan escaped Deborah's lips. At the sound, Philemon looked
toward her with a frown. "I s'pose we'll have to listen to her
caterwauling now."

I scowled at him in disbelief. Did the man have no sympa-
thy? I hurried to Deborah's side. Seeing me, she moaned again.
"Kit?"

"It's me, Deputy Moore. How are you doing, Deborah?"

"Where's Kit?"

My chest constricted.

"He's not here right now. I'm going to give you some more
medicine so you can rest until we can get you to the doctor."

She began to thrash, but the movement caused her pain and
she let out a bleat.

"Shh, you'll be all right. We just have to wait a short while
before leaving here."

"Where's Kit?"

The combination of laudanum and pain had made her
unaware of Kit's death. I dared not remind her of it while the
laudanum was still playing tricks on her sensibilities, so I had to
think of something that might placate her.

"Do you need more laudanum?"

She moaned loudly. "Yes."

I needed to mind the amount I gave her. If the raft was
finished soon, we needed her to be awake and alert so we could
assist her getting onto it. I confess a part of me wanted to ask
her a few questions, too, before she again became incapable of
coherent speech or thought.

"Deborah, do you remember why you're here?"

"Where?"

"In the Brewsters' house. The lighthouse."

"The storm."

"Yes. What do you remember about the storm?"

"I remember coming here. With Kit." She whimpered. "To make sure Henry and Abigail had what they needed to ride out the storm." She paused to take a tremulous breath. "I brought more food because Abigail was sick."

"Anything else?"

She groaned and shook her head from side to side. "Please help me. The pain is terrible."

I reached for the laudanum and gave her a very small dose. She swallowed it and lay her head back on the cushion. Tears seeped from her eyes and rolled toward the floor, wetting the hair at her temples. There was nothing more I could do for her until the raft was complete.

"Deputy, can you find us something to drink? It's hot work putting this raft together." Otto wiped his forehead with his sleeve.

"I'll say it is," Philemon said.

I went into the kitchen and found a fresh jug of cider and several cups which Deborah had washed since we last ate and drank. I took them to the parlor and set them on the table.

"Any food out there?" Otto asked.

"I'll check."

On the wooden slab table in the kitchen, I found bread, butter, pickles, and potted beef. The remainder of the beef soup still bubbled on the stove, but Deborah had taken the mushroom soup off the heat. It was on the wooden table, cold and unappealing. I put the cold food and the beef soup, along with a ladle and utensils, on a large tray and set it down next to the jug of cider. "Eat your fill, men. We're going to need our strength in the coming hours if we're going to get out of here on that raft."

Otto nodded and helped himself to a large piece of bread

slathered with butter and potted beef. Philemon filled his cup with cider, drained it, and filled it again with the hot beef soup. He ate that quickly, then returned to his work. Otto ladled the rest of the beef soup into a bowl and drank it, slurping loudly. I frowned. Even in these dire circumstances, he gave no thought to the hunger of others in the building, consuming everything for himself. I had told him to eat his fill, to be sure, but I hoped he would leave some for the rest of us.

While Otto and Philemon worked on the final stages of the raft, I returned to the kitchen with the tray. I put more food on it, including bowls of the congealing mushroom soup. I wished I had a way to warm it quickly, but I had a feeling neither Henry nor Jeremiah would mind eating it cold. I took the tray up to the tower. Both men thanked me for the meal, which was the least I could do for them. I left quickly so they could return to their critical tasks.

After being told by Otto and Philemon that they didn't need my help with their tasks, I sat and watched them work, trying not to notice the degree to which the cottage floor tilted. I didn't realize until that moment how desperate I was to get out of the lighthouse. I had been holding my own fears at bay by doing what I could to keep up morale and spirits, but with nothing to do but sit idly, I suddenly felt apprehensive.

I hoped we would all make it to dry ground before the rising waters consumed the cottage.

# CHAPTER 37

*T*he cottage was quiet, save for the sounds coming from my companions as they lashed Philemon's buoyancy frame to the planks that Otto had secured into one large platform. It was taking some time, since they had to carefully saw away pieces of wood that kept the frame from sitting flush against the rest of the raft.

They were nearing the end of their work when the sound of footsteps racing down the stairs made all of us turn around. Henry dashed through the parlor and into the bedroom where Abigail, Kit, and August lay. A moment later we could hear violent retching sounds coming from within.

Otto and Philemon and I exchanged glances. I stood and walked to the bedroom door.

"Henry? Are you all right in there?"

"Yes," he rasped. "Give me a minute."

I sat down again and waited. Presently Henry came out of the bedroom looking pale and qualmish. He ignored us and walked a bit unsteadily toward the stairs, but before he could take a step he turned around and ran back into the bedroom, from which more sounds of sickness echoed.

When he exited the room again and walked slowly toward the steps leading to the tower, I stopped him. "Henry, you look terrible. Sit down and I'm going to bring you some cider."

"I don't want any."

"You have to drink something. How about a bit more soup?"

"I don't want any more. 'Twas that soup what made me sick, I know it. I disgorged all the mushrooms."

"I'm getting you cider."

Henry hesitated for a moment, then sat in the chair I indicated with my hand. "Be quick. I have to get back upstairs. We're coming along with the light."

I hurried to the kitchen and poured him a large measure of cider, then returned to the parlor. Otto and Philemon were talking in low voices while Henry glowered at them. I set the cup in front of Henry. "Drink this. You'll feel better."

With trembling fingers he raised the cup to his lips, then set it down without taking a sip. He shook his head. "I can't drink it."

"Stomach too roiled?"

Henry nodded. "I'll take it up with me. I'll drink it while I work." He stood and picked up the cup. His hands continued to shake and a bit of cider sloshed onto the floor.

"You sure you're going to be all right?" I asked.

He nodded again. He held the cup with both hands and made his way up the staircase slowly, stopping every few steps.

Philemon spoke up. "He doesn't look good."

I nodded, my brows knit together. I didn't know how much more calamity the people left in the cottage and the lighthouse could withstand.

THE RAFT WAS COMPLETE. It was a hideous thing, but that didn't matter as long as we could rely on it to get us away from the cottage and onto dry ground. Otto and Philemon had worked hard to build it so quickly. Sweat ran from their faces and the pungent odor from their bodies permeated the air in the cottage, even with the windows open. What a relief it would be to get out of here, I thought.

"We got to get this thing outside," Otto said.

"Shouldn't be hard," Philemon said.

"If the water hasn't risen as far as the door yet. I'll take a look," Otto offered. He strode to the door, with Philemon and me in his wake. He eased the door open and no water rushed into the cottage. It was the one fortunate thing that had happened since I arrived. From my vantage point behind both men, though, I could see the water. It lapped and sloshed within a few inches of the canted threshold.

"Otto, you'll have to get in the water and hold the raft steady while Philemon and I get Deborah out of here," I said. It wasn't going to be an easy task. She was still asleep.

Otto frowned. "You'd best rouse her in a hurry." He closed the door. I shook Deborah's shoulder while he and Philemon looked on.

"Deborah, you have to wake up. It's time to leave."

She moaned once and didn't move. I shook her shoulder again. "We have to leave, Deborah. Let's go."

Her eyes fluttered open, closed, and then opened again. When she spoke, her mouth sounded dry and hoarse. "I can't. It hurts too much."

"You must try, Deborah. We're all in danger. The cottage is going to crumble and we aren't going to leave you here."

She finally opened her eyes fully and stared at me. "What about Kit? Where is he?"

I could feel Otto and Philemon watching me, wondering what I was going to say. I took a deep breath. It was time to remind Deborah what had happened to Kit. I didn't want to be cruel, but I couldn't let her go on thinking Kit was alive and would join us when we sailed away from the cottage.

"Do you remember anything else about the storm?" I asked her.

Her eyes held a faraway look. She shook her head.

"I'm afraid Kit passed away during the storm, Deborah."

Her bottom lip began to quiver and she blinked several times. "During the storm? Kit is gone?"

I nodded.

"Why do I not remember this? Are you telling me the truth? Are you sure he died?" Tears fell from her eyes.

"You don't remember because of the medicine I had to give you. For your leg." I gestured toward her injury with my chin. I couldn't bear to look at it—it was swollen and deep purple. The bone coming out of her leg was dark red with dried blood.

She looked at her leg and gasped. Her eyes rolled back in her head as if she were going to faint, but I was able to catch her before her head fell back. When I lurched forward to brace her head, she opened her eyes again.

"Don't look at it, Deborah. Look at me instead," I commanded her. "You have a job to do. We need to get you out of here." I gave Otto and Philemon the responsibility of getting the raft out the door. My plan was to enlist Philemon's help to carry Deborah and place her on the raft. While building the raft, Otto had set aside planks to be used as oars, so the three of us men would take turns rowing to land once we were all aboard.

It was a simple plan, but I did not expect its execution to be simple. Deborah weighed hardly more than a sack of corn, but with her injured leg, we would have to keep her still. Maneuvering her onto the raft was sure to be an exercise in pain for her and frustration for us.

Otto and Philemon each took hold of one end of the raft and tilted it so it was standing sidewise. It looked much bigger now that it was no longer on the floor. They made their way slowly to the door and I opened it for them. The water lapped near my feet in the doorway, closer than it had been just a few minutes ago.

"Hurry," I urged them. Both men glared at me.

They struggled to fit the raft through the door. The raft wasn't even wide enough for two men to sit abreast, but it was heavy and cumbersome. Otto and Philemon pushed on it, straining and sweating. When that didn't work they tried turning the raft ninety degrees, but that didn't work, either. Finally Otto let out a roar of anger. He grabbed the closest axe and while I watched in morbid fascination, he swung it around the back of his head and smashed it into the side of the open door. I stopped myself from cautioning him not to do any more damage when I realized that was the least of the damage that would eventually befall the cottage. It wouldn't be long before the water started seeping in.

Otto sat on the threshold and slid into the water beside the cottage. He lost his footing on something beneath the water and he came up sputtering and swearing. "Push!" he yelled to Philemon and me. He pulled on the edge of the raft while Philemon and I pushed on it with all the force we could muster.

Finally, with a great cracking noise, more wood splintered down one side of the doorway and we were able to free the raft from the confines of the cottage. Philemon and I leaned against the wall, panting from the exertion. I watched as Otto clambered onto the raft and lay there, his chest heaving up and down.

Deborah watched us struggling, tears streaming from her eyes. I wished I could comfort her somehow, but getting people out of the cottage was the most important task at hand. The poor woman had been through Kit's death mere hours before— now she was experiencing it afresh. It was as if Kit died twice. Several times I turned to look at her from the doorway, and each time I was struck by how small and frail and scared she appeared.

Alas, I did not have time to console the new widow. The water was rising. I hurried to where Deborah sat, beckoning Philemon to follow me. I told Otto to get into the water again and hold the raft steady.

When we reached Deborah, I directed Philemon to support her under her arms. I positioned myself near her knees.

Philemon bent and placed his hands under Deborah's arms, then looked at me to tell him when to move. But when I reached for her knees to lift her lower body, she screamed.

"I'll try not to touch your shin. Is that what you fear?" I glanced at the water outside the door.

She nodded, her neck stretched taut and tears running down her face. She seemed too overcome to speak.

"We must leave here because the water is just outside the door. We don't have much time. I know you're in a great deal of pain, but you have to work hard for just a short time so we can get you onto the raft. Otto is waiting and he will help you. The moment we reach dry land, we'll send for the doctor to take care of your leg."

She shook her head and gasped out a breath. "I'm not leaving without Kit."

Philemon and I exchanged glances. From outside, Otto shouted. "Come along now! No more waiting!"

Deborah covered her face with her hands. "No!" she shrieked. "I'm not leaving without my husband!"

I crouched beside her and spoke in as soothing a voice as I could muster. "Deborah, I promise you I will come back for Kit. But first we have to get you to the doctor."

She looked at me with red, puffy eyes. Despite the tears that had been falling, her gaze was like iron. She swallowed and spoke calmly now, her voice low and measured. The sound of it sent chills down the nape of my neck.

"I told you I am not leaving Kit behind."

"But—" I began.

"That is my final word on the subject." She winced in pain.

I locked eyes with Philemon, who shook his head in apparent disgust. "I'm getting out of here, woman, with or without you." He scowled at her. "Your husband is already dead. You can either join him or come out with us. But I'm not going to die because of you."

She clenched her teeth in pain and a hiss escaped her lips. Its intensity startled me. "Deborah, if you're going to get out of here alive, you have to come with us now."

"I don't care if I die here."

"I'm not going to let you die. Not while I'm in charge here."

She let out a strangled laugh. "Who said you're in charge here? It's Henry's lighthouse."

"That may be so, but I'm the one who has to make sure everyone gets out safely. This cottage is going to crumble into the water and if we don't leave very soon, we're likely to go down with it. I am not going to allow that to happen." I understood her reluctance to leave her husband's body. If we could not safely return for all the bodies, they would be lost to the sea forever. But I would not be able to live with myself if I didn't do everything within my power to save the survivors in the cottage.

Otto's shout sounded as if it came from far away, but he was only outside the door. I turned to see him struggling to hold on to the raft. "Get out here, all of you! I can't hold onto this much longer!"

I turned back to Deborah. "Come along. We're getting you out of here."

# CHAPTER 38

$\mathscr{I}$ bent down again to grasp Deborah's knees. Philemon still had his hands under her arms. "We'll lift on my count of three," I said. "One, two, three." We heaved Deborah up from her position on the floor.

Suddenly her entire body convulsed in a violent, thrashing motion. She screamed. "I'm not leaving!"

"Hold onto her," I barked at Philemon. I took hold of the underside of her legs in an attempt to keep them steady, but they seemed possessed of an unnatural strength. Her good foot caught me on the face and I tasted blood in my mouth. She continued kicking my head and torso with one leg. Philemon was shouting and Deborah was squalling and I could not ignore the sharp pains in my chest and head. I inadvertently dropped her legs and she screamed as if the very Devil were pursuing her.

I reached for her legs again, but she kicked my arms away. Philemon yanked his arms away from her in surprise. She fell none too gently onto the wooden floor. Philemon and I stared at each other. Otto continued to shout exhortations for us to hurry.

Next I knew, Jeremiah thundered down the stairs. "What goes on down here?" he demanded.

"Deborah won't leave Kit." My voice was grim, angry. I had been subjected to enough of Deborah's foolishness. She could not jeopardize the lives of everyone in the lighthouse and cottage because she refused to leave a dead man behind. I understood her agony, but my priority was the living.

I opened my mouth to speak to her, but she shocked me and, I suspect, all the others, when she pushed herself to a standing position using only her arms and her good leg. She reached for a chair and yanked it toward her. As we watched, she used the back of the chair as a crutch and hobbled into the bedroom at an astonishing speed. I think Philemon and I were too surprised to chase her. I glanced at Jeremiah to see if he was going to run after her, but he was staring after her, mute.

I was the first to recover my wits. I strode through the bedroom door, assuming I would have to pry her away from Kit's body, when there was a terrific shattering of glass. I stopped short.

Deborah had used the chair to smash the bedroom window and was lifting her bad leg onto the window frame.

"Deborah, no!"

I reached for her good leg to wrench her away from the window, but she kicked me with such force I was knocked into the bureau.

By the time I was upright again, she was leaning out the window. Something fell from the pocket she was wearing. I blinked and heard a splash.

Everything had happened in only a few seconds. I wouldn't have thought she was sufficiently alert from the effects of the laudanum to behave so. Philemon had come up behind me.

"What do we do now?" he asked.

"We try to get her out of the water." For just a moment, I considered diving into the water after her, but what would I do then? Who knew how strong the currents were under the surface of the water? I might be doing more harm than good by pursuing her in the water. I made my decision quickly.

"Get on the raft. I'll go with you," I said. I looked at Jeremiah, who had come into the room behind Philemon. Without thinking, I bent to retrieve the object that had fallen from her pocket and stuffed it into my own shirt pocket. I spoke quickly, striding toward the cottage door. "Otto and Philemon and I will take the raft to try to save Deborah. We'll take her as far as land. You and your father be ready to leave when I get back."

Otto was still fighting to keep the raft steady. Philemon only had to step down a few inches to reach the raft, and I followed. Otto looked at us in surprise.

"Deborah threw herself out the bedroom window." My voice was terse. "Let's get around to the other side of the cottage. We have to find her."

"Deputy, don't go."

The words were shocking. I turned around to see Jeremiah standing in the doorway.

"What are you saying, man?" I reached for an oar. "Otto, help me get around the front of the cottage. Now."

"George, by the time you get around to the place where she jumped in, you won't be able to find her." Jeremiah's expression was indecipherable. "This is what she wanted."

First Abigail, and now Deborah? "Jeremiah, you're talking rot. Otto, now." I pointed to an oar.

We all looked up as the building shuddered. I watched in horror as the doorway, with Jeremiah in it, listed suddenly. He gripped the door frame, his eyes showing concern for the first time.

"Jeremiah, get your father. We're leaving. All of us."

"No. I'm staying here with him. Get yourselves to dry land." Jeremiah, his feet and ankles underwater, turned away. He splashed through the water that was now seeping quickly into the cottage and disappeared around the corner where the stairway was located.

"What are we doing, George?" Otto asked. "We can't stay here."

Jeremiah's appalling words still hung in the air. And I knew, somewhere in my mind and in my heart, that he was right. I knew we wouldn't find Deborah.

But still, we had to try.

"Start paddling around to the other side of the cottage. If we don't see her, we'll head for land," I told Otto. "It's not safe for any of us to get into the water to look for her, not with the cottage sinking further."

Otto and I rowed in tandem until we reached the place under the bedroom window where Deborah had thrown herself into the water.

There was no sign of her. I stood on the makeshift raft, my knees and ankles quivering with the exertion of keeping my balance, and shielded my eyes from the sky's gray glare on the water. I scanned the waves in each direction. Otto and Philemon did the same, though they remained kneeling. It was safer that way.

After several futile minutes, I sat down, too. "We'd better head for Cape Island," I said in a dull voice.

I felt as though I had failed Deborah. She had not led an easy life. She was married to a man who showed her no respect. One who, I suspected, beat her on occasion. And yet, despite her husband's treatment of her, she was bound to him for support. She had probably felt taking her own life was the only solution in the face of his death.

The three of us stared at the place where Deborah had hurled herself into the water, underneath the bedroom window. I watched for any sign of her until my eyes watered with the strain of my stare. Finally, I turned to the men with a sigh. Four deaths now. Four deaths during the storm, and on my watch. I longed for a large measure of cider to take away the sting of my shortcomings. I dreaded telling the sheriff that I had not been able to save any of them.

As I turned my back on Deborah's watery grave, I saw Otto and Philemon exchange pointed looks, nodding once at each other. My eyes narrowed. Damnation. Whatever they were communicating between themselves, I had a hunch I didn't want to know what it was.

# CHAPTER 39

*I* took up an oar and thrust it into the water, and we managed to turn the raft around. A stiff wind had blown in from the west and the force of it was as great or greater than our combined strength. We struggled against the massive gusts that blew toward us. In time, we managed to row close to the cottage, but instead of heading west toward Cape Island and dry land, Otto and Philemon propelled us toward the door.

"I told you we're heading for Cape Island. This wind is not going to stop us." I spoke calmly, though a feeling of apprehension was causing my heart to thud a bit faster. They were acting as one, and I didn't have the strength to row us in the opposite direction from the one they were taking.

"We're going back for August," Otto said. The set of his chin defied me to disagree, but disagree I did.

"We are not going back for anyone until we three have gone for help in Cape Island. That is an order."

Philemon shook his head. "We're through taking orders from you, George. We're going back for August or you can swim to Cape Island."

Anger and trepidation warred within me. How dare they usurp my authority?

But what was I to do? We were on a raft a long way from dry land. I was opposed by two rough men who, I suspected, would render me immobile without compunction and with violence, if necessary. I sat up straighter. I spoke as though I had made a decision, but in reality there was little option for me. "Very well. We'll go back for August, but be quick. It's not going to be easy to get him out if the water has gotten into the cottage."

The two men maneuvered the raft as close to the cottage door as possible. Otto stood unsteadily on the undulating raft and took a giant step toward the house. Using his hands to grip the sides of the splintered doorway, he managed to stay upright. He stood unsteadily on the threshold for a moment before disappearing inside.

I glared at Philemon. He smirked at me. It was clear they had planned this before the raft ever left the cottage. They had always intended to bring August with them.

"I need some help," came Otto's voice from inside.

Philemon looked toward the open door and back at me. "I'll stay with the raft. You go."

I much preferred to stay with the raft, but Philemon couldn't swim. And the longer it took us to bring August aboard the raft, the more harrowing the situation would become. I exhaled loudly. "Very well. I'll go."

Like Otto had done, I stepped into the doorway and grabbed the sides of it to pull myself into the cottage. The floor had indeed disappeared under several inches of water. Judging from the amount covering the floor near the base of the stairs and the greater amount toward the kitchen and main bedroom, I knew the cottage had continued pitching forward at an alarming angle. The building was clearly unstable, and I feared too much movement might cause it to tilt further into the water. Or worse.

I splashed through the water to the bedroom, where Otto had hold of his cousin's body under the arms. He was straining to pull August off the bed. He looked over his shoulder as I waded into the bedroom. "Grab his legs," he said. "No, over on this side of the bed."

I stood next to him and tried lifting August's feet as Otto hefted his upper body. It took a strenuous effort, but at last we managed to ease his long frame off the bed. Small step by small step, we made our way out of the bedroom and into the parlor of the cottage. Otto was moving backward and I was moving forward holding August's legs. I mistakenly let one of his feet fall into the water covering the floor and Otto shouted an oath at me. I gave him my severest frown, but I fear that did nothing to deter him from raising his voice to me again.

When we reached the door, Philemon was waiting for us. He pulled August's arms while Otto and I pushed and maneuvered and cajoled the rest of the body onto the raft. When August was finally recumbent on the wooden craft, the two sailors and I sat panting and perspiring for several minutes before any of us took up an oar to row for shore. I dreaded the idea of coming back to retrieve Kit's body—it would be much heavier than August's.

The thought occurred to me that we might lay Kit to rest in the water, where his wife died, but I could discuss that with Henry and Jeremiah when I returned for them. At the moment, of course, it was imperative that the raft reach dry land so August's body could be properly prepared for burial. Once that was accomplished, I could turn my worries to the people left in the lighthouse and the cottage. I also planned to officially arrest Otto for the attack on his cousin, but that could wait until everyone was safely away from the lighthouse.

We rowed for what felt like weeks, but was probably only an hour. I traded places to assist Otto and Philemon when one of them needed a rest. The wind and waves pummeled the raft, making our way slow and laborious. It was with a great sigh of relief and a flood of emotion that I saw several people from Cape Island waving to us and yelling greetings as we approached shallower water. We were much farther inland than the normal low-lying area along the coastline, and I wondered uneasily how other citizens in the area had fared. I continued to fret about Aces and about Abe Bradford.

Several of those who watched us advance through the water waded out to meet us. Many hands took hold of the sides of the raft and pushed us forward, toward the blessed drier land. Some of the men, upon seeing that one of our party on the raft was deceased, appeared shocked. Others seemed to accept it as a natural consequence of the storm.

Little did they know August's death had been at the hand of one of the other men on the raft.

Otto and Philemon and I also slid off the raft into the water when it was shallow enough to stand. Otto took up his station next to his cousin, and refused to let any of the helpers take his place. Limp with exhaustion, we finally slid the raft onto the marshy grass and let it rest there while we three sat on higher ground for several minutes to recover from the grueling exertion. By now a small crowd had gathered and exclamations of dismay over August's death, as well as many anxious questions as to the fate of the lighthouse, were directed toward us. Finally I put my hand up.

"I'll answer your questions as soon as I can. But right now, we need food and drink. I must return to the lighthouse so I can bring the Brewsters to land."

Another woman bustled forward with a large cloth-covered basket. "Joseph saw you coming on the raft. He ran home and asked me to fix this for you," she explained, thrusting the basket at me. Bless me, it was Joseph Whitman's wife.

I took the basket with a smile. "Thank you, Hannah. This is

very kind. How is your son from the licking he took from old Abe Bradford yesterday morning?"

"He's doing better, Deputy. Thank you for asking after him."

I lifted the cloth to find cheese, bread, and honey. I broke three pieces of bread from the loaf and handed two of them to Otto and Philemon. Philemon hadn't looked up since sitting down on the ground. He merely stared at his hands in his lap as I ate and answered some of the people's questions.

As I handed him the bread, he looked up and his eyes scanned the crowd for a brief moment. Joseph's wife gasped.

"What is it?" I asked in alarm.

She pointed at Philemon, her face drained of all color. "It's not possible! Are you a ghost? Are you bewitched?"

"What are you saying?" I asked. I could not honestly describe Philemon as a virtuous or upstanding man, but a ghost? Bewitched? That was ridiculous.

She pointed at him with a trembling finger as everyone else in the crowd hushed and stared at her.

"Karl!" she cried.

"You're the bewitched one, woman!" Otto cried. He leapt to his feet and charged at her, but several of the men ran forward and threw him to the ground before he could reach her. He put up a struggle, but was overpowered by the number of men holding him down. Philemon sat motionless, staring at the woman who had accused him of trickery, then he glanced toward me.

"Karl?" I blinked in confusion. "Why is she calling you by the name of Karl?"

"Karl Schuhmacher." Hannah Whitman was now standing at my elbow, still pointing at Philemon. "That's him. I would swear to it."

I could only stare dumbly. She was suggesting that Philemon and Karl were one and the same person.

"Karl's gone, you know that," came Otto's voice. It was angry, accusing.

The woman shook her head. "No. No. I would recognize Karl Schuhmacher anywhere. He must have used a charcoal dye in his hair, and it's much longer than it used to be. He's fatter than he was all those years ago, too, but that's him. There can be no doubt of it."

"What is she saying?" I asked Philemon.

It happened in an instant. Philemon was on his feet, running away from us with the speed of a hawk with a mouse in its sight. But he was tired from rowing and from getting very little sleep over the past twenty-four hours, so the men who ran after him caught him quickly and dragged him back to where I stood, still bewildered. Philemon kicked and yelled the entire time.

Joseph Whitman came striding up to the group of men surrounding me. He nodded at me. "Glad you made it through the storm, Deputy."

"Can you tell me what's going on here?" I asked him.

He turned to his wife, who spoke to him in a low voice. He stared at Philemon for several long moments, then nodded toward Hannah and turned back to me. "Yes, I can tell you. This here is Karl Schuhmacher, sure as the sun shines."

"How do you know?"

"The set of his chin, those eyes that look like he's come straight from he—"

"Joseph!" His wife glared at him.

"Anyway, there's no mistake," Joseph said. "Everyone thought he'd died."

"Is that true?" I directed my question at Philemon, but it was Otto who answered.

"And suppose it is?" He lifted his chin as if he were challenging me. "He's not done anything wrong to any of you." He tried to sweep his arm, but several men still had hold of him and wouldn't allow him to move.

"Perhaps not, but he's been accused of killing Abigail Brewster's brother, Horatio," I said. "And his own wife and her unborn child."

Philemon looked at me balefully. If so many people weren't nearby with their hands ready to restrain him at any moment, I might have expected him to attack me, so fierce was the look on his face.

"Tie his hands and feet," I ordered several of the men standing near him. "And tie up Otto, too." I was met with blank looks. "I'll explain later. I'll take both of them to Cape May Court House at the first opportunity. As long as they're not going anywhere, I need to get back to the lighthouse." I turned to Joseph again. "Can you keep them in your barn until I get back?"

"Your horse is in there, and I don't want to put them in the same place as your horse. I'll put one in the root cellar and the other in the privy." Joseph grinned.

"You got Aces?" I blinked quickly so no one would see the tears of relief that pricked the backs of my eyes.

He nodded. "Soon as that storm began, I remembered you had left her in your paddock. I went and got her. Rode her pretty hard for a lame horse, but we had to get back to my house quickly. She's fine."

"Thank you, Joseph."

"You're welcome. Your house, your stable, and the cell all sustained some damage. Not too bad, but it'll need to be cleaned up." Joseph hitched a thumb toward Otto and Philemon. "We can keep these two at my place until you can get them up to Cape May Court House."

"Do you know how Abe Bradford fared during the storm?"

"By the time I got the horse, Daniel had gotten to him in the cell and let him out." Joseph grinned again. "He was scared near to death, from what I hear. I'd lay bets he won't risk being put into that cell again."

# CHAPTER 40

*O*ith Otto and Philemon in the custody of my trusted friend, I turned to Mrs. Whitman. I ate quickly and gratefully from the basket she had brought and washed the food down with a small jug of cider. I asked one of the men in the crowd to fetch me a sturdy rope. As soon as he returned and hefted the rope onto the raft, I climbed aboard again and pointed it in the direction of the lighthouse. Several men had offered to accompany me, but I knew they had homes and property to take care of after the storm and I didn't want to impose. Besides that, there was a good possibility that two men and two corpses would be sharing the raft with me on the trip from the lighthouse and I dared not risk more people.

The lighthouse wasn't even visible from where I started out, but after rowing for some time, it came into sight. I gasped at my first look at it from this distance—it was listing toward the southeast. As I got closer, the cottage was visible, too. It had partially torn away from the rest of the structure and tilted dangerously toward the water.

The afternoon was lengthening by the time I pulled the raft alongside the cottage door, which was now halfway underwater.

Thankfully the westerly wind that had opposed us on the first trip to Cape Island helped propel me back toward the lighthouse. The cottage looked as if God had reached right down and tipped it toward the ocean.

Gingerly, I slipped off the raft and into the water, then used the rope to tie it to the door handle. Looking through the door, I was dismayed to see how deep the water was inside the cottage. The only way I was going to get through the parlor and to the lighthouse stairs was by swimming. Perhaps I could find a foothold somewhere indoors. I thought about the bodies of Abigail and Kit, wondering if they were where we had left them. I couldn't afford the time to look, though. I needed to reach Henry and Jeremiah as quickly as I could.

I half-swam, half-groped my way to the staircase leading to the tower. My feet found the floor of the cottage, but the water was almost up to my chin. I started yelling for the two men as soon as my hand touched the railing. "Henry! Jeremiah! You up there?"

"Yes," called Henry. "It looks bad from up here, Deputy."

It was a lucky thing the staircase was still intact, though it, too, tilted dangerously. I reached the first step that wasn't underwater and sat on it for a moment, catching my breath. "It is bad," I called back to him. "You two need to leave. There's no telling whether or how long the lighthouse is going to remain standing."

I waited to hear their tread on the stairs, but the sound didn't come. "What's going on up there?" I shouted. "I told you, you need to leave."

"I'm writing in the lighthouse logbook," Henry responded. "We need to leave a record of everything that happened here so my superiors know I did everything I could to save the light."

I shook my head in exasperation. I understood the need to document their efforts, but not at the risk of losing their lives. And perhaps mine, too. Exhausted, I slowly climbed the steps.

When I reached the top, Henry and Jeremiah were bent over the logbook. Henry was scrawling in it with a pencil. I took a step toward them, but tripped. I let out an oath, and the two men looked at me.

"I've tripped over that thing at least twice now," I said angrily, pointing to the nail in the doorway.

Henry nodded, then both men returned to the task at hand.

"It's time to leave. Now."

They turned to look at me, then glanced at each other. "The deputy's right. We should leave." Henry nodded at me. "We're coming with you."

"Good. Make haste, please, but be careful. The stairs are wet."

"What about Abigail?" Henry asked.

"And Kit?" Jeremiah added. Henry looked sidewise at him.

"We'll do what we can to get them out, too. But we don't have time to stand here prattling on."

I started down the stairs, then looked over my shoulder to make sure they were following me. They were, but they both wore scowls.

When we reached the part of the staircase that descended into the water, I put my hand on the railing and turned around to face them. "The water in the cottage is deep. Reaches to my chin. It's best if you try to swim. I'll go first and you two follow. We'll go into the bedroom and make a decision about taking Abigail and Kit."

I reached the bedroom door and stared inside in shock. The bodies were gone.

I must have looked ashen, because Henry swam over to where I was treading water. "What's the matter?" he asked.

"The bodies. They're gone."

"They're not gone. They sank. We have to pull 'em up."

"How do you know they sank?"

"Because I've seen dead bodies in the water before. They sink. After nigh on a week, they float."

I had never seen a dead body in the water. I assumed they would float. I hoped Henry was right.

"Who's going under to get them?" Jeremiah asked.

"I think it'll take at least two of us to get each body up. It's going to take some time because we have to get one of them on the raft and come back for the other one," I said. "Henry, I've done a mule's work today and I'm fit to fall asleep right here in the water. Can you and Jeremiah do it?"

"Yes. Jeremiah, get over here and help me."

Jeremiah spoke up. "I can't yet. I left my spyglass in the tower. I have to go back and get it."

I shook my head. "You don't need a spyglass and you can't go back up. We don't have time."

"Mother gave me that spyglass and I'm not leaving here without it."

# CHAPTER 41

*I* shook my head at Jeremiah. "You can't go back up to
the gallery. We don't have time." I repeated.

"And I told you Mother gave me that spyglass. I'm not
leaving here without it. It belonged to Horatio."

Henry and I exchanged glances. I sighed. "Very well. I'll get
the spyglass and you and your father work on getting Abigail—
or Kit—up to the surface of the water and onto the raft. Where
is the spyglass?"

Jeremiah told me I could find it in the storage room up in
the gallery. I turned and made my way through the water to the
stairway. For the second time, I emerged from the water and
trudged up the slanted steps as best I could. It wasn't easy with
sodden clothing and shoes. I was only a few steps down from
the top when I had to sit down to catch my breath. I turned
around to stretch my back, which was starting to cramp from
the exertion and swimming. As I did, I caught a glimpse of the
nail sticking out of the door jamb. It was the nail I had tripped
on twice. There was a tiny piece of dark green cloth snagged on
it. I peered closer and saw a bit of brown twine tied around
it, too.

That was odd.

My trousers were brown, so it wasn't my clothing that had been snagged on the nail, even though I had stumbled on it.

I placed my palms on my knees and pushed myself into a standing position, then went up the last few steps into the gallery and the storage room where Jeremiah had said his spyglass would be.

A quick visual search of the storage room did not reveal the spyglass. Grimacing, I stepped toward the box where I had found the wax earlier and lifted the cover. Amid the rags, hand tools, and string, I found the spyglass wrapped in a clean cloth. It was smaller than I expected it to be. I picked it up and buttoned it into one of my shirt pockets. I turned to leave and as I did so, noticed a thin piece of twine lying on the table. It was neatly sliced on one end and frayed on the other.

I stared at it for a moment, my mind working. Something was bothering me, tickling the corners of my mind. With the spyglass secure in my pocket, I headed toward the stairway to return to the others. I wondered if they had succeeded in bringing Abigail's or Kit's body to the surface of the water.

There was a loud scraping sound and I felt a stirring under my feet. The lighthouse was shifting, sliding away from its sandy foundation. I feared the stairway would buckle at any moment. I needed to get everyone out of the building and onto the raft as quickly as I could.

But as much as I wanted to hurry, I had to descend the stairs carefully lest I slip and provide Henry and Jeremiah with one more person to drag onto the raft.

It was that thought—that I might slip—that caused me to inhale sharply.

Kit. He was wearing dark green trousers. Jeremiah had lent them to him after the rescue of the three men in the boat. Could that scrap of fabric caught on the nail belong to those trousers? And the twine with the frayed end … was it possible that twine had been tied to the nail in the jamb? The nail had brown fibers on it.

I turned around and hastened back up the stairs as quickly as my body would allow. At the top step, I bent down to examine the nail more closely. Yes, those fibers were indeed a match to the twine in the storage room. I plucked the fibers and the scrap of green cloth from the nail and buttoned them into another pocket.

I was forming a hunch—one I did not like one bit. I moved to the other side of the step and bent down to examine that side of the doorway.

The small head of a nail protruded from the jamb. I hadn't noticed it before because it was camouflaged in a knot of wood.

Two nails, one with a small bit of twine tied around it. A piece of twine in the storage room, one frayed end and one neatly sliced end. I could practically see what had happened: the twine was sliced from one nail—the nail with the fibers and cloth on it—and ripped from the other one—the nail hidden in the knot of the wood.

There was something else. I squeezed my eyes closed, trying to recall if I had seen a nail in the doorway when I first went up into the light early on in the storm. No, I had not. I remembered now. I had tripped on the top step and looked on the floor, hoping in my embarrassment to find something to blame it on. Instead, I was forced to admit to myself that I had tripped due to my own inattention and clumsiness.

That meant the nail had been placed there after my first trip up to the lighthouse.

And suddenly I knew how Kit died.

He was tripped, and deliberately so. I recalled hearing light hammer taps after my humiliating stumble. Henry had said he needed Jeremiah to fix a barrel stave, but the hammering hadn't come from any barrel stave. Someone was hammering two nails into the door jambs.

But who had done it? My thoughts sped on, coming to a halt when I called to mind the letter Deborah had written. In it, she hinted at a secret. She planned to share the secret with Henry and she implored him not to discuss it with Kit.

Deborah had been in the parlor when Kit fell. I had a clear recollection of that. She was desperate to see her husband as the other men and I carried his body into the bedroom.

That left two people—Henry and Jeremiah. Which one of them could have wanted to hurt or kill Kit? And why?

"Deputy, can't you find the spyglass?" It was Henry. "We need help getting Abigail's body onto the raft."

"I found it. I'm coming down now."

I recalled how perturbed Kit was when I spoke to Deborah alone about the history between the Brewsters and the Schuhmachers. Kit had warned me to include him the next time I wanted to talk to her. What happened between Kit and Deborah Archer? Deborah wanted assurances from Henry that he wouldn't tell Kit what Deborah was going to say to him, while Kit made no secret of the iron fist of control he maintained over his wife.

And now that Kit and Deborah were both dead, there was only one way to find the answers I needed.

# CHAPTER 42

*I* kept my eye on the water level while my mind spun —two more steps and my feet would be submerged. I needed to focus on the task at hand, which was helping Henry and Jeremiah get the bodies of Abigail and Kit on the raft, but I couldn't help formulating theories about everything I had learned so far.

My best guess was that Deborah had a secret about Kit that she needed to share with Henry.

But why share a secret with Henry? Why not Abigail? By her own account, Deborah did not have much contact with Henry. It seemed odd that if she had a secret, she would choose to share it not with her friend Abigail, but with Abigail's husband.

Was it possible the secret also involved Abigail somehow?

A slight shudder ran through the structure again. Small ripples spread out from the steps. The building was continuing its descent into the water and we were running out of time.

I rounded the last bend in the stairway, my legs and waist descending into the water, to see both men treading water and holding Abigail's body between them. Henry was trying to support her upper body under her arms and Jeremiah held her lower legs.

"We need to coordinate our movements so we don't lose her," Henry said to Jeremiah, panting. "George, we can move her body toward the door and onto the raft, but we'll need you to hold the raft steady for us."

A few strokes through the water brought me to the door and out into the daylight. There might be monumental flooding, but least there was no more rain. I placed both hands on the raft to keep it stable and kicked my legs furiously to stay in the same spot.

Getting Abigail's body across the parlor and to the raft was easy compared to sliding her body onto it. After much cursing and labored breathing and barked instructions by all three of us, we managed to roll her onto the raft. She lay face-down. Henry, still treading water, attempted to turn her onto her back, but Jeremiah told him (rather curtly, I thought) to leave her be. They needed to retrieve Kit's body before we could leave for dry land.

Henry heaved his upper body onto the raft and lay his head down on his crossed arms. Jeremiah grimaced. "What are you doing?" he asked gruffly.

Henry lifted his head up and looked from Jeremiah to me. "Do you think we need to get Kit's body? His wife is under the sea. Should we let him join her?" I did not mention I had asked myself the same question.

Jeremiah looked at his father as if he were daft. "Of course we have to get Kit's body. The man deserves a Christian burial even though his wife deliberately took her own life."

Henry heaved a long sigh and didn't answer for a long moment, but finally he spoke. "I suppose you're right. Very well, we'll go." He slid off the raft and swam around it slowly to the door.

Someone had to stay with the raft and Abigail's body. I

volunteered to do it. I needed some time without Henry and Jeremiah to make sense of everything I had learned.

Henry and Jeremiah left me at the doorway to the cottage and swam back inside. Both men looked haggard and worn.

I was glad I couldn't see Abigail's face as she lay there on the raft. I was still haunted by the look of her the last time I saw her alive.

Time was of the essence. If I could reach a reasoned theory about Kit's fate, and perhaps even Abigail's, I might be able to officially question Henry and Jeremiah by the time we reached land.

We had two bodies, Abigail's and Kit's. If my new hunch was correct, someone had strung up a piece of twine at the top of the stairway and tripped Kit by design, killing him. There were only two possibilities—Henry and Jeremiah, who I now recalled had both been with him in the lighthouse at the time of his death. Perhaps the perpetrator's intention was not to kill the man, but merely to scare or perhaps maim him, but that was not my concern at the moment. I needed to know the facts so I could present them to the sheriff if necessary.

And if my other hunch was correct ...

A light was beginning to emerge from behind the veil of mist in my mind.

Abigail and Kit. Both educated, both from Philadelphia. It was becoming more common, of course, to see people from as far away as Philadelphia in these parts, but it was unusual for two people of affluent upbringing, of education, to end up here, both married to spouses who were simple and ordinary.

Was it possible Kit and Abigail had known each other before both arriving in Cape Island? Was it coincidence that they were both here now? And living not far from one another?

I needed to find out why Kit had moved here from the city. Henry might know.

Another thought was forming in my head, too. I needed to give it a bit more thought.

My musings were interrupted by sounds of splashing from inside the house. I looked in to find Jeremiah sputtering and cursing. "I can't get a hold of him," he said, spitting water out of his mouth.

"I'll do it." Henry sounded furious.

I waited and some thirty seconds later, Henry came up also sputtering. "His foot is caught on something. The bureau, I think. The longer it takes to get him out of there, the less likely we are to survive this. The building is going to crumble around us."

Father and son agreed to attempt just one more time to get Kit's body free. Henry disappeared under the undulating waves.

To my surprise, he was successful at extricating Kit's foot from its trap. His head bobbed above the water another thirty seconds later. "He's out. You go down there and pull him up," Henry told Jeremiah.

Jeremiah dove down and burst above the water's surface after what seemed like many minutes. He gasped for breath. "Help me," he snarled at Henry.

Kit's body was as large as, if not a bit larger than, Jeremiah's. And now it was waterlogged. It must have weighed as much as an ox.

"Have you got hold of him?" I called.

"Yes," came two angry voices in unison.

The structure shuddered again, and this time it was loud enough for me to hear its movement. "Hurry!" I shouted. "We've got to get out of here!"

A cacophony of splashing issued forth from the parlor of the cottage, and only a few seconds passed before Henry and Jeremiah struggled out of the bedroom with Kit. Henry was swimming backward at Kit's head, and Jeremiah was pushing his feet.

As soon as they were near enough, I slipped into the water,

grabbed one of Kit's arms, and helped Henry pull. I still held one side of the raft with my other hand, trying to steady it to receive Kit's body. The three of us heaved and grunted and swore until the top half of the body was on the raft, facing the sky. His legs dangled in the water.

"We're leaving now," I said. "I want to be far away from here if the lighthouse falls. Henry, get on the raft and hold Kit's arms so he doesn't slip into the water."

"You do it, Jeremiah," Henry said.

I didn't care, as long as one of them did it. Jeremiah hoisted himself out of the water and climbed onto the raft. He tugged under Kit's arms while Henry and I shoved the raft away from the cottage doorway. When we were twenty feet from the structure, Henry and I hauled ourselves up to join Jeremiah on the raft.

Henry and I grabbed the oar planks and rowed while Jeremiah kept Kit's body steady on the raft. We had only gone about a hundred yards when a thunderous noise boomed behind us. We all jerked our heads around.

I'll never forget that dreadful sight as long as I live. The lighthouse and the part of the cottage still attached to it were crumbling before our eyes, collapsing into the sea with a terrific roar.

"Hold on!" I shouted. I let the plank fall between my legs and grasped the side of the raft closest to me with an iron grip. Henry did the same. Jeremiah let go of Kit's body and reached frantically for the edge of the raft.

Seconds later, a wave the size of a large house engulfed us. Then another, and another.

I WAS surprised by how quickly the water stopped its furious roiling. After only a few moments, the huge waves lessened and we bobbed on them as we had done before the building fell. I wondered how long it would take the lighthouse and the cottage to sink and settle on the sea floor below the spot where they had stood for years.

None of us spoke. There was nothing to say—not yet. The shock of what we had witnessed was still too ghastly. The three of us could only stare at the place where the lighthouse had been standing only minutes before.

But we could not gander for long. I had gripped Abigail's arms as the raft undulated, which kept her body from slipping into the water, but we had nearly lost Kit. Only by a great effort and struggle were Jeremiah and Henry able to wrestle the top half of his body back onto the raft. Thereafter Jeremiah held Kit's arms for the rest of the way to Cape Island.

As Henry and I propelled us toward land, I revealed what I had learned about Philemon. Both men stared at me, mouths hanging open.

"Are you sure?" Henry asked.

"Joseph Whitman and his wife certainly seemed sure. And the way Philemon acted after I found out he was Karl, well, that proved it."

"I can't hardly b'lieve it," Henry said.

"You didn't recognize him at all?" Jeremiah asked his father. The young man wouldn't have known who Philemon really was —he was just a tiny lad when Karl disappeared.

Henry shook his head slowly. "It was so dim in the house the whole time, I never got a good look at him. Prob'ly Deborah didn't, either. The only time I might have recognized him was just after we rescued those three mongrels. And what with the water and the wind and being so tired from being out in the water, I s'pose I wasn't paying enough attention. When I knew him, he was a skinny thing. That was years ago, of course, and I never did know the man well. And he must have dyed his hair."

We rowed in silence for a long time. As if by unspoken

agreement, there came a time when Henry and I both held our oars still and drifted a short way. The rest felt good. I closed my eyes for a few seconds, wondering when I might get a good night's sleep. When I opened them, the first thing my eyes landed on was Kit's face. I gazed at him for a full minute. His eyes were open in a white mask of death. The sight sent shivers up and down my spine. I looked at Henry, who was staring straight ahead at the shoreline, then at Jeremiah. He was gazing back at the place where the lighthouse had been.

Something was bothering me, but I could not name it. It ate around the edges of my thoughts, but I could not coax it to the forefront of my mind. I closed my eyes again, thinking perhaps I might be able to grasp it if I weren't focused on the sights around me.

But that didn't help. Try as I might, I couldn't summon a solid idea of whatever was troubling me. I opened my eyes and looked around again—at the shore, at the place in the distance where the lighthouse had so recently stood, at Kit's grotesque form, at Henry staring ahead glumly, and at Jeremiah looking worn and wearied.

And suddenly I knew what had been making me uneasy— what with the storm and the darkness we had endured, I hadn't given it any thought before.

It was Jeremiah. More precisely, it was his eyes. They looked exactly like Kit's.

# CHAPTER 43

*I* couldn't help staring at the young man, feeling like I'd just stumbled onto the key to everything happening at the lighthouse before and during the storm.

Jeremiah glanced at me before I could look away. "What makes you stare so?" He didn't sound inquisitive. He sounded accusatory.

I shook my head. "Nothing. I suppose I'm just tired."

Jeremiah frowned and looked away.

It wasn't just the similarity of the eyes, I realized. I had noted to myself several times just in the past thirty hours how large Jeremiah's body was, especially when compared to that of his father. Henry was of small stature, stocky but diminutive. It seemed odd to me that such a man could father a son who grew up to be as large as Jeremiah was.

And now that I looked, Jeremiah had the same dark hair as Kit, too. The same nose, the same brows.

If I were forced to make a guess, I would say Kit was Jeremiah's father.

Suddenly, things were starting to make sense to me: the physical similarities, the possible connection between Kit and

Abigail in Philadelphia, and even the letter about which Henry and Jeremiah had lied to me. But I had other questions.

First, who else knew this? Did Henry and Jeremiah know? Did Deborah know? I suspected the answer was yes.

Second, if in fact Deborah knew Kit was Jeremiah's father, how did she find out? Was this the information she was keen to share with Henry? Is that why she wrote the letter asking him not to tell Kit? I had a hunch the answer to the latter questions was yes, too. And if that was the case, what was the likelihood either Henry or Jeremiah had killed Kit? The letter had been dated near the end of August, a little over a week before the storm. If either Henry or Jeremiah had known for a long time that Kit was Jeremiah's real father, they would have had plenty of opportunities to kill Kit. But they didn't do it until the storm, which suggested to me that they had only recently become aware of the information Deborah may have given them.

And third, what of Abigail's death? I could rule out Otto, August, and Philemon since they were only at the cottage accidentally and hadn't had anything to do with the Brewster family in many years. But any one of the other four—Henry, Jeremiah, Kit, or Deborah—could have killed Abigail. If Henry found out his wife had been unfaithful to him and that Jeremiah wasn't really his son, he could have killed her out of anger. Or revenge, or shock, or shame. If Jeremiah found out his father was someone other than Henry, he could have killed his mother for any of those same reasons. Deborah's motive for killing Abigail might have been as simple as womanly jealousy.

Could Kit have killed Abigail? I doubted so. Why would he kill her so many years after their presumed indiscretions? It was agreed by all parties that Kit and Deborah only visited the lighthouse once a week to check on the Brewsters, and Deborah slightly more often to visit Deborah on social calls. If Kit and Abigail were still involved somehow, he or she probably would have made excuses to be absent from their homes or to visit each other's homes more often. Now that I thought about it, there had been no mention of Abigail ever visiting Kit and Deborah, only the other way around.

Then there was the mushroom soup. I knew, of course, that poisonous mushrooms grew in these parts. Mushrooms that might taste good, but that could be deadly. One had to know how to forage for mushrooms correctly in order to avoid the dangerous ones. I remembered the book that had fallen from Deborah's pocket as she hurled herself out the window earlier and took it out of my pocket.

And there it was: *American Fungi, Illustrations and Descriptions*

The pages were too wet to separate without damaging them, but I had a strong feeling Deborah had taught herself to identify poisonous mushrooms in contrast to edible ones.

According to Henry, Kit and Deborah visited the lighthouse with supplies every week. Also according to Henry, it had been about a bit over a week since Abigail initially became quite ill. Her health had improved for several days after that, but she had become sick again, running to the privy countless times.

I wondered if Deborah had given food to Abigail during her last visit and if that visit had taken place after the date of the letter to Henry. If so, and if the food contained poisonous mushrooms, that would explain Abigail's sudden and acutely dangerous illness.

There had been a cup of soup on Abigail's bedside table at the time of her death, suggesting that someone had given it to her earlier. She had consumed at least part of it, she said.

And it was mushroom soup Henry had eaten in the wee hours of the morning and again several hours ago. After the first sampling of it, he felt unwell. Shortly after he ate it the second time, he rushed downstairs to vomit into the chamber pot. Vomit, he said, that consisted of mushrooms.

There was no doubt that Deborah had prepared the mushroom soup. She was the only woman in the house besides

Abigail, and Abigail was too sick to cook. Henry certainly hadn't cooked it—he almost never set foot in the kitchen, and if he had prepared it, he would have known not to eat it himself. I recalled Deborah serving soup to the men trapped in the lighthouse and the cottage—she had served only the beef soup.

With both Deborah and Abigail dead, I might never know the answer for certain. But I was confident I now knew what had transpired. Poison is a woman's weapon, and I surmised Deborah had used it to exact her revenge on Abigail for having relations with Kit. I sighed. Two women, two wrongs, two deaths. Only one had been a murder, though. As I thought through what likely happened between Kit and Abigail years ago, I became more confident in the accuracy of my guesses. And as my confidence grew, a great weight lifted from my shoulders. There would be no earthly justice for either woman, and my role in their deaths was at an end.

Now my thoughts returned to my immediate circumstances, that of being on a raft with at least one and possibly two murderers and their victim. Deborah and Abigail were gone and I could not ask them any questions. I hesitated, thinking perhaps it would be wise to wait to make my inquiries at a later time, but I knew once we arrived on land there would be many people around and I might miss my chance to talk to the men alone. As long as they were sitting next to me, I would seek the information I needed.

"What will you do with Abigail's body?" I asked suddenly. Both men jerked their heads toward me, as if my voice had startled them.

"Bury her. What else would we do?" Henry asked. He dipped his oar in the water again and started rowing. He nodded for me to do the same.

I rowed while I talked. "She was from Philadelphia, wasn't she?" I directed my question to Henry.

"Yes. What of it?"

"I wondered if you would take her there to be buried with the rest of her family."

"She never spoke to her family, except for Horatio, after she came here to live. And Horatio's been gone for many years, so there's no reason to take her up there. She can stay right here."

"Kit hailed from Philadelphia, too, didn't he?"

Here Henry and Jeremiah looked at each other as Henry answered. "Yes."

"He must have come from an affluent family."

"What makes you say that?" Jeremiah asked.

"It's obvious, isn't it? He was reading 'Precaution' earlier. He's clearly been well-educated."

"I reckon," Henry said.

"Did that book belong to one of you or to Abigail?"

"It was Abigail's book. I have no use for anything like that," Henry said. I had expected that answer. If Henry knew how to read at all, he didn't have the capability of reading and comprehending all the words in a book like the one Kit was reading.

"When did Kit move to these parts from Philadelphia?"

The two men exchanged glances. "I reckon it was about twenty years ago, maybe more," Henry said.

"Why would he come here, when he lived a life of wealth in Philadelphia?"

Jeremiah's eyes narrowed. "Why are you asking us?"

"I was just sitting here thinking. Do you suppose Abigail and Kit knew each other in Philadelphia?"

The muscles in Henry's jaw clenched. "Are you trying to say something, Deputy?"

"Me? No. I was merely speaking my thoughts aloud."

"Kindly leave your thoughts unspoken," Henry said.

"But don't you agree it's an intriguing question?" I persisted. "It would be quite a coincidence, do you not agree? That is, if Abigail and Kit were acquainted when they lived in Philadelphia."

"My father asked you not to speak your thoughts."

"I do not take orders from your father."

"I will make you shut your mouth if you keep talking," Jeremiah said in a low voice.

"You would do well to stop threatening me." My questions were riling the two men, of that I was sure. I hesitated again—I was putting myself in a precarious situation by asking them personal and probing questions, but I felt I was getting close to a revelation. I feared I would lose my advantage if I waited to get answers when we reached land.

Besides, I had just one more thought to put to them.

I chuckled as if what I were about to say was humorous, though it was anything but. "Do you know something? It's amazing how Jeremiah resembles Kit. If I did not know better, I would say he was the young man's father."

A moment later I was sputtering for breath in the waves behind the raft.

# CHAPTER 44

My head broke the surface of the waves. "I will not forget that when I speak to the sheriff, Henry." The raft hadn't moved forward more than a few inches after Henry swung at my head and pushed me into the sea, so I gripped one side and hauled myself onto the raft. I kept my eyes on the men, in case either tried to push me back into the water. I took up an oar and held it with both hands, prepared to strike either one of them if necessary.

"It's time you told me what happened when Kit fell down the stairs."

"He fell," Jeremiah said. "What else could have happened?"

Henry swallowed and opened his mouth, but no sound came out. He swallowed again. "If you know so much, why don't you tell us?"

"You two were the only ones up in the tower with Kit when he died. I think one of you, perhaps both, stretched a rope across the bottom of the gallery doorway leading to the stairway. I found what remained of the rope. Your intention was for Kit to trip and fall down the stairs. Your intention was for him to die. And I think you did it because you

learned he had relations with Abigail. Relations that culmi-
nated in Jeremiah's birth. And I think Deborah was the one
who told you."

Neither man spoke.

"I believe Deborah intended to tell only you, Henry. But
Jeremiah found the letter she sent you asking you to meet her
and to say nothing to Kit. Then he either persuaded her to tell
him the secret, too, or he persuaded you, or he found out by
eavesdropping on your conversation with her. That's why he's
been so ornery and ill-tempered." I paused. "Please tell me if I
am wrong. I wholeheartedly hope I am wrong, but I do not
believe I am."

Jeremiah moved toward me with a face that betrayed his
hatred of me, but Henry placed a hand on his son's arm. "Jeremiah, do not make matters worse."

"Was it Jeremiah?" I directed my question at Henry. "Did he
kill Kit?" All the sounds around us seemed to stop. I didn't hear
the lapping of the waves or the caw of sea birds or any of the
other sounds I knew were present. I was focused solely on
Henry as I awaited his answer. He finally spoke.

"It was not Jeremiah. It was me."

"That's not true!" Jeremiah erupted. "It was me. I killed Kit. I
strung that twine to trip him. And it worked."

"Deputy, he's trying to protect me. I was the one responsible
for Kit's death."

"He's lying," Jeremiah insisted. "I wanted Kit dead for what
he did to my mother. I hate him."

I stared at each man in turn. I had expected them to deny
any wrongdoing. I was shocked, though I did my best to conceal
my thoughts. "Is it possible you both participated?"

Henry shook his head emphatically. "No. I told you I did it.
Jeremiah had naught to do with it." He looked into the water,
avoiding my eyes.

Jeremiah's fists were curled into white balls of knuckle and sinew. I half expected him to strike me, but as the silence on the raft lengthened, his fists unclenched.

"You know I'm going to have to take both of you up to the sheriff to be questioned since you both confess to killing Kit."

"Please, Deputy, leave Jeremiah out of it. He's a young man. He's never done anything wrong. Imagine learning your father isn't the man you thought he was. What would you do? Jeremiah was angry, of course, but he didn't kill anyone."

"Not even Abigail? To punish her for what she did?" I asked. My eyes swept between the two men. "Or was it you, Henry, embarrassed and ashamed that you'd been fooled into thinking Jeremiah was your son all these years?"

Both men looked aghast. Henry paled and his mouth slackened. Jeremiah's eyes were saucers.

Now father and son stared at each other, and I watched their expressions shift from unity to mistrust in front of me.

Henry squinted and tilted his head as if he were trying to figure a particularly troublesome question. "Deputy, I've told you I loved Abigail. No matter what she did."

"You think I would harm my own mother?" Jeremiah asked in disbelief. It was interesting to me that neither man admitted to killing Abigail, but both insisted upon shouldering the blame for Kit's death.

These two men were confirming what I had suspected already—that Deborah had killed Abigail. I knew neither Otto nor August nor Philemon had killed her, and I had a strong hunch the men on the raft with me were telling the truth.

"When Deborah told you that Kit and Abigail had had relations," I said to Henry, "did she blame anyone?"

"She blamed Abigail entirely. She said Abigail had seduced and bewitched Kit."

"And do you agree?"

"I think both of them were equally at fault for breaking the marriage vows. But Abigail deserved a better husband than me. I don't blame her for what she did."

I know when a man is being sincere and when he isn't, and Henry was being sincere. He was serious and thoughtful. He looked directly into my eyes as he spoke. He didn't fidget or fuss or try to distract me from the course of my questions. He was telling the truth, of that I was sure.

And Jeremiah? I took my eyes away from Henry's face for a moment and was shocked to see a tear rolling down the young man's cheek. He caught me looking at him. "I'll miss her." He wiped his nose with his wet shirt sleeve. "Believe me, Deputy. I would never do anything to hurt my mother."

And I believed him.

# CHAPTER 45

*A*s we approached land, the good folks of Cape Island who had helped us before were there again, this time with lanterns as darkness was quickly approaching. And they had recruited more people. I was reassured and grateful for the people lighting our way.

"We need to speak now with haste," I said gravely. "I believe that Deborah was responsible for Abigail's death. We may never know why, but I will tell the sheriff I think she did it. Tell me, Henry, did Deborah bring mushroom soup for Abigail the last time she visited? The last visit before the storm?"

Henry thought for a moment, his mouth pursed. "Yes, I believe she did."

"And was that after she wrote the letter asking you to meet her?"

Henry nodded, then his eyes widened. "Yes, it was. Is that what made Abigail sick? Mushroom soup?"

I nodded. "I believe it was. Did you or Jeremiah eat the soup the last time she visited?"

The men looked at each other and shook their heads. Henry

spoke up. "She brought a small amount of the soup and asked Abigail to taste it."

"And Abigail ate it." I could see everything clearly now. "What pretense did Deborah use when she asked Abigail to taste the soup?"

Henry let out a tremulous breath. "I believe she told Abigail she would make more if Abigail liked it."

"And did Abigail like it?"

"Yessir. Abigail has always liked mushrooms."

I knew my theory was correct. But where normally I would feel elation at having solved a crime, this time I could feel only sadness. "How long after that visit from Deborah did Abigail begin to exhibit signs of illness?"

"The next day, I believe it was."

"You've both heard of death cap mushrooms?" I asked them. They nodded.

"I've seen them near here." I paused to gather my thoughts.

"I think Deborah made a soup with them and gave some to Abigail to see what would happen. Then she brought more mushroom soup yesterday when she visited before the storm. Her plan must have been to give Abigail enough soup to kill her."

Henry started to speak, but I held up my hand and continued. "I've heard about what can happen when someone consumes those mushrooms and Abigail had all the signs—sickness followed by a period of feeling better, then acute sickness again."

This time I let Henry speak. "Are you sure of all this?"

I nodded. "Deborah had on her person at the time of her death a book entitled *American Fungi, Illustrations and Descriptions*. She knew what death cap mushrooms could do. Her actions were deliberate and planned."

I paused again while Henry and Jeremiah stared into the distance over the water. "I am truly sorry I didn't make the connection between the mushroom soup and Abigail's symptoms until just a little while ago. But if it's any comfort to you, Henry, there was nothing you could have done to prevent Abigail's death. Once the mushrooms have been consumed, it is only a matter of time before death befalls the victim."

"I ate some of that soup and got sick," Henry said. Then I watched as realization dawned on him. "Do you think I'm going to suffer the same way Abigail did?"

"Only time will tell, but you disgorged the mushroom soup shortly after you ate it. We'll tell the doc what happened and have him look you over. How do you feel now?"

"Same as usual."

"That's good. Hopefully the mushrooms are out of your stomach."

Henry looked at me grimly as I went on.

"I'm quite sure that my hunch about Abigail's death is correct. And now, what I need you both to do is tell me the truth about Kit's death. Only you know what happened, and you're both accepting blame for it. Is that how you wish me to proceed when the sheriff begins his investigation into all the deaths in the lighthouse?"

The men exchanged glances and nodded.

They were exasperating, this father and son. But I understood what they were doing and I could not find fault with them for refusing to point the finger of blame at each other. "When we get to land, you'll both accompany me to Joseph Whitman's house. I'll borrow his wagon if he's agreeable to that and tomorrow I'll take you and Otto and Philemon to Cape May Court House to see the sheriff. I'll let him figure out what to do with you."

The men from shore were getting closer. Jeremiah cleared his throat. "Deputy?"

"Yes?"

"Deborah told me I should have been her son."

Henry's breath caught. "She told you that?"

Jeremiah nodded. "She said she could never have children. She hated Kit because he provided my mother with a child. She hated my mother because she was able to give birth."

I did not know what to say. I could only imagine the jealousy that must have raged within Deborah's heart when she learned her husband had fathered a child with another woman, especially given her own barrenness. It must have been doubly humiliating for her.

I finally found words to speak. "Did Deborah tell you how she found out Kit was Jeremiah's father?"

Henry nodded. He took so long in answering I thought he was going to stay quiet, but finally he spoke. "The day before she wrote the note to me asking me to meet her, she found a letter, an old one, written by Abigail and addressed to Kit. It was in Kit's bureau. He had kept it all those years. In the letter she apologized for turning to him in a moment of weakness. She told Kit that he was Jeremiah's real father."

"I'm sorry," I said. I meant it truly.

"I wish I had never found out." Henry's face darkened.

"I assume Kit followed Abigail here to Cape Island from Philadelphia all those years ago? Why did he marry Deborah?"

Henry answered. "I think when Kit realized Abigail was going to marry me, he decided to marry Deborah. Deborah used to be much prettier and more lively, but daily living on a farm, especially one far from almost everyone else, has a way of souring people. And of course, she was barren. Theirs was not a happy union."

I wondered if Henry and Jeremiah had spared a thought for their own responsibility in Deborah's death. Surely they knew how hard life would be for her following Kit's death— could they have surmised that she would take her own life at the prospect of living out the rest of her days, bitter and alone?

Henry spoke into the silence. "May God have mercy on her soul."

"For killing my mother? May He show her no mercy at all." Jeremiah spat out his words with ragged force.

Henry looked away.

"Henry, I presumed you had done something to harm Abigail because she didn't want you to come near her in her final moments. But in fact, she was the one who wronged you. Why do you think she wanted you to stay away as she neared the end?"

Henry shrugged. "I'll never know for certain, but I believe it's because she was ashamed of herself. I confronted her after Deborah told me the truth about Jeremiah's father, and Abigail was right distressed. She cried and apologized and begged my forgiveness. I forgave her, of course, but that doesn't matter anymore, does it?"

Henry's words were the last ones spoken among us before the men from shore tumbled into the water to offer the fresh strength of their arms and backs. I was glad to let my oar fall while we rode the rest of the way to land, and I suspect Henry was, too. We were almost to the marshy land where it would be easier to get off the raft and push it the rest of the way. The men who had come out to rescue us exclaimed with shock and surprise at the loss of the lighthouse—and the loss of life within it.

"What in tarnation happened in that lighthouse?" one of the men asked me. I pretended not to hear his question in the confusion.

When the men had helped Henry and Jeremiah and me onto land, they returned to the raft for Abigail's and Kit's bodies. I instructed them to take the corpses in a wagon to the doctor's house. He would be able to deal with them better than I.

I turned to the group of men standing nearby. "Can one of you take us over to Joseph Whitman's house?"

Several minutes later the lighthouse keeper, his son, and I were in the back of a wagon heading for Joseph's house. No one said anything in the gathering darkness. As soon as we were let off, Joseph came out of his house wearing a look of surprise. "Why, Henry Brewster. What are you folks doing here?"

"Joseph, do you have room for Henry and his son to stay here? I need to go check on my house and the cell."

"I reckon we can keep them in the house with us."

Henry and Jeremiah waited off to the side while I spoke to Joseph. "You can keep them in the house if you like, but I would recommend you keep them locked up. I can help you tie them up if you prefer." Joseph looked at me in some alarm, his eyes wide. "They'll be going up to Cape May Court House with Otto and Philemon. That is, Karl Schuhmacher. I don't trust Henry and Jeremiah to stay put. If it would help, I'll deputize you until I can get back here and you'll have the same authority as I do over them."

Joseph agreed to be deputized. I administered the oath and gave him my badge temporarily. After that I helped him tie up the father and son, then I departed for Decatur Street.

MY HOME and those nearby sustained some damage in the great storm, as Joseph said. A tree fell on the roof of a small room in the back of my house, and the land around me was underwater. It was salt water, so I knew the vegetables I had planted that were still in the ground would not survive the deluge. The paddock was a sea of mud, but the stable was relatively unscathed. Water, of course, covered the stable floor, but that would subside before long and Aces would be in her pen again.

The cell, located in a small depression off the side of the street, was filled with approximately three feet of water. Abe Bradford would certainly have survived if he had been left in the cell during the storm, but I was glad my neighbor had let him out.

I returned to my house, exhausted, and climbed the stairs to bed. Had it really only been thirty-two hours since I was last at my house? It was early in the evening, but I slept soundly until the sun rose the next morning.

I was fortunate to find a pair of high boots I used for walking in the snow. I pulled them on and waded through the water and mud toward Joseph's house. In every direction I saw evidence of the damage the storm had wrought in Cape Island. Crops were underwater, houses were listing in the mud or completely torn apart, and trees lay on the ground everywhere. It would be a long time and require a great deal of work to restore the New Jersey cape to the way it had been only forty-eight hours previously.

I was lost in thought when I heard someone shout my name.

"Deputy Moore!"

# CHAPTER 46

*I* turned around to see Titus running toward me. He wore his red shirt and a worried look.

"Slow down, Titus. What's the matter, young man?"

"It's me and Edwin and Flora, sir." Edwin and Flora were Titus' younger brother and sister. "I tried to get your attention yesterday morning, sir."

I recalled Titus waving to me early in the morning the day before. I thought he was merely being friendly. "What about you and Edwin and Flora?"

Titus bent at the hips with his hands on his knees as he caught his breath. I placed my hand on his shoulder. "Take your time, Titus."

He straightened up several seconds later and took a deep breath. "Yesterday morning, sir, before the storm started—even before the sun was up—someone came right into our house and tied up me and Edwin and Flora and put us in the back of a wagon and took us straight out of town." Titus's eyes were wide with fear.

I frowned. "Who did that?" A prickle of unease ran up and

down my arms. I had a feeling I knew where this conversation was headed.

"I don't know, sir. Two people. They musta been men. They were strong. They stuffed our mouths with rags so's our mother and father wouldn't hear us hollering."

I recalled a wagon racing out of town before the storm. It was the sound of the wagon that had awakened me. My chest constricted—I should have waited when Titus tried to get my attention yesterday morning. I should have realized he was in trouble. I should have questioned why that wagon was hurrying so.

"What happened next?"

"A ways up the road, I jumped out of the wagon and ran straight back to town. That's when I saw you. But one of the men, he was chasing me, and I needed to hide right quick."

"And did you get back to your house?"

"No, sir. The man caught me and gagged me again and dragged me back to the wagon. The wagon had turned around and come almost all the way back to town. I got thrown right into the back of it. Then they drove us north, sir. They put us on a boat and another man got on the boat to help them. And they took us right out in the ocean."

A cold stone dropped into the pit of my stomach.

"You and your sister and brother must have escaped, am I right?"

"Yes, sir. The storm came up quick. I'll tell you something, sir, we were afraid for our lives."

"I am sure you were. Were you still tied up? Still gagged?"

"Yessir."

"What happened?"

"The men, they needed our help to keep the boat from sinking. They set us to bailing water. They had to untie our hands for that. They hadn't tied our feet because they needed us to walk through the water to get in the boat, so that was a stroke of good luck. While we bailed, the men talked. While they talked, me and Edwin and Flora looked at each other and the water and we agreed to jump in and swim away as fast as we could. We're good swimmers, sir. Our father taught us to swim."

"You three jumped out of the boat?"

"Yessir, and we swam fast."

"Did the men swim after you?"

"No, sir. They had their hands full what with bailing the water out of the boat."

"What were they talking about while you and Edwin and Flora bailed out the water?"

"They were arguing about where to take us to sell us. One said Virginia, one said farther south. One said New Orleans." He took a shaky breath. "If that storm hadn't happened, we'da been separated and sold, sir. My poor mother and father woulda rather died than see that happen."

"What did the men look like?" I had a sickening feeling.

"Mean. One—a fat one—had hair the color of midnight. The others weren't quite as dark. One was taller'n the other. They wore kerchiefs around their faces the whole time so's we couldn't tell who they were."

"Did you recognize their voices?"

Titus thought for a moment. "I don't know, sir."

"Did you look behind you as you swam?"

"Once, sir."

"And what did you see?"

Titus smiled for the first time. "They were strugglin', sir. That boat wasn't any good. They had their hands full of bailing."

"Was it you I saw on a raft earlier today?"

"Yessir. When we told my father what happened, he was afraid. He gave me and Edwin and Flora some money and told us to take our old raft up the river to Philadelphia, where we would be safe. He wanted us to travel only in the dark, but he was so afraid those men would come back that he sent us out this morning at daybreak. He said the wind would push us quick. He told us to find a place to hide the raft until nightfall, then head out again."

"So why are you here?"

"We couldn't do it, Deputy. We couldn't leave our mother and father behind. We went back home. Me and Edwin and Flora will all be free before too awful long, and we'll stay where they are."

"Titus, I want you to go home. Tell your family I'm looking into this. I have a feeling I know who was behind this and I'm going to see that they're punished for it. I don't take kindly to anyone kidnapping the people under my care."

Titus grinned. "Thank you, sir. I'll do as you say. You're a good man, Deputy."

"Go on now."

Titus turned around and ran again, this time in the direction of his house. With a determined gait, I continued on my way to Joseph's farm. When I arrived, I found Henry and Jeremiah, with their feet still tied, sitting in the kitchen. Joseph's wife was putting plates of food in front of them, under the watchful eyes of her son.

"Thanks for looking after the Brewsters," I said, doffing my hat. "Where might I find Joseph?"

"He's in the privy, making sure that heathen out there is still tied up tight. There's one in the root cellar, too. He's tied up good."

I nodded. "I'll be back."

Joseph was coming out of the privy when I arrived. Philemon—Karl—took to yelling as soon as he heard my voice. "Sheriff's going to hear about this, Deputy!"

"You tell the sheriff anything you please, Philemon. Karl. I've a hunch I'll be able to share more information with him than I had even last night."

There was a momentary silence from the privy. Then, "What's that supposed to mean?"

"It means, I think I know why you and Otto and August were in that boat yesterday."

"I'll bet."

"You were taking three negro siblings south to sell them, weren't you?"

More silence, then "Goldarn that Otto. Did he tell you everything?"

"He didn't need to. But you just as much as told me yourself."

"What do you mean by that?"

"I'm tired, Philemon. I've heard enough out of you. You'll do the rest of your talking to the sheriff."

I followed Joseph to the barn, where I do believe my horse was as happy to see me as I was to see her.

# CHAPTER 47

*A*n hour later I was sitting on the rumbler of Joseph's wagon. Otto, Philemon, Henry, and Jeremiah were in the wagon, their feet tied up and their hands tied to the sides of the wagon. Joseph sat beside me, the horse's reins in his hands. It took us quite some time to get as far as Cape May Court House, but I was glad to deposit the four men in the sheriff's office.

All through the storm and its aftermath, I had been concerned about what the sheriff would say when he heard four people lost their lives under my watch at the lighthouse. And I was right. He demanded to know what happened and the steps I took to protect those people. To his credit, though, he let me talk.

He listened while I explained what happened to Abigail and Kit and August and Deborah. I explained my theory behind each victim's death and shared with him all the evidence I had found to support my speculations. I was forthright when it came to Kit's death. I told him I was responsible for letting Kit go up those lighthouse steps when I knew he had consumed too much cider too quickly. And I told him I was accountable for not realizing Titus needed my help the morning before the storm began in earnest. He said such a mistake could have happened to anyone.

Like me, the sheriff was confounded by the confessions of Henry and Jeremiah, each one insisting the other had nothing to do with Kit's death. And I believe he was as relieved as I not to have to determine the innocence or guilt of either man. At least one of them was guilty—the judge would be the one to resolve that dilemma.

The sheriff and I talked for over an hour. Before I left his office, he shook my hand and told me he was proud to have a deputy like me. I may have exercised poor judgment in allowing Kit to go up the stairs just prior to his death, he said, but I had solved two murders and arrested the man responsible for inadvertently killing August. In addition to that, the sheriff praised me for figuring out that Otto and August and Philemon had been kidnapping young slaves to sell further south. He suspected the three men were responsible for several such kidnappings that had taken place up and down the New Jersey coast recently. Thankfully, the sheriff and I held the same ideals when it came to the ownership of other human beings, and I was pleased to hear he was going to ask the judge for the severest penalty for the two surviving slave merchants.

I was never so glad to get back to Cape Island as I was that night. Joseph and his wife invited me for dinner, then offered to keep Aces for me until my stable dried out. I walked home with a full belly. On the way, I was surprised to run into Abe Bradford, who was as sober as a judge.

"How are you feeling, Abe?"

"Fine, Deputy. Fine. I heard you had a time out at the lighthouse."

"And I heard you had a time here in town. I'm glad you got out of that cell."

"You won't need to put me in there again, Deputy. I'm a changed man."

"I believe you, Abe. Make sure you stay changed."

He nodded and continued on his way.

I spent the rest of the evening cleaning out the stable so I could bring my horse back. My house could wait. I needed to fix that roof over the back room, but it would be there tomorrow.

Unlike the lighthouse.

Before retiring, I sat in my parlor with a mug of cider. I closed my eyes and sipped my drink as I finally allowed myself to remember Evelyn. Her delicate features, her soft hair, and her bright, inquisitive eyes. It had been a long three years without her. I rubbed my hand over my own eyes, wiping away the moisture that threatened to spill over my lashes. I was glad she didn't have to live through that storm. She hated storms. I missed her more than ever, but then I thought of Deborah's words following Kit's death: work helped. Keeping busy helped. And there would be plenty of work to do in Cape Island in the coming months.

Everything, eventually, was going to be all right.


THE END

# AUTHOR'S NOTE

~

The Great September Gale (also known as the Norfolk and Long Island Hurricane) struck Cape May on Monday, September 3, 1821, with sustained winds of 135 miles per hour and gusts of 200 miles per hour. In modern parlance, it would be called a Category 4 hurricane, and it was one of the strongest storms ever to assault the New Jersey cape. It was a fast-moving storm, though I have slowed it down somewhat for the purposes of this story. The raging tempest resulted in a 10+-foot storm surge that cut off Cape May from the rest of the county. Roofs blew off buildings, ships sank, homes and wharves collapsed, and trees blew miles away from where they once grew.

As in previous books in the Cape May Historical Mystery Collection (*Cape Menace, A Traitor Among Us*), I have taken certain liberties with the language used by the characters. Language in 1821 was more formal than that which we use today, so for the sake of clarity I have used description and dialogue that are more readily accessible to the modern reader.

With that being said, I have used some 1821 vernacular for color and zing.

I hope you've enjoyed reading *The Night the Light Went Out* and I hope you'll consider leaving a review. Reviews are important for authors because they increase a book's visibility in the marketplace. It's easy—just a couple sentences will do. Consider the following if you need some inspiration:

Did you like the characters? Did you care about what happened to them?

Did you like the setting? What did you like best about it?

Did you learn anything about nineteenth-century Cape May?

What was your favorite part of the story?

Remember, the best way to help an author is to leave a review and tell someone else about the book.

Thanks for reading!

# NEWSLETTER SIGN-UP

~

I invite you to visit www.amymreade.com to explore my website and join my newsletter. You'll receive updates, promotions, contests, recipes, and more. As a subscriber, you'll also get access to exclusive content!

ALSO BY A.M. READE

∿

THE CAPE MAY HISTORICAL MYSTERY COLLECTION
*Cape Menace*
*A Traitor Among Us*

WRITTEN AS AMY M. READE

∾

THE JUNIPER JUNCTION COZY HOLIDAY MYSTERY
SERIES

*The Worst Noel*
*Dead, White, and Blue*
*Be My Valencrime*
*Ghouls' Night Out*
*MayDay!*
*Fowl Play*
*St. Patrick's Fray*

∾

## STANDALONE BOOKS

*Secrets of Hallstead House*
*The Ghosts of Peppernell Manor*

## THE MALICE SERIES

*The House on Candlewick Lane*
*Highland Peril*
*Murder in Thistlecross*

WRITTEN AS A. DIANNE READE

∾

THE LIBRARIES OF THE WORLD MYSTERY SERIES

*Trudy's Diary*

∾

STANDALONE BOOKS

*House of the Hanging Jade*

# ABOUT THE AUTHOR

∿

Amy M. Reade is the *USA Today* and *Wall Street Journal* bestselling author of cozy, historical, and dual timeline mysteries and domestic suspense novels.

A former practicing attorney, Amy discovered a passion for fiction writing and has never looked back. She has so far penned seventeen novels, including standalone mysteries, the Malice series, the Juniper Junction Cozy Holiday Mystery series, the Libraries of the World Mystery series, and the Cape May Historical Mystery Collection. In addition to writing, she loves to read, cook, and travel. Amy lives in New Jersey and is a member of Sisters in Crime and the Alliance of Independent Authors.

You can find out more on her website at www.amymreade.com.

Made in the USA
Middletown, DE
02 September 2024

60245873R00165